ALSO BY NATHANAEL LESSORE

Dropping Beats

KING
OF NOTHING

NATHANAEL LESSORE

LITTLE, BROWN AND COMPANY
LARGE PRINT EDITION

This book is a work of fiction. Names, characters, places, and incidents are the product of the author's imagination or are used fictitiously. Any resemblance to actual events, locales, or persons, living or dead, is coincidental.

Copyright © 2026 by Nathanael Lessore

Cover art copyright © 2026 by Kingsley Nebechi. Cover design by Gabrielle Chang.
Cover copyright © 2026 by Hachette Book Group, Inc.
Interior design by Amanda Kain.

Hachette Book Group supports the right to free expression and the value of copyright. The purpose of copyright is to encourage writers and artists to produce the creative works that enrich our culture.

The scanning, uploading, and distribution of this book without permission is a theft of the author's intellectual property. If you would like permission to use material from the book (other than for review purposes), please contact permissions@hbgusa.com. Thank you for your support of the author's rights.

Little, Brown and Company
Hachette Book Group
1290 Avenue of the Americas, New York, NY 10104
Visit us at LBYR.com

Originally published in 2024 by Hot Key Books in Great Britain
First U.S. Edition: March 2026

Little, Brown and Company is a division of Hachette Book Group, Inc. The Little, Brown name and logo are registered trademarks of Hachette Book Group, Inc.

The publisher is not responsible for websites (or their content) that are not owned by the publisher.

Little, Brown and Company books may be purchased in bulk for business, educational, or promotional use. For information, please contact your local bookseller or the Hachette Book Group Special Markets Department at special.markets@hbgusa.com.

Library of Congress Cataloging-in-Publication Data
Names: Lessore, Nathanael, author.
Title: King of nothing / Nathanael Lessore.
Description: First U.S. edition. | New York : Little, Brown and Company, 2026. | "Originally published in 2024 by Hot Key Books in Great Britain." | Audience term: Teenagers | Audience: Ages 12 and up. | Summary: "An unlikely connection forms between two very different teen boys as they grapple with crushes, toxic friendships, and the meaning of masculinity." —Provided by publisher.
Identifiers: LCCN 2024060293 | ISBN 9780316588560 (trade paperback) | ISBN 9780316588577 (hardcover) | ISBN 9780316588638 (ebook)
Subjects: CYAC: Interpersonal relations—Fiction. | Masculinity—Fiction. | High schools—Fiction. | Schools—Fiction. | London (England)—Fiction. | England—Fiction. | LCGFT: Novels.
Classification: LCC PZ7.1.L473215 Ki 2026 | DDC [Fic]—dc23
LC record available at https://lccn.loc.gov/2024060293

ISBNs: 978-0-316-58857-7 (hardcover), 978-0-316-58856-0 (trade paperback), 978-0-316-58863-8 (ebook), 9780316610483 (large print)

POUR MA KIKINE

FIGHTS ARE NEVER like what you see on TV. The hero punches one guy once, and they get knocked out immediately. In real life, there's all this wrestling and trying to floor each other. The other guy's zip scratches your face, and the blows never land like they should. The movies are a lie.

The only reason people don't mess with me and the crew is because they know we'd win any fight. Still, every now and then, someone disrespects us and we have to prove a point.

Like this afternoon, something got said in the schoolyard that we couldn't let slide. Femi said that girls find Kehinde so creepy his nickname should be Friday the 13th. So when Kehinde came in after lunch, he spat on Femi's journal, kicked his chair, and raced to the back of the class before Femi could even react. I don't have nothing against the guy, but when Femi stood up like he was gonna retaliate, he forgot one simple rule: You step to one of us, you're stepping to all of us.

It don't matter who spit on who first. What matters is that if someone starts something, I'll be the one to finish it, unless it's a marathon or a salad. And that's what I did. Kehinde didn't even have to move; one quick nod to me and Caleb was enough. I pushed Femi away, and Caleb flung him over a table. Marcus was filming because we like to watch stuff back; otherwise, what's the point? When we're all thirty, we're gonna look back at these videos and laugh at the antics.

Nobody can square up to us here, and I prowl these corridors like my kingdom come. When kids see me, they ten-toes it, like antelope at a watering hole. If they ain't scared of me, then how they gonna respect me? Quick math, fam.

The only problem with being top of the food

chain is that people are rooting for your downfall. If it ain't Year Eights getting mouthy or Year Tens getting edgy about starting their subject exams, it's teachers tryna prove a point, show you they're still boss. There are one or two who are calm, but the ones who take out their failed dreams on us are still dotted about. Ain't my fault you wanted to be an astronaut and got stuck in a South London classroom. Dreams are for Sleeping Beauty and Martin Luther King. I don't need none of that. I'm king of the school, already living my best life. Nothing else matters.

Right now, though, I'm on my way to detention with Marcus while Kehinde and Caleb are off somewhere eating their chicken and chips. They're supposed to be coming with us. They don't care, though. Caleb's parents stopped answering calls from the school some time ago, and Kehinde just does what he wants. I'm cool with that, even if we're only here because of what he did to Femi.

We're strolling down the corridor when Marcus's phone rings. He starts fumbling with it, panic in his eyes. It's his mum—she's the only one who can strike fear into his heart like this.

"Anton, I beg you, don't say anything about detention." He says it so fast, getting the words out before quickly answering, "Hi, Mummy." His voice is so high-pitched I have to bend down and hold my breath from laughing. He waves me away and tries to walk off. "Yeah, no, I got soccer today; I won't be home till later."

"Mummy, I love you, Mummy," I whisper.

He stops dead in his tracks and turns away to avoid my smirking. "I'm sorry, Mummy. I forgot." There's another pause before he responds. "No, I'm not in trouble at school again. I swear, I just got soccer today." Bro, the way this guy is sweating like a ham sandwich in the sun, it's not even funny. It only ends when, mid-apology, she hangs up. Man doing the whole "I'm sorry, Mummy. I—hello? Mummy?" and then when we hear the phone cut, he bows his head like a child, defeated. No respect.

"Did...did your mum just hang up on you?" This time I can't hold it in; I start screaming with laughter. "Bruv, you just got finished. Man said she left you a one-star review like Tripadvisor." I'm still laughing when we get to the classroom door.

He gives me side-eye. "Whatever, fam. You don't know what she's like," he says quietly.

"Nah, I know I ain't never been disrespected like that in my life. How you gonna let her toss you aside like a nonrecyclable?" I've met his mum; she's not one to be messed with. But that level of contempt, though—that's how you know she don't treat him like a main event. "I heard she asked the maternity ward for a refund."

"What about you?" He frowns. "I'm not the only one going to this detention. If you weren't scared of your mum, you wouldn't have come. You'd be out with the others."

"I ain't scared of my mum, and I could never allow her to do me like that. I just don't want the aggro. There's a difference." Can't lie; my mum would end my world and release a four-track diss EP if she knew I was in detention for fighting.

"How is that different?"

"Because man needs to focus and stay tops out here. I can't do that if she's on my case like

Sherlock." Besides, Mum already thinks Kehinde's a bad influence, and this'd just give her more ammo. She makes it a big deal whenever he comes over that he never says hello to her, and he's always raiding her fridge. But she don't see that Kehinde's like me, just on a higher volume, and he don't care about what anybody thinks. When I started secondary school and all the kids were mocking the fact my dad was doing time, talking about how we can dress in matching orange jumpsuits for Halloween, Kehinde had my back. He showed me how to turn that reputation into respect, and if that means occasionally landing in detention, then it's water off a duck's back, fam. Like hoisin sauce.

When we walk into the detention classroom, I look to Marcus to tell me this isn't a joke. Mr. Benjamin is sitting at the desk at the front. I don't actually believe it. This guy's always coming for me. He once gave me detention for coming to school in my slides. Well, he offered me sneakers from lost and found, and I threw them in the bin. Kehinde still laughs about that to this day. I would've done the same to Crocs and anything

PUMA. Even now, Mr. Benjamin starts on me the second I walk in.

"Ah, gentlemen, thank you for gracing us with your presence. Please take a seat." This guy's voice is so slimy. He thinks I don't get his sarcasm, but I ain't no punk. I pick up the chair closest to me.

"Take it where?" I say innocently.

Marcus is slyly grinning. He knows I'm just getting warmed up like cookie dough. There's a couple of other kids in here with us: two girls in the third row near the window, and some dorkus I don't know. They know me, though, and they're looking up because they know they're in for a treat. Still, I wish the others were here to see it.

"Ah, you think you're funny, don't you, Mr. Charles? How funny does another detention tomorrow sound?" Man's smirking at me like the *Mona Lisa*. Marcus raises his eyebrow, waiting for me to respond. I can't speech him about disrespect and let this teacher finesse me immediately after.

"Not as funny as your shirt," I tell him. "Why is it so small? Out here looking like LeBron James in a crop top."

"OK." Mr. Benjamin has got a fake grin, trying to play it off like a joke, and I would let him off, but I spot Marcus's phone in his hand, subtly recording. Can't stop now; the crowd wants a show and I ain't one to let them down. Can't look weak in front of my loyal subjects, and I pay back their respect by entertaining them. So I look Mr. Benjamin up and down for extra effect.

"Nah, for real, that shirt is a main event. I can see the outlines of your vital organs, that shirt is so tight." I pretend to squint at his stomach. "Sir, are you digesting a bagel? I can literally see your heartbeat."

"Right, that's enough." He's gone bright red, and I can't tell if it's anger, or embarrassment, or that Ken doll–sized shirt cutting off the circulation to his face.

"When you're done with it, you can donate it to the dog rescue. There's small dogs in there that need winter clothes, shout-out chihuahuas."

"Right, that's another detention. You want to try for a fourth?" Mr. Benjamin is so angry his voice is quivering like he's warming up for an R & B feature. It's only because Marcus ain't filming anymore that I decide to lay off this nobody. How's he gonna start on me when all I did was turn up to a stupid detention? I could've ditched it like Kehinde and Caleb. Now I'm here and I'm catching negative vibes like Henry VIII in a group chat with all his ex-wives.

Me and Marcus take seats at the back of the class, and Mr. Benjamin hands us all a blank sheet of paper and a pen. He starts pacing around at the front of the classroom.

"Detention is a time of reflection, or at least it should be. So I'm asking you to reflect; write down where you see yourselves in five years." I roll my eyes as far back as they can go and Marcus snorts. Bruh, I hate that question. I'm in the here and now, fam, top dog like an alpha wolf. Who cares about stuff that ain't even happened yet? The only future I wanna know is what Mum and Nanna are making me for dinner tonight. If it don't bang, I'm going rogue like a stray eyebrow hair you can't stop staring at.

After ten minutes of me not writing anything, Mr. Benjamin narrows his eyes. So I write down that in five years' time, I see myself as taller. I almost put down "definitely not a teacher," but my uncle Fred is a teacher, and it doesn't feel fair to him. And a lot of the teachers in this school are harmless; it's only Mr. Benjamin who makes me feel like I'd rather lick a cheese grater than be in his lessons. So, instead, I write that I always had dreams of being a gardener, planting roses, palm trees, aloe vera. Now I'm just listing plants, even though I've never picked up a shovel in my life.

When I look over, I see Marcus has written serious answers. Talking about how he wants to go to college, graduate in graphic design, become an animator and that. Like, what is he thinking? This guy watches too much anime; it's putting ideas in his head. When he catches me looking, Marcus covers his paper with his elbow like we're in an exam.

"Maybe you could draw a series about a guy called Marcus whose mum disrespects him whenever she calls," I say, grinning.

"Yo, chill," he says, and shifts to cover up even more of his answers.

When Mr. Benjamin comes over to pick up

our papers, he pauses as he reads mine. Then he scowls and folds it up into his pocket. My eyes follow him back to his desk. I know what he's gonna say before he says it. Please don't call my mum. Don't do it, you complete loser, don't call her, don't do me like that.

"I'm sure your mother will be very interested to know how productive you've been today." He sneers. I knew he'd say it. Still, it proper makes me tense up. I can't show him that, though.

"Do you." I kiss my teeth at him and get up, throw my things in my bag, and walk out the classroom.

When I get home, I hang out downstairs by the trash bin outside my building for a while. I don't wanna go inside just yet. I know Mum'll be stressing.

When I can't stay out any longer, I take a deep breath and finally head up. The lights in the elevator flicker like it's haunted, but we're used to it by now. The elevator is out of action every few weeks, and then we have to walk up four flights of stairs. The lady next door with the baby carriage always asks me for help, which I do sometimes. Other times I'm not feeling it, so I wait for her to go inside without me. It's character-building.

When I get to my front door, I take a deep breath, take my keys out, and head inside. I can hear Mum playing Celine Dion; that's the white side of her family escaping from her soul. What will the neighbors think? I'll have to play loud drill music later to even things out.

I'm sneaking down the hallway when her head pops around the kitchen door. Swear this woman's got a sixth sense. She's got those yellow cleaning gloves on and she's wearing the joke apron I got her for Christmas. It says FRY ME TO THE MOON, and it's got a picture of an egg on the moon. It was funny at the time. Not so much now when her face looks like that.

"Anything you want to tell me?" she asks.

I know that she knows that I got in trouble again; it's almost like she wants me to lie to her.

"No, I'm good. Why? What's up?" My acting is Vin Diesel levels of terrible.

"You really want to play this game?" she huffs.

"Do what?" I can't stop it at this point. Even if I wanted to, something in me tells me to see it through. Mum pulls off her gloves and puts her hands on her hips. Battle stations ready. I guess we're doing this.

"Anton, I can't keep having this conversation over and over again. Mr. Benjamin called and told me exactly what happened." Of course he did. That guy would snake out his own mother for a can of beans. "Detention. Again. For fighting. And why do I have to hear it from a teacher? You've got a phone; why didn't you just ring and tell me?" Yo, she is spewing, spitting embers like Pompeii, fam. I just have to grit my teeth and wait for it to be done with. "When are you going to start taking responsibility for yourself? Did I raise you to be disrespectful?"

"No, Mum." I tell her what she wants to hear.

"And did I raise you to be a liar?" Her voice is getting higher.

"No, Mum."

"And surprise, surprise, I then have to find out your friend Kehinde was involved." I automatically roll my eyes. I can't help it; she always goes there. "You can roll your eyes all you want, Anton; that boy drags you around by the skin of your nose." This is when I get defensive, when she acts like I'm his sheepdog or something, like I'm not my own person.

"Kehinde wasn't even in the classroom with Mr. Benjamin when I got in trouble." Now *my* voice is getting high-pitched.

"Great. So he gets you in trouble and doesn't even turn up to face the consequences. That's the type of person you want to be around, is it?"

I shouldn't have said anything. I get out a feeble, "You don't know what you're talking about," but we both know she just finished me with my own words. Let's just skip to the part where she gives me my punishment; hopefully she's too busy with work to follow through with it anyway. Mum's been working on this big project, some women's shelter or charity or something, I dunno.

After a tense standoff, she drops her hands by her sides. "No internet for a week."

My jaw clenches and my hands ball into

fists. *Don't answer back, don't answer back....* Last time I tried to argue, she upped it to two weeks and changed the Wi-Fi password to "AntonIsSorryAndLovesHisMummy123." She totally mocked me; the numbers were so unnecessary. She blocks my data allowance, too. My phone is on a rolling contract, so she just calls them up and caps the internet. No joke, she might be small, but my mum can be an evil genius sometimes. "And you're taking your grandmother to the hospital tomorrow."

"No way, tomorrow's Saturday; I got plans." I'm meant to be meeting the boys for a park sesh; we're going to Telegraph Hill. Besides, I've taken Nanna to the hospital loads recently. She keeps needing appointments because she's complaining she gets dizzy very easily and has stomach issues. The stomach issues I can vouch for—you can tell when Nanna's been in the bathroom because she leaves remnants of her soul in there. She don't need a doctor; she needs a priest to exorcise the bathroom demons when she's done.

"You're taking her, and that's final. Now go and wash up before dinner." Wash up? Does she think I'm a scullery maid? I didn't know I was living in *Downton Abbey*. Mum goes back to cleaning the kitchen, so I slink off to my room, avoiding the bathroom on the way. Before I even get there, my phone buzzes with a text from Kehinde.

> Yo, fam. You chillin tomorrow? Parklife

I start typing out my response.

> Got something with my nan but feeling to ditch her and just come out

Before I can hit Send, though, I see the internet bars disappear. She's changed the password already. I bite my bottom lip in frustration and stomp into my bedroom, slamming the door behind me as hard as I can. The noise echoes through the apartment. From the kitchen, I hear Mum's voice call out, "That's one month no internet."

ON THE BUS with Nanna the next day, my phone keeps pinging with messages from Kehinde.

> Why you text messaging like an old man?

> Mum capped my data and changed the Wi-Fi pword on some human rights violation

> Don't even get me started

> Lol you send out

> When you coming park?

> > Not sure yet

> > Taking my nan to hospital

> Forget her dusty ass

> She's grown, she can take care of herself

> Come park

> I'll see you in a bit.

This guy has no chill. He is sort of right, though—she don't need me with her the whole time. But even if this is long, I do love Nanna.

When my dad went inside, Mum started university less than a month later, so Nanna was looking after me most nights, and she moved in proper when Mum went into her second year. It's been the three of us ever since.

I lock my phone and stuff it into my pocket. It carries on vibrating, so I pull it out to see what else he has to say. But just then, Nanna taps my hand excitedly. "I love these little excursions. You know, when I was a girl, and my grandpa would take me to church, he'd always hold my hand for the entire journey. I wore my favorite white dress. It had little purple flowers on it that I'd sewn on myself."

"Cool." I usually love hearing her stories, but right now they're just a reminder that I'm stuck here while the homies are waiting for me in the park.

"It *was* cool," Nanna says as she glances at my phone. "Stop pretending like you've got friends," she says. Then something hits my senses, a stench that only Nanna's cabbage stomach could achieve. Pungent, evil, like fermented sins. Her eyes gleam when she clocks I've smelled it. Before

I can call her out on it, she loudly says, "And stop farting like that in public; there's other people on this bus." She's loud enough for everyone around us to hear. Then she leans over and mutters, "You can put that away now, unless you want another round with my stomach gas."

I'm cringing so hard. She did not just do that. Tucking my nose and mouth into my T-shirt, I dare someone to look at me. I slide my phone into my pocket and sink low into my seat.

"Sorry, did I embarrass you, sweetie? Farting is perfectly natural. A little toot here and there never hurt anyone." Tell that to the inside of my nose. Breathing in her ancient particles like we just opened a pharaoh's tomb. She's fully enjoying herself now. Checking her nails like she's so proud, while I'm dying on the inside. I swear, if she wasn't my nan, I would've yeeted her out the window.

Luckily it's our stop next. When we get off the bus at London Bridge, the hospital is right there, but it still takes us ten minutes to do a two-minute journey because of Nanna's hobbling. Some people are giving us dirty looks as they overtake us on the sidewalk. Even though I feel their pain, I do find myself glaring back. For real, though, this woman's so slow she's got all the urgency of a dead leaf falling from a tree. I've seen houseplants grow at a faster pace than she walks.

Once we finally get to the hospital, I navigate us to the waiting room, and time slows down even more. My phone is buzzing away in my pocket, all messages from Kehinde, but I'm so agitated from waiting that I can't even be bothered to read them. The room is packed out—it looks like there's only one doctor for all these people—and the man next to me keeps coughing and spluttering like an old lawn mower. I cover my mouth with my sleeve and look over at Nanna. She's sitting uncomfortably, leaning forward. She don't care too much, though; she's happily fixated on a TV in the corner that's playing one of her awful shows. Ironically, it looks like it's set in a hospital. And it is dreadful. When the episode ends and another starts, I kiss my teeth loudly and throw my head back.

"Nanna, you don't need me here, do you?" I try to say it gently. She frowns but doesn't take her eyes off the screen. "If you give me your phone, I can schedule an Uber to come pick you up in an hour."

"Why on earth would I pay all that money for a taxi when I have a free bus pass?" She turns her attention to me, raising her eyebrow. "Wait. You're not trying to ditch your poor old grandmother, are you?"

"No. Well, yeah. My boys are at the park and we might have a kickabout," I tell her. "I would invite you, but you ain't a baller like that. You're too much of a liability on corner kicks. If I cross it in, I know you're not an aerial threat."

"Huh," she huffs. "I'll have you know I was the under-sixteen team captain back in my day. I was known for my headers. I could leap higher and had a stronger neck than you and any of your gang ever could. In my prime, you wouldn't have stood a chance."

"So can I go?" I grab my hoodie from the chair beside me.

"No." She goes back to looking at the TV. "I need you to take me home after. You know the bus schedules confuse me."

I slump back into my seat and scroll through old videos. There's one where Marcus keeps fake-coughing to cover up the sound of his fart, but the cough is always a split second too late.

After a million years, we're finally called in to see the doctor. Dr. Alice has got bags under her eyes; she looks like she ain't slept in three months, and her hair is all ratty with sweat. But when she sees Nanna, she has a huge smile on her face.

"My favorite patient! How was the journey in? Everything OK?" No, I want to tell her. It was about as OK as having a stone in your shoe. And then having your shoe robbed at gunpoint.

The doctor gets her to lie down and starts gently pressing different parts of Nanna's stomach, saying stuff like, "Yes, that does look sore; there's still some swelling." Nanna giggles at the more tickly part, and they both laugh softly. Dr. Alice says it's likely a digestive issue, maybe a bug, which would explain the nausea. Nanna's farts explain my nausea. "I'm a little concerned your body hasn't fought it off by now, but that's not completely uncommon for someone your age." Cool, if it's not uncommon, then we can dip now, go live our lives. Me in the park, Nanna in front of the TV getting the answers wrong to *Countdown*. She has a pen and paper while she watches; there's no excuse.

"Ah, I'm getting old." Nanna sighs and then grins. "Seventy-nine, and I don't look a day above twenty." Lol, yeah right. I'm just picturing Nanna putting "twenty years old" in a dating profile and then hobbling off to a mini golf date with her teeth in her pocket. Dr. Alice plays along with her, though.

"You're still a spring chicken, and once we figure out the source of the pain, you'll be as spry as ever. I'm going to book you an MRI, looking for any abnormalities we might've missed, just to be safe. Depending on availability, it might be a few weeks away, but I'll redo a prescription for those stronger painkillers in the meantime." Doctors be doctoring. I could do with some of those painkillers, too, for the journey back.

I try to ignore my phone urgently buzzing away in my pocket. It's bad enough that I'm sitting here in some dingy hospital. Never mind coming back in a few weeks; Mum can do the

MRI trip. We thank the doctor and head back out to the waiting room. I try to not make eye contact with the sick people we're passing, the hospital corridors cleaner than a same-day skin fade.

In the elevator, I check my phone. Three missed calls and seven text messages. The most recent ones are from Kehinde.

> Yo, wasteman, you still on granny daycare duty?

> It's a vibe out here, Caleb brought his speakers and we just seen some hotties checking us out

> Bell me

All right, he's probably lying about the girls; this is Kehinde. But what if he's not? Girls and music. You know what, forget this. Park sesh is calling. I can't help ignoring Nanna all the way to the bus stop. She's still chattering along, talking about why the supermarket sometimes has better deals on certain days, stuff that is so insignificant to my entire life. OK, this is it, Anton, her bus is approaching. I ignore her squinting at the route number above the driver.

"Hey, Nanna, this is you. I'm gonna get the 343 to go chill with the guys." The more casual I sound, the less she can moan.

If she's disappointed, she does a good job of not showing it. Hopefully I can trust her not to rat me out to Mum that I didn't take her home.

"OK, poppet." She bites her lip. "And where do I get off?"

"Southampton Way. Press the bell when you see the Morley's. And try not to rob any banks or start a riot or anything," I tell her.

"No promises." She half chuckles and nervously shuffles as her bus pulls up. Then she quickly turns to me and reaches into her bag, pulling out her purse. "Oh, I almost forgot." She takes out a ten-pound note and shoves it into my hand. I stare at it for a couple of seconds and then quickly put it into my pocket. As a stranger helps her on, I whip out my phone to text Kehinde.

> OMW, don't ever say I dont come thru

There they are, sitting on the wall just outside the football pitch, dressed all in black like it's our uniform outside school. They were easy to find; I just had to follow the loud music playing from Caleb's speakers. His hair is growing out again; he's been begging his sister's friend to do his braids because she's the only one he trusts. Kehinde keeps his short and clean; man's not changed his style in years. It's funny, cuz Kehinde has a twin, Taiwo, who lives with their mum now and has a giant afro. We've learned not to ask Kehinde about his family; he pretty much acts like they don't exist.

"Yo, there he is." Kehinde grins up at me as I stroll over. I'm looking around and there's not a single girl in sight. I knew it. I had hope that he wasn't lying, but deep down I knew the truth. Oh well. I shake it off as he reaches out for our signature fist bump. See, this is the side of him that Mum never gets to see. "You finally ditched your nan, huh." He nods in appreciation.

"Yeah, don't even get me started," I reply. "That was so long, man; she's so frustrating." The ten-pound note in my pocket burns with guilt, but the feeling doesn't last long. In my defense, a chicken drumstick could cross the road faster than her, *and* I proved that she could do the journey without me. No regrets.

"Is she all right, though?" Marcus asks, barely looking up from his phone.

Kehinde snorts. "Why, you want her number? She's too old for you."

"Yeah, she's fine," I reply to Marcus. I take a seat, careful not to step on Caleb's new sneakers. "Man with the fresh kicks." I nod down at them.

"You know it." He beams with pride. A parent couldn't love their baby as much as Caleb loves his shoe collection.

"What if I did this?" Kehinde pretends like he's about to pour his Coke on them, and Caleb instinctively jumps up out the way. He's half laughing, but you can still see the fear on his face. Kehinde laughs and I join in.

"Nah, you play too much." Caleb admires his babies, making sure they're still spotless. "You can't mess with a man's trainers like that. What's it called when you're allowed to hang people for really bad crimes?"

"Capital punishment," I tell him. Man pays attention in history. Low key, the teacher catches me sometimes and I have to look away. But yeah, history is kinda lit; the Romans were on a wild one. Shout-out *Gladiator*.

"*P*," Marcus says. We all turn to him expectantly. He shrugs, confused that we're confused. "The capital of punishment is a capital *P*," he explains.

There's a couple of seconds before we start screaming with laughter. Kehinde snorts and coughs up his drink at the stupidness. Caleb takes a big leap back to avoid the splatter.

"You're actually stupid, bruv." Kehinde's still choking. "Man said *P*."

We're all mocking Marcus, who pulls his hat down in embarrassment.

"Whatever, fam, it wasn't that funny." He goes back to his phone.

"Funny with a capital *F*?" I ask, and we all start laughing again. This is almost as bad as the time he tried to spell *onion* with a *u*. We carry on kicking it for a bit, Kehinde DJing off Caleb's phone, ignoring the people shooting us looks for playing music so loud.

Caleb requests a song; he's loving Ghetts, who he says is a distant cousin or something. Kehinde pretends to queue it; I can see the screen. Three songs later, Caleb's still pestering for his track. Kehinde's ignoring him, though. He's got his eye on the kids playing football, and after watching for a while, he goes over with Caleb.

"Yo, it's us two versus the rest." Kehinde just walks in and picks up the ball, all confident. Lol, this guy don't even care that they were in the middle of a game. As soon as they start, these two are unstoppable. They're outplaying everyone, the ball glued to their feet. Caleb gets a couple of goals in and me and Marcus make noise, fully hyping him up. Some of the other kids are confident enough to try to tackle him, but he barges them out the way pretty easily. Nanna would've never stood a chance.

Kehinde does a lot less running; he ain't on

that vibe. He's just an antagonist. When Caleb flattens one guy who calls for a foul, Kehinde tells the kid, "Hit the gym, bruv."

Only when Caleb's pretty much floored or scared the other team away, Kehinde bursts forward and smashes the ball into an open net. "That's five-nil," he calls out, high-fiving Caleb.

"Actually, it's only three-nil," one of the kids on the other team corrects him. Big mistake.

"What did you just say to me?" Here we go.

"It's three-nil," the kid repeats.

"Are you calling me a liar?"

Me and Marcus stand up, ready to jump in. We recognize that look in Kehinde's eyes, when his bottom jaw clenches like that. Caleb is already having trouble holding him back. The kid has a death wish, though. Anyone else would drop it and apologize.

"I'm not saying you're a liar; I don't know you well enough. I'm just saying you're misinformed." Too late, the damage is done. He shouldn't have answered back. Kehinde sidesteps Caleb and fake lunges.

"Caleb, I beg you put hands on this kid. You don't wanna see what happens if I catch him," Kehinde says.

Caleb does as he says, holding Kehinde off with one hand and clawing at the guy's T-shirt with the other. The kid manages to tear free. T-shirt torn, and shaking with adrenaline, he sprints for the fence and leaps over like a gazelle. You can see it in his face; his life just flashed in front of his eyes, trembling like he's about to cry.

"Come back and say that again if you're brave," Kehinde shouts after him.

"I'm not that brave," the kid squeals back, making us chuckle. All the others just stand there, staring awkwardly. So weak, they didn't even try to stop their friend getting roughed up. No loyalty, that's the difference between us and them. Kehinde's always got our backs, and we're in his corner.

We go back to the bench with our speakers, and Kehinde eventually joins us, sitting down in a huff. He got called out and still didn't lay a glove. The opportunity's in the wind now, boy.

He's tenacious, though, I rate that. No joke, fam. Tap water, no ice.

We spend the rest of the afternoon chilling out, playing music and watching Kehinde's favorite podcast on his phone. This one's about power and money, and how the trick is to always stay free and back yourself, no matter what, because no one else will. The hosts show us their lambos, so they must be doing something right. After a while, they start listing things girls do on a first date that's unattractive, like when they talk about themselves or try to correct you on stuff. Kehinde's nodding along and agreeing, even though we all know he lyin'. He's never been on an actual date.

It's only when it gets to around 7:30 PM and Kehinde says he's hungry that everyone starts thinking about making a move. Mum hasn't messaged me yet, which means Nanna hasn't sold me out for ditching her at the bus stop, so I'm not too worried. We walk down the hill toward the main road and split off to head home.

Mum's still working when I get back, even

though it's a Saturday. She's got all these papers laid out in front of her talking about some place called St. Luke's. This is how boring her job is: She's a project manager. Two words that combine into something even more dull, like *Architectural Digest* or *New Hampshire* or *dairy-free*. St. Luke's must be her latest project, that run-down community center she's turning into a women's refuge or something. She asks my opinion on it, trying to bring me in while I sort myself a drink in the kitchen. I just give her air-time, hammer-time, time-square, bruv; there ain't no multiverse crossover where I care about something like that. I do want new Jordans, though, so I might show a little interest tomorrow.

SCIENCE IS OUR first lesson of the day on Monday. Kehinde and the others are taking their time to get there. Normally I don't care about being late, but in the back of my mind I'm picturing Mum getting another call from the school. I feel exposed without internet on my phone; a single day feels like Nanna's entire lifetime. I'm walking ahead of the others, hoping they'll catch up. We're already four minutes late.

"Yo, Anton, what's the rush?" Kehinde is strolling behind me with Marcus and Caleb.

"I ain't tryna go longer without internet, fam." It sounds weak even as I say it.

"Yeah, your mum's a snake for that, still." It's hard to argue with that. I didn't even do anything that wild. I slow down my pace, fall back in line with the others. We're already late, so no point hurrying now.

"Excuse me," a little voice comes behind us. This damp kid in our class, Matthew, is trying to skirt around Caleb. He's running late for the same lesson.

"Look at this little weasel," Kehinde says, trying to block his path. I tell Kehinde to allow him. Matthew is a disaster of a human being, the type of guy who probably wears a cape after school. This kid's always by himself, like he was engineered to be a victim. But he went to my primary school, and when everyone found out about my dad, he didn't mock it. Probably because he didn't have any friends to mock it with. The others laugh as he squeezes against the wall to get past us and goes racing on to the science lesson.

When we do finally get there, Mr. Young's already started.

"Ah, good afternoon, gentlemen, nice of you

to turn up." He checks his watch to emphasize the fact that we're late. It don't matter how late we are, thirty seconds or two hours, he'd still make the same joke. Swear these teachers are as inventive as Dwayne Johnson's hairstylist. Still, as we make our way to the back of the classroom, I silently plead with him not to call Mum.

The lesson's pretty boring, other than Marcus laughing at the word *hormone*. Kehinde laughs, too, like, really loudly, even though it's not that funny. Things take a turn when Mr. Young assigns us some group work, though.

"Now, you're going to partner up for this exercise. On your worksheets you'll see a periodic table of elements. Together, I want you to name as many as you can in five minutes." He goes around pointing at people, two at a time. "You and you. Steph, you'll be with James. Rochelle and Jessica." When he gets to our table, Kehinde automatically shuffles toward me. Mr. Young's not having it, though. "Hah, nice try. No, today, Kehinde, you'll go sit with Caleb. And Anton, you'll be with…" He looks around the room. There's only one person without a partner.

"Matthew." Instant groan. Some of the heads in front of us turn around to see my reaction.

"Allow me, sir, can I join another group?" Any other group will do. Yeah, he didn't make jokes about my dad being locked away, but Matthew is some weird kid. He's got this stupid floppy hair and big eyes like one of those ventriloquist puppets. And I've seen him in classrooms during lunch painting little figurines with a paintbrush.

"No, now get on with your work," Mr. Young says, and walks off.

Sigh. Any other day, I wouldn't move, I'd just refuse and put my head down on the desk, but Mum's face and those empty internet bars flash up in my mind. I get up slowly and drag my bag across the floor to Matthew's table.

"Hello, friend," he says.

"No." It's bad enough I have to sit with him; I ain't about to start engaging in chitchat. Kehinde and Caleb are sneering at me from our table. I sink low in my chair, watching Matthew pull the worksheet toward him.

"Heh, periodic table." He looks up at me.

"The only element I recognize—" he lowers his voice "—is the element of surprise."

I immediately put my hand in the air. "Sir, I beg you, let me switch places."

Mr. Young ignores me and says to the entire class that anyone who doesn't complete the task in time won't go to break until they have.

Matthew does a little gasp and starts scribbling away at the worksheet. He does work pretty fast.

"These are all the ones I know." He pushes the worksheet toward me. "Can you think of any more?"

"No," I reply, even though I can see he forgot copper and zinc. He sits there biting his lip while he tries to think of more. I don't wanna lose my break, so eventually I tell him the ones he's missing.

"Thanks." He winks at me.

"Nah, don't do that."

"Do what?"

"Don't wink at me like I'm a girl sitting across from you at a bar."

"I was being whimsical."

"Well, be something else. That was weird."

Something soft taps me on the back. A scrunched-up paper ball. I turn around and see the others are making kissing noises at me and Matthew. I'm biting my tongue as I shake my head at them. Kehinde pulls out his phone and taps out a text message. A couple of seconds later, my phone buzzes.

> This winky weak male brudda wants to braid your hair in a tree 😉

My guy's mocking it. I wanna throw something back at him, but I'm already a month without internet. I turn back to Matthew, who's done filling out the spreadsheet. Now he's drawing something in his notebook. It's a picture of himself dressed as a medieval knight. Even though I groan inside, it's actually not bad. He sees me notice it.

"That's me brandishing a sword. *Brandish* is a funny word, isn't it? Why can I brandish a sword, but I can't brandish a fish or a sock?"

"Yeah, I don't care." Another paper ball comes

flying over. This time it hits Matthew on the shoulder. He flinches and lowers his head, but he doesn't turn around. Totally pathetic. Caleb is grinning, goaded on by Kehinde.

Mr. Young didn't see it, but I can tell from the way he's scowling that he's on high alert. Meanwhile, Rochelle, the smartest know-it-all in the whole year, is shooting evils at Kehinde. I think she's decent; her long braids are always on point, and she's got a wholesome smile when she isn't frowning at us. Kehinde says her personality lets her down, though, and that females are all wired to want attention. He's the only person I know who calls girls "females." He gets it from that podcast he's always listening to. If I called my mum a "female," she'd be shocked for a split second and then I'd be in boarding school till I'm thirty. Anyway, Kehinde says Rochelle's always trying to prove how smart she is by answering questions in class, chatting to teachers, and making friends with everyone.

Barely a couple of seconds pass before another paper ball hits Matthew, this time on the back of the neck. He ignores it and hunches his shoulders as he sinks even lower in his chair. Man's gone all quiet now. I bend down discreetly and pick up the scrunched paper. I can't let them get away with all the fun, not when I got the best aim out all of us. This thing needs an upgrade, though. I take my bottle of water out my bag and pour it over the paper ball. Mr. Young's got his back to us, so he can't see it dripping all over the floor. Once it's all nice and soggy, I wind my elbow, aim it right at them, and with an extra flick of the wrist, I launch it like an arrow. Kehinde just about ducks out the way in time, and it goes crashing into a beaker on the counter behind him, which goes flying. The group of girls in front of it scream, as three or four glass beakers smash to bits. The noise and the commotion are immediate, that whole section of the class jumping onto their desks and chairs to avoid the explosion of glass that's spread to all four corners of the classroom. And Mr. Young is fuming. But surely even he has to admit that was pretty epic carnage. Maybe he'll see it as a science experiment: how to turn a sheet of paper into a lethal projectile while ignoring potential harm to classmates.

"What on earth do you think you're playing at?" he shouts. No such luck. "That's it. Pack your stuff away and get out of my classroom." Everyone's gone silent as they wait for my reaction. On the one hand, I can't get in any more trouble. But on the other, Kehinde and Caleb are grinning, and I know I can't go soft right now. The whole school knows who I am, who my dad is; I can't let some teacher make me look weak. Sorry, Mum.

"This is some dead class anyway." I stuff my books into my bag, knocking my pencil case on the floor. Matthew picks it up and hands it to me.

"You dropped this," he whispers. Man's not helping. I snatch it from his hand and storm out.

I barely get halfway down the corridor before the adrenaline evaporates and what I've just done sinks in. Mum's going to hit the roof. I'm just picturing her face when she bans me from the internet until I'm forty-five. But then my phone buzzes. A message from Kehinde.

> You got that teacher rattled!

Football pitch at lunch

I grin and pocket my phone, gassed that he rates me.

Suddenly, I hear footsteps approaching from behind. It's Mr. Wall, the head teacher, some little bald guy in a stern suit. My legs freeze. This guy's always been kinda cool, and I ain't about to disrespect the one person who can expel me. He marches right up to me, completely violating my personal space.

"Anton, what are you doing out here?"

"I got kicked out of class, sir." He hates it when you don't call him sir. Man thinks he's one of the knights of the Round Table.

"Well, I can see that. Why'd you get kicked out?" This is the headmaster of the school. I can't tell him it's because I smashed the science lab and mouthed off. I guess it was hella dangerous—if those girls didn't jump out the way, it would've been curtains for them. I feel bad for whoever has to clean up that mess; that'll take ages. "Did you deserve it?"

"Yeah, I kinda did, still." I look down at the

ground. There's no point lying; Mr. Young's just gonna tell him the truth anyway.

Mr. Wall's frown becomes less severe. "Good. A bit of accountability, you hold on to that. You're still young enough to learn new lessons. How old are you?"

"I just turnt fourteen."

"You just *turned* fourteen."

"Yeah."

"Say 'turn.'"

Oh my days, this guy's not serious.

"Turn," I repeat. This is humiliating.

"Now say 'Tina Turner.'"

Is this guy for real?

"Tina Turner."

"Now say, 'I love Tina Turner.'"

"I love Tina Turner." I can't help but smile at this foolishness. He quickly grins at his own joke and then goes back to being serious.

"What year are you in, Anton?" He leans in to hear the answer.

"Year Nine," I reply.

"Good, good. Have you thought about your options for next year? You'll need to decide soon."

For a hot second, I think he's talking about girls. Surely, that's not what he means. Do I tell him I'm keeping my options open? Seems a bit inappropriate. In the end, I just shrug. Feels like a safe response.

"Your exam options," he clarifies. "You have to take two noncompulsory subjects with you into Year Ten. It's important for your future. You know that, right?"

Oh, OK, that makes way more sense. Still, the last things on my mind are my exams or the future. I get the feeling Mr. Wall knows that; he's scanning my face like a self-checkout.

"We're going to make time to talk about this, you and me. I might have some space in my calendar in the next couple of weeks. You can come to my office."

Allow it, that's so soft. What are the guys gonna think if I'm sipping tea with the headmaster, talking about subjects?

"Sir, I think I'm good, you know. I can think about it some more and make a decision on the day." By that, I mean, "I'll see what the others are doing and pick the same options as them."

Mr. Wall's not having it, though. He smiles and shakes his head. "I'm going to say to you what my wife says to me every year when she invites her parents for Christmas: It's not optional."

Wow, just like that, I'm holding another L. Why give me the illusion of choice, fam? I feel like Poland before WWII.

He goes all serious again. "Listen, you don't realize how important these years are until you're looking back at them. When I was your age, all the troublemakers around me went on to lead unremarkable or challenging lives, with very few exceptions." My stomach does a quick jolt at that one, but I keep straight-faced like it doesn't affect me. "If I were you, I'd start thinking long and hard about the company you keep. Just a word of advice. I'll be in touch about our chat, so do have a think about those subjects. And Anton?"

"Yes, sir?"

"Don't ever let me find you wandering through my corridors during class time again." With that, he goes striding back toward his office. I check the clock on my phone and start slowly making my way over to the football pitch.

SITTING ON THE little wall in the corner of the football pitch, I can see the others laughing before they even reach me. I ain't gonna tell them about Mr. Wall; all that is hella weak.

"Yo, there he is." Marcus greets me like a Roman emperor. "You ended that teacher's soul." We fist-bump, although they're unaware of how Mum's gonna erupt like a volcano when I get home. It's gonna be fatality, dun-dun-dun movements when I step through the door. One small step for Anton, a giant leap for thugkind.

Kehinde joins in. "You need to work on your

aim still. I can't believe you smashed that equipment with a wet paper ball."

"Yeah, did you film any of it?" I ask. Marcus always has his phone in his hand. Part of me wants to do a watchalong, just for the laughs. Although, if Mum ever sees it, I might as well pack my bags and join a convent. Sister Anton on the run, fam—that's the only place she might not find me.

"Which part? You're gonna have to be more pacific," Marcus says.

"Specific," I correct him. "How can a man be pacific? Come on, bro. We literally go to the same school."

The other two chuckle, shaking their heads.

"What? What did I say?" He looks around, proper salty, always reacting to their reactions.

"You said 'pacific,' man; that's an ocean."

"OK, Aquaman," he says all sarcastically. "I didn't know you were king of the seas."

"Nah, don't do me like that; man said Aquaman." My face scrunches up like I just bit a lemon. All the superheroes, and he chose the only one who would marry a seahorse. We carry on laughing, though, "pacifically" at Marcus, until suddenly the football the Year Eights are playing with hits Caleb on the side of the leg. He looks down and sees a little dirt mark on his pants.

"Yo, don't have that," Kehinde says, egging him on. The kids come over, chasing the ball. Caleb reaches it first. With a scowl on his face, he picks it up, calmly walks over to the fence, and kicks it over into the street. Kehinde's cackling like a *Macbeth* witch. The kids start protesting, but as soon as me and Marcus stand up, they pipe down and accept the ball is lost.

We really do make the perfect team for running the school. Kehinde is the instigator, and kids respect me because they know about my dad. Caleb will throw hands with anyone; man would fight both the Paul brothers if Kehinde told him to. And Marcus is loyal.

Across the schoolyard, I spot Rochelle and her friends, who just witnessed what Caleb did. She shakes her head and goes over to help the Year Eights. They're all calling to people walking past our school to throw the ball back over. I wonder what would happen if I went over to help them out. The fallout would be devasting, and besides, Rochelle keeps shooting us evils.

Kehinde sits down, and we carry on chatting like it never even happened.

School only finishes at 3:30 PM. So why is Mum belling up my phone at 3:34 on the dot? Oh yeah, Mr. Young kicked me out of class this morning. I have to remember that she can't punish me any worse than a month without internet. Or maybe she can? I picture her walking me to school in front of everyone or replacing all the snacks in the house with dried apricots and quinoa. The others are waiting for me to go get hot wings and fries, but I let them walk ahead and duck to the side to call her back. I don't want no dusty apricots.

"Hello?" I say when she picks up. *I'm brave*, I tell myself. *It's just a phone call.*

"I want you home, right now." She's not playing about. She usually says hello and asks how I am. But today is not that day.

"Actually, I was gonna chill with the guys. We're gonna get chicken and—" No, she did not just hang up on me. No respect. What am I—Marcus? How is she treating me like a substitute teacher? I got that sinking feeling in my stomach, like *Titanic*. Maybe if I run home, I can explain to her the situation and it won't be that bad. She might let me off if she knew I was throwing that paper ball at Kehinde.

"Yo, I'm gonna have to head home," I say as I catch up to the others. "My mum needs help with the shopping."

I almost feel bad for lying, until Kehinde says, "Females are so weak. Tell her next time she should just buy what she can carry." I feel suddenly defensive, little prickles of anger in my chest, but I shake it off. I know he doesn't mean it in no type of way, but he's still talking. "Just come to Morley's; your mum can wait. It's only ten minutes more. You can't stay scared of her for the rest of your life."

He does have a point. The food at Morley's is quick to make anyway, and I can eat it on the way home. And Mum's already taken my internet; it's not like things can get much worse. Fine, I'll join them.

"My guy." Kehinde grins as he puts his arm around my shoulder.

When we get to the chicken shop, there's a bit of a line. I keep checking my phone. She hasn't called me again yet, but those minutes are adding up, boy.

"Boss man, where's my sauce?" Kehinde's the first of us to get served. The guy behind the counter slides a small tub of burger sauce toward him. "Nah, gimme more than that. What's with these baby portions?" The guy huffs and slides another tub toward Kehinde, who kisses his teeth and steps out the sweaty shop.

When it's finally my turn to order, they've run out of hot wings. Of course they have. That's like Starbucks running out of coffee or IKEA running out of meatballs. But I can't wait four minutes for them to make more; I've wasted enough time.

"Just wait, bro. It's not that deep," Kehinde says when I come out empty-handed. Oh but it is. I just got a missed call from Mum. The panic sets in, and I start walking away. Marcus fist-bumps me as I leave.

"I'll see you man tomorrow," I tell them. The second I'm around the corner, I break into a sprint. It's a quarter past four.

When I get home, I make sure to take off my shoes as soon as I'm through the front door. Maybe I can sneak to my room and pretend like I've been here the whole time. I barely make it a couple of steps before she calls me into the kitchen. My head drops. But I straighten, roll up my sleeves, and go in to face the smoke.

Mum's sitting at the table surrounded by all her work stuff again. Her lanyard is swinging from her neck and she's got these dark bags under her eyes. She's going all in on this one, boy. I ain't never seen her work this hard.

"Anything you wanna tell me?" She doesn't even look up from her paperwork. Proper cold out here.

"Listen, Mum, it wasn't my fault."

She holds up her hand to stop me. "It's never your fault, is it, Anton? So whose fault is it this time? Whose fault is it that you didn't come home straightaway when I asked you? Whose fault is it that you're in detention, messing around in class? And don't think I didn't notice Nanna coming home alone on Saturday, while you were off gallivanting with your friends."

I don't even have an answer. I just have to sit there and take it, even when she uses dumb words like *gallivanting*.

"You wanna act like a baby, then I'll treat you like one," she goes on. "Starting from tomorrow, you'll come straight home the second school finishes." I picture the others' reaction when I tell them no more chicken shop, or park sesh, or gaming sessions. I can almost see Kehinde's smug face, like, "I told you your mum was a problem."

"Mum, you know I can't do that. I got a reputation."

"Your reputation?" Her voice gets louder. "Lord help me, you did not just say that. Where's the hidden cameras?" She looks up at the corners of the ceiling, so theatrical. "Your reputation? You know what your rep means to my life?" I try to get a word in, but she interrupts me. "Less than nothing. Take it, double it, and throw it in the trash." Her eyes are huge right now and her voice erupts. "You'll be home whenever I tell you."

"And what if I don't?" Famous last words. But if she thinks she can just ruin my life and I'll stay silent like Hollywood before the #metoo movement, then she's got the wrong guy.

"If you don't?" she screams. "You know what, Anton? You want to carry on ruining your life, be my guest." I glare at her. This woman needs to stop shouting. Why's she in my grill like Gordon Ramsay? "Do you really want to end up like—?" She stops mid-sentence, mouth wired shut. But it's too late—we both know what she was going to say.

"End up like my dad?" Now we're both breathing heavy. "That's what you were gonna say, wasn't it?" How is she dropping it like that? We never talk about him, and this is how she brings it up? I know she ain't fond of the guy, but he's my dad, and even if I can't remember much about him, a part of me looks up to him still. "What if I *wanna* be like my dad?" I say. I'm proper annoyed now. She's kept me from him ever since he went inside, and now she's saying I'm like him, like it's an insult, when she's never given me the chance to get to know him! "The guy made a mistake, years ago, and he's still rent free in your head. You're the one I don't wanna be like," I spit at her.

Mum looks like I've just thrown up on her. She shuts her eyes for a second, shakes her head, and takes a deep breath. "Crimes and mistakes are not the same thing, Anton. But this isn't about him; this about you and the path that you're on."

I hear some shuffling behind me. Nanna's come out of her room to try to defuse the situation. We've never argued like this. I'm shaking, though, and I'm still feeling petty. "Well, you're the one who had a baby with the guy. You chose a criminal and now you're taking it out on me; it's pathetic."

"Anton...," Nanna warns.

Mum stands up suddenly, knocking some of her papers to the floor, but then she composes herself. When she speaks, her voice is the calmest it's been all week.

"Your father is the biggest mistake I ever

made, but from that came the greatest gift I ever received. And you can bet that I'll guard that gift with my life. I won't let my baby become a failure. My job is to take care of you." Great, I can see tears starting in her eyes. Now my stomach is bubbling with acid guilt. "And if that means I have to treat you like a baby right now, then I'll do it a million times over." She turns her head from me. "Now get out of my sight; I don't want to see you for the rest of the evening."

I stand there shaking as Mum goes back to her work without giving me a second glance. Nanna shuffles into the room and quietly takes me by the arm.

"Come now, give each other some space." She leads me out.

"I'm sorry, Nanna," I whisper when we make it to the hallway. I don't want her to be upset. Mum's the one on a crusade to ruin my life; Nanna don't need to catch stray bullets. She pulls me in for a hug.

"I know." Her little wrinkly hand caresses me behind the ear. She's always done it since I was a kid. "Oh, Anton," she sighs.

Later that evening, I head to the kitchen for a glass of water. Without internet, there's not much to do except watch TV in my room and take a million trips to the kitchen. Passing by the living room, I overhear my name. Through the crack in the door, I can see Nanna on the couch, with Mum sitting legs crossed on the floor in front of her.

"What am I doing wrong, Mum?"

"He's a good child; he'll find his way," Nanna replies, stroking Mum's hair.

"But what if he doesn't? How do I get him on the right path? I keep getting these horrible images of his face on the six o'clock news. I just wish there was a way to set him on the right track. He has no empathy, no direction, like he only sees two meters in front of him. He's not helping himself." She rests her head on Nanna's knee.

"You think you weren't just as bad at his age?"

"Was I?" They both chuckle.

"Kids respond well to love. I know you did. And you turned out all right."

"Just 'all right'?" Mum teases.

"Fine, you turned out much more than all right," Nanna concedes. She pauses, then, "You know he's not his father."

"I know, Mum."

"He's a sweet boy. And he's got a brain in him, too. He's *your* son."

"I know, Mum."

My eyes are stinging as I head back to my room. They think I'm just some loser with no potential. Well, I'm not. And comparing me to my dad as if it's a bad thing? Get outta here. It's the only reason people at school respect me.

I drop to the floor and do push-ups. It keeps me competitive, little tip from Kehinde's podcast, and it'll show them I'm not some pathetic little waste kid.

It don't really help, though. Mum and Nanna's words keep circling in my head. In the end, I go to bed angry. And as I fall asleep, I don't even know if it's them I'm angry at.

BREAKFAST THE NEXT day is awkward. Mum's got her back to me and has the radio on louder than usual. As I walk into the kitchen, she puts a bowl of cereal in front of my chair at the table. A peace offering. I mumble some thanks, and she goes back to making her lunch.

I can't lie; I'm not looking forward to school. The entire journey there, I'm flip-flopping between having a normal day with the squad and thinking of ways to stay out of trouble.

We've got English as our first lesson, and when I get there, I avoid eye contact with the crew. They're doing the most, right next to me.

Caleb's got his feet up on the desk, and Kehinde's tryna throw Skittles into Marcus's wide-open mouth. Can't lie; I do wanna join in, the king of the schoolyard shouldn't be sidelined like this, but everything that happened last night is real, too. In the end, I stay quiet and chill, nodding at their antics, but I ain't tryna get involved. One of Rochelle's friends nudges her, and they both turn around to look at me. Even the teacher's eyes linger on me for a sec; she can see I ain't hyped like the others. I've barely looked at them. The only person who doesn't notice is Matthew; he's got his finger on his nose, trying to cross his eyes. Like clockwork, my phone buzzes in my pocket. It's Kehinde.

> You good, cuz?

I don't reply. I'll catch him up later. Another ping.

> Why you not joining?

I can feel their stares on the side of my head when I still don't reply.

Miss Lilly gets up then to start the lesson. She's all right. She don't always control the class, but you can tell she cares. Today we're doing Shakespeare; I guess we're still pretending like he's relevant. In front of us, we've got one of his old poems.

"So what do we think he means when he says, 'Shall I compare thee to a summer's day'?" Miss Lilly asks the class.

Rochelle's hand is the first to go up. "I think it's romantic. His love is deeper, more desirable than a day of summer." She clutches her pen to her chest, and for a split second, I'm strangely jealous of that pen. Then Kehinde mutters something to Marcus and Caleb, and they all snigger and I snap out of it.

"Kehinde?" Miss Lilly frowns. "If you have something to say about the poem, please share it with the rest of the class."

He smirks and shakes his head. "Yeah, I was just saying it's garbage, all that 'summer days' stuff. Most girls don't like a guy who writes whack poems."

"Most girls don't what?" Rochelle turns around with a dirty look. I can see the shock on Kehinde's face when he gets called out. He's not used to that. He notices the rest of the class looking at him, too, and he kinda sinks back into his chair.

"Nah, you know what, I'm not even gonna." He don't want the smoke; Kehinde's not great at confrontation. To be fair, he doesn't usually have to be, not when people are already scared of us.

Rochelle's not letting it go, though. I think she can tell she's got him on the ropes. "No, say it with your chest, go on. Most girls don't like what? You got girls here; let's hear from you what most of us like."

Kehinde grins sheepishly and shakes his head. Man's rattled, and I don't know how I feel about it. It's kinda awkward.

Miss Lilly calls for everyone to calm down. Rochelle kisses her teeth and turns to face the front.

"The lesson here, Kehinde, is to do more listening than talking," Miss Lilly says. "You might learn something." I know that hurts him. Out of all of us, Kehinde thinks he knows most about talking to girls. These YouTubers got him gassed up; he thinks he's a Grammy winner, but he ain't even Eurovision quality, zero points on the scoreboard. Always going on about how Rochelle and her friends are a lost cause, and how they hate guys, which is why he caught all this heat to begin with. Part of me thinks Kehinde complains about girls to us much more than they complain about guys.

He's still spewing when we're out of the lesson. And for the rest of the day, all the way through to the final bell.

"You see girls like her, yeah, the ones who spend all their time talking about 'standards' and that, goin' on like you need to be a millionaire to chat to them; she's part of the problem." Everyone nods along. If I'm being honest, though, it don't really make sense. If all girls only wanted to date millionaires, then 99.9% of guys in our hood would be single. The math ain't mathing. Deep down, I know he's just salty because she called him out.

We're only distracted when Mr. Wall passes us in the hallway. He makes eye contact with me and steps in our way.

"Oy, you ragamuffin. You keeping out of trouble?" He's always so animated. I don't get why this guy's insults always sound like he's on a pirate ship.

"Yeah, I'm good, sir, still," I reply. I hope he doesn't mention that meeting he wanted to organize. If he says it in front of them, I'll get roasted. I'll have to do a no-show, and then it just becomes a whole thing. Behind me, I notice Marcus slowly start tucking in his shirt. He can't ever call me out for being some mediocre loser. Even Kehinde has the common sense to pause his rant.

"You're not good, you are *well*," Mr. Wall corrects me. OK. I stare at him blankly. What's the difference? "Whether you're good or bad is a matter of opinion, whether you're well or unwell is a matter of fact. Have some conviction. The English language is your friend." He looks at me and nods, and I can tell from the look on his face that he hasn't forgotten about our meeting. He's just not bringing it up right now. Fair. He continues on his way, ignoring the others.

Through that entire interaction, I could feel Kehinde watching me. I know he's still not over the fact that I wasn't messing around with them in English class this morning. But there's no time to bring it up. It's almost 3:40, and I have to race home to Mum. What is she doing to my life?

When I come in, Mum and Nanna are giggling away in the kitchen over a cup of tea. The conversation stops abruptly when they see me, and Nanna looks at me sheepishly. This can't be a good sign. Last time she looked at me like that, she put her fake teeth in my hot chocolate when I wasn't looking. Mum seems way too happy as well. When she tells me to sit down, she's got a worrying twinkle in her eye. Nanna conveniently leaves the room. These two are cooking something, and I ain't gonna like what it is.

"How would you like your internet back?" Mum catches me off guard with the question. I thought she was gonna ask what I want for dinner or something, and whatever my answer is she'd make gizzards. Seriously, I'd like my internet back very much. But wait. This isn't how she operates. Like, what's the catch? "No, first tell me, what are you willing to do for it?" Ah, there it is.

I don't care. I take the bait. I tell her I'll do all the chores, I'll take Nanna for her MRI in a few weeks, and I'll even ditch the crew for a couple of weeks if it means I can have my data back and the Wi-Fi.

"Anything," I conclude.

"Anything?" She raises her eyebrow. What is this, *Oliver Twist*? "Promise me."

"Yeah, fam, just tell me what it is." She pulls a face when I say that; Mum doesn't like when I call her fam.

"Well, as luck would have it, I've got a few volunteers to help me out with the St. Luke's project." Her smile gets wider. Wait, is this to do with her work? What have I just agreed to? "They're part of a local club called the Happy Campers." I don't like where this is going; they sound like flower-picking dorks. How is this relevant to my life? "The man who runs it, Rob, said it's a great place for young people to figure out who they are. Sounds like just the kind of thing you need, after our little chat last night, don't you agree?" She smiles at me, all innocent- like. Disagree. Strongly disagree. But before I can protest, she carries on, "And they've agreed to let you join! Tomorrow night's your induction. If you stick with it, you can have your internet back before the month is up." She's got to be kidding. No. No way. I'd rather have no internet. "Did you hear him promise?" Mum calls out to Nanna.

"Yes, I did," Nanna calls back from the living room. Snake. I hear her chuckling away from her armchair.

I ain't joining no Happy Campers; my mum needs to get G-checked for that one. If anyone at school found out, I'd be done out here. Man'd have to go on the run, become a wood carpenter in a small town, live off the land and start a new life eating berries, fam. I'm not doing it.

6

WE ROCK UP at the local community center at a quarter of seven. It's just a really large hall with scratchy wooden floors and heavy bars on the windows. Mum comes here for dance classes sometimes, and from all the notice boards with leaflets and flyers dotted around the entrance, it looks like they do other stuff, too. It's just around the corner from our place. I'm sure she only walked me here to make sure I go inside and don't bunk off to do literally anything else in the world.

"Don't look at me like that," Mum says once we're outside. "You'll be OK; I'll come back when it's over. And I expect to you to be here." Is she slyly grinning as she turns to walk away? Fam, there's an actual spring in her step.

As I enter the main hall, my world comes crashing down even further. It's worse than I thought. A group of kids are sitting on the floor in the corner. They're silently concentrating on their sewing. Another group sits around a foldout table, shouting and squealing while they play cards. One girl is eating asparagus from a little food bag she just took out of her pocket, and nobody is calling her out on it. Yeah, these are not my people. There are only two adults. One is a bubbly gal with a Northern accent. She's showing a couple of youngers how to tie a rope in different ways. The other one is some gangly dude with curly hair, who sees me and comes bounding over. He looks like an allergy kid who grew up and stopped eating vegetables. Those iron deficiencies, boy. God, I hate his grin. And I'm sure if I get to know him on a level, I'll hate his entire life, too.

"Ah, you must be Anton; your mum told us you'd be coming." Of course she did. That serpent. "Campers, how do we greet newcomers?" He calls out to the room. "Toot, toot!"

"Hoot, hoot!" they all call back, imitating owl sounds. Nah, what the hell is this? I'm questioning reality right now; they did not just do that. The lady comes over then, and they do this weird double act where they introduce each other.

"I'm Rob," she says.

"And I'm Jess," he says. Then they shuffle around to switch places.

"Actually, I'm Rob."

"And I'm Jess." They both laugh at their own stupid choreographed joke. I'm disgusted. I just want Mum to come get me out of whatever fever dream I'm in.

"We're super excited to have you join us, Anton, and we're super excited to be a part of your mum's project. Volunteering is a big part of what we do here at Happy Campers." Yeah, if you say so, Rob. "We meet on Wednesdays and every week here is different," he says. "Like last week we had a talk from the head of the garden society, teaching us all the tricks and perils of local vegetation." What is this guy on about? What perils? I live in a project; the only way "local vegetation" is hurting me is if someone throws it off the balcony. I just stare at them disgusted.

"Ohhh, that was a good one," Jess jumps in. "We also try to incorporate some skill-learning into each of our sessions, like how to tie knots, how to build a fire, how to gain tools for life." None of what they're saying sounds like tools I'll ever need. Someone needs to show them YouTube—they'll be out of a job. "And then of course there's always time for socializing, too, building on your people skills and inclusivity. A few months back, we had a couple come in and give lessons on ballroom dancing. Honestly, it was just fab!" Dancing with these pasty little weirdos? I'd rather take another look at the garden society. "It's really just a safe space to chill, to learn, to…just be." They're acting like this is some profound sanctuary, not just a dusty hall in South London.

Once that hellish introduction is over with, Rob steers me by the shoulder toward a table with a single kid at it.

"Seeing as you're new here, we've decided to

partner you up with one of our more... experienced campers."

Oh no. Oh no, no, no.

I recognize the back of that head; I've been sitting behind it since primary school. This can't be happening.

Matthew turns around, and his mouth drops to the floor when he sees me.

"Anton, this is Matthew. He'll show you the ropes, show you how we jive up in this hang." Rob puts on this "cool" voice. I think all my organs just cringed.

Matthew just nods, his mouth still hanging open. He hasn't blinked once.

"I'll let you two get more acquainted," Rob says with a big smile, and then he moonwalks off toward the kids playing cards.

I stare at the edge of the table, wondering what my life has become: Anton Charles, one of the scariest guys on the playground, sits with Matthew the weirdo and these Happy Campers.

Matthew is first to break the silence. "Hello, friend. Have you seen this weather recently?" he says with a strained smile.

"We're not friends. Please don't talk to me." I just need to make it through the next couple of hours. He bites his bottom lip and goes back to drawing unicorns or whatever he was doing. After a few minutes, another boy with short hair and rosy cheeks comes over to introduce himself. Matthew looks relieved to see him, and they do the toot-toot, hoot-hoot owl exchange from earlier.

"This is Sebastian," Matthew tells me. "Sebastian, this is Anton. He's my... We know each other from school."

"Hello, Anton. Toot, toot," Sebastian says. He waits for my response.

"No." He must be out of his goddamned mind.

"Right." He looks like I just canceled Taylor Swift. "Well, I was just wondering if you wanted to come join our sewing tutorial. Jess is leading." He looks over, and Jess grins and gives him a thumbs-up. Sigh.

"What's your name? Sebastian, is it?"

"Yes."

"Sebastian, you're a disgrace."

"Err..." He glances back at Jess, who's started her tutorial.

"Boy, get the hell outta here. I'll join your tutorial if she teaches me to sew my eyelids shut. That way I won't have to see you disappointments."

"Oh my." Sebastian looks helplessly at Matthew and then scuttles away like a turtle. Boys and girls shouldn't be sewing together; this isn't an H&M clothes factory.

When it's just the two of us again, I turn to face Matthew. I feel like I need to take control of the narrative, address the giant elephant in the room.

"Look, my mum forced me to come here, OK? Nobody at school can find out. If they do, I swear to God, Matthew, I'll destroy everything you love." I use my big-man voice for this one; I can't risk this getting out.

"You can't destroy my hopes and dreams," he says. He clutches something hanging round his neck, but I can't see what it is under his T-shirt. He's testing me. I can't lay a finger on him, otherwise those *Elmo and Friends* wannabes might tell my mum.

I decide to change tack. "Look, Matthew. I just wanna sit here, wait for my mum to pick me up, and pretend like this ain't happening. I'm asking you, man to man, to let me sit here in peace. Just...pretend I'm not here. Pretend I never walked in here today, and do what you usually would on any other day." I go and sit in the far corner over by the door and pull out my phone to text Mum.

> I've learned my lesson, they're making owl noises at me

> Please don't be late picking me up

Out the corner of my eye, I can see Matthew looking at me, but I hold firm and ignore him.

At twenty past eight, Matthew comes over for another attempt at friendship. If he's this brazen about chatting to me now, what if he's brave enough to do it at school? I've lived in the projects my whole life; I've seen things that no kid should ever see, things my mum shielded me from the best she could. But right now, the thought of Matthew talking to me in front of the others, or letting slip that I'm being forced into the Happy Campers, has got me more shook than anything I've ever lived through. I thought I was just gonna come here a couple of times, help Mum with St. Luke's, get my internet back, and this whole chapter would go completely under the radar. But Matthew's a liability to all that; if the king of the school gets caught with the biggest loser, my rep is done out here. Even with the crew, that's not something I could ever come back from.

"How did you find your first meeting?" Matthew's voice is really soft, so different from the people I'm used to chilling with that I have to strain to hear him.

"Bruh." I stare him down a bit. "You can't talk to me. I mean it; if people see you chat to me at school, they'll come for you." They'll come at me, too, but I don't tell him that.

"Why?" he asks, and for a second, it scrambles me. Why am I part of this crew? Why is this the way things are? Honestly, I don't know and I don't care. Matthew's a clumsy, heart-eyed liability.

"We're just not on the same level," I say. "People will think you're begging to be with me; it puts a target on your back. It'll make your life miserable." I think back to his reaction when they threw paper balls at him in science. "More miserable than it already is."

"Fine, I get it. I won't talk to you at school." His shoulders slump and his lips pout as he finally gets the message. Can't lie; the wave of relief is immense. I feel like I've just been reborn, until… "Can I talk to you here at the Happy Campers?"

"I mean, I'd rather not."

"Cool beans." There's a glimmer of hope in his eyes that I'm tryna ignore. "So, are you coming on the annual camping trip this weekend?" There's a new excitement in his voice.

"I'm gonna go with 'hell to the no.'"

"But what could be better than a holiday with the Happy Campers?" He beams.

"Anything. Anything would be better. Honestly, bro, I'd rather eat hot sand than go anywhere with you fools."

"You don't mean that." He's too bubbly; it's aggravating. "I can read between the lines."

"There are no lines." He's clearly not getting this. "Matthew, I'm telling you straight up. Anywhere you are is a place I don't want to be. Like, I can't make that any clearer."

I can tell my words are stinging, but it's the only way he'll get the message. He opens his mouth to respond, probably something dumb, when I spot my mum across the room. I jump to my feet and go running over. OK, she's had her fun, now let's get the hell out of here.

She's grinning when I approach. "You been enjoying yourself then?" She's mocking it. I'm trying to drag her out, and we're almost at the door when she starts resisting. She's seen Rob, Jess, and Matthew coming over.

"Mum, please," I whisper. "These people aren't normal; I beg you, don't engage." I'm still tryna get her to leave when they crowd around us.

"Hi, Miss Charles," Rob says. "It's so nice to

see you again. Anton and Matthew here have been basically inseparable all evening. We've had a fun little time, haven't we?" Cap. This is insulting.

Mum raises her eyebrows like she knows they're chatting from their no-no zone. She plays along anyway. "Oh really?" She's got her fake enthusiastic voice going.

"We won't talk at school, but Anton implied that the possibilities are endless in the Happy Campers," Matthew tells her. I roll my eyes. Aggressively. "And we can explore our friendship on the upcoming camping trip." Pause. Facepalm.

Rob and Jess chime in. "Oh yes, I forgot to mention it to you yesterday, Miss Charles," Rob says as I mentally fall into the sunken place. "It's a fun getaway, great for team bonding, which I think will help before we all pitch in with the St. Luke's renovation."

"We'll send you the details," says Jess. "We're leaving on Friday evening, back Sunday evening."

When Mum says she'll "consider it," I'm scanning her face like a Terminator. She said she'd "consider" getting me the Air Max 90s, and that never happened, but this feels different. And it's getting me shook, bruv. Nah, relax, it's calm. If I can talk a KFC worker into giving me extra sauce for free, I can make Mum see sense on this one.

"Laters, po-taters." Jess waves as we head out. Mum waves back. I just pull my hood up and grit my teeth.

SCHOOL THE NEXT day feels hella strange. It's like I got this dirty little secret that no one knows, a bit like wearing the same boxers for three days and you hope you don't have PE that day. My heart starts beating proper fast when I spot Matthew walking toward me and the crew in between periods. Thankfully, he passes with his head down like he always does. I'm grateful that he doesn't do anything to hot me up.

Sitting with the others during class, I'm still feeling proper nervy. Keeping secrets from the guys is tough, and I don't wanna give them any reason to suspect anything. I'll just treat it like

Jaden Smith's rap career and pretend it never happened. That's the only way to make them less suspicious, less likely to ask questions and that.

The day goes on as normal, with Marcus and Caleb acting up, being loud, both desperate to impress Kehinde. Rochelle and her pals keep turning around to silently give us dirty looks. I don't care about them; I'm too busy keeping an eye on Matthew, who's got his head down over his work in the corner. He's proper different here than he was last night, way less chatty. If he wasn't such an easy target, he'd be basically invisible. That's the realistic best that someone like him could hope for.

During lunchtime registration, my homeroom teacher pulls me aside and hands me a note. It's from Mr. Wall; he's scheduled our appointment for two weeks' time.

"What's all that about?' Kehinde gestures at me; he must've clocked me quickly putting the note in my pocket from across the room. I might as well tell them; it ain't a big secret. Especially not next to my other big, *big* secret.

"It's Mr. Wall; he ran up on me after that

science class. Man wants to talk about my future and that, something about my exams. It's better than getting in trouble," I add quickly, make it seem like it's not a big thing. Which it isn't.

"Who cares about exams?" Kehinde says, scowling. "Soon as I leave school, I'm gonna get rich, drive a lambo, land me a loyal female, and keep that cash rolling in." He leans back, super proud of himself.

"How you gonna do all that?" Marcus asks, more like he's asking for advice than questioning the logic.

Kehinde taps the side of his head with his finger, saying, "As a man, I'll be able to do anything I put my mind to. The only thing that can stop me from achieving my dreams is me." The others are nodding like that means anything. I'm just glad we skipped over my meeting with Mr. Wall, so I'm not gonna speak. Although in my head, I'm confused, like, "do anything I put my mind to"? What about time travel, magic, immortality, and triangular Rubik's Cubes? And why "as a man," as if the same dumb logic wouldn't apply to women? We need to switch up the type of videos we been watching, for real. If being a millionaire was that easy, there'd be a lot more success stories in the comments.

"Anyway, what you guys saying for Harry's on Saturday?" Kehinde says. "His mum's away, and I heard Jen and her friends are going."

Kehinde's been pursuing Jen for some time. But you can tell from the way she acts that she's not on him like that. I tried to tell him, for real, and he just wasn't having it. The way he's obsessed with her, we used to laugh about it, but now it's just uncomfortable. She started taking a different way home just to avoid him. I think Marcus noticed, too. We've never talked about it, though, and Kehinde has no idea. Right now, he's way too excited to see her. I don't know what's worse, camping with Matthew and those dweebs or babysitting Kehinde at a party. You know what, it's camping. Camping is much worse.

I'm in a hurry to get home after school. I dawdled a bit too long with the others. Caleb's money got stuck in the vending machine and it didn't feel right to leave him. But if I wanna persuade Mum not to make me go camping this weekend, I need to get home quick. So I decide to get the bus for four or five stops, cut a bit of time off the journey, and it looks like I'll make it home before four. The bus is packed, hella armpits in my face like a Dove commercial. I spot a space at the back and race over before some old lady can sit down. If I don't look at her, it's like she's not there. Same rules apply to dirty dishes—and babies who stare at you. Always creeps me out, and you can't even say nothing to them.

As I get closer to the free seat, my chest does a little jump. Rochelle is in one of the seats, and I recognize her cousin in the year below sitting next to her. She sees me see her, says something to her cousin, and goes back to looking out the window. I can't back down now; they saw me eyeing up the empty seat, and it'll look like I'm scared if I don't sit there. Rochelle doesn't even acknowledge me as I sit down. She's acting like I'm invisible, and her cousin is staring straight at me with the dirtiest look on her face. I playfully look around, pretending to search for who she's giving evils to.

Rochelle notices and whispers, "Grace, leave it." Grace rolls her eyes, and I smile at her to annoy her even more. Petty, I know, but I'm not about to start beefing with two girls on the bus. I've seen the way it looks, and it's never cool.

From the way this girl is frowning at me, I can't believe her name is Grace. Must be one of those ironic names. Like Little John or Tyler, the Creator. Seriously, she's so grumpy and scowling like life gave her lemons instead of a loving home. Acting like she just woke up from a nap. Some angry kid.

This is officially the most awkward bus journey I've ever taken in my life, including the one where Nanna blamed her farts on me. We're all aware of one another, and the situation's getting tense. I can feel myself building up to call out Grace-less for giving me dirty looks. Rochelle's still looking out the window with a determined look on her face, and her cousin's angrily scrolling through her phone. I haven't done anything to either of them. Kehinde's the one she had a confrontation with; Rochelle should be angry with him. And Grace, well, she should sue whoever stuck her lashes on like it was pin the tail on the donkey.

The awkwardness levels rise when I press the button to get off the bus. There's no goodbyes or nothing like that, not that I want any from these two. Still, Rochelle's in my class; least we could do is be polite. Once I'm off the bus, I look back at the window, and suddenly they're happily chatting again.

Am I that bad to be around? Whatever, fam. They don't know me.

A tiny part of my brain is rethinking if it's the right idea to get out of this camping trip. Change of scenery or something, maybe I need to mix things up. Mr. Wall wants me to be better, and maybe Rochelle would stop glaring at me. Life with Mum would be much easier, that's for sure; all I have to do is spend a weekend away. A weekend with the Happy Campers. Yuck. What am I talking about? Of course I don't wanna go camping. I shudder at the thought of spending time in the middle of nowhere with those dweebs. My chest tingles uncomfortably when I picture Kehinde, Marcus, and Caleb's reaction. Screw that; I'm not going. Why is Mum doing this to me?

At dinner, Mum and Nanna are chatting away over their bowl of dumplings. I decide to sit with them; there's nothing good on TV and I still obviously can't stream anything. Just a couple of more Happy Campers meetings and everything goes back to normal. It'll be worth it. Man's counting down the days like a calendar.

"Have you packed a bag for tomorrow?" Mum asks, as if she's reading my mind. Nanna picks up her bowl and starts drinking the tasty sauce at the bottom. I know she's doing it so she doesn't have to see my reaction. She knows the Happy Campers isn't my scene. I was hoping that if I didn't mention it, Mum might forget about the trip, but who was I kidding? When it comes to me and my movements, she's omniscient, bruv.

"Nah, not yet. But, Mum, I was thinking, what if I didn't go? I could wash the car and clean the house instead? It's a win-win." I cross my fingers under the table. Nanna raises an eyebrow at Mum. She's an ally to the cause, always was.

"Anton, the point isn't for you to win, it's for you to *learn*," Mum says. "Life is richer when you step out of your comfort zone, meet a variety of people, experience new things." Why's my mum ruining my life? Nanna's quietly nodding along. Treacherous serpent. I always knew it, fam. "Besides, if you're going to be helping out with the St. Luke's project, getting to know these people better will help. Wow, look at that, I guess it is a win-win after all." She chuckles. Win-win for her maybe. Her Mother's Day gift just got demoted from flowers and chocolate to a bag of peanuts and a used light bulb.

I huff and lean back in my chair. I even look to Nanna for support, but she's cleverly avoiding eye contact while she ladles herself another helping of dumplings. Judas.

After dinner, I make my way back to my room, defeated, like Mufasa in that stampede. Flipping camping trip. Honestly thought I could talk my way out of it.

It takes me ages to fall asleep, thinking of all the horrors that tomorrow will bring. I don't wanna leave London, don't want to sleep in no tent. Every time I check my phone, I've wasted another thirty minutes not sleeping. This is gonna be a long weekend, fam.

FOR THE FIRST time in my life, I'm wishing for school to go slower. Bruh, I'm really not looking forward to this trip. I'm extra quiet around the guys today, too; the more I talk, the more opportunity I have to let something slip.

I've still got my eye on Matthew in the classes we share. The idea of spending an entire uncomfortable weekend with him is honestly quite devastating. The way he's looking out the window, staring at the clock, willing time to go faster, is a huge contrast to how I feel. Once or twice, I catch him glancing in my direction. Sigh.

"You good, bro?" Kehinde asks me at lunchtime. "You ain't being your usual self. It's Friday; you should be more excited, fam." If only he knew. I crack a couple of jokes, to throw them off the scent and that.

And then before I know it, we're sitting in the last lesson of the day. Every second that edges closer to 3:30 PM has my insides tingling with nerves. Once or twice, I tell myself, *I'm Anton Charles. I ain't afraid of nothing. People are afraid of me.* Those moments of bravery don't last very long.

The bell rings and I pack my stuff away in slow motion. Caleb and Marcus are chatting excitedly about this party tomorrow. Kehinde is smiling along, but I notice him wiping his sweaty palms on his lap. Wow, Jen's really living rent free in his head, utility bills included.

I decide not to get the bus today. Nothing to do with Rochelle and what happened yesterday; I'm just not in a rush to get home.

I'm barely through the front door before Nanna starts provoking me. Mum's not back from work yet, which means Nanna's reached for the sugar on the top shelf and freely pours it into her tea. She doesn't snitch when I'm home late, and I keep my mouth shut about her sugar intake when Mum's not about. It's our silent agreement. Doesn't stop her from teasing me, though.

"You looking forward to your trip?" She hides her cheeky smile behind her massive mug of diabetes. I saw the amount she stirred in; that drink's sweet enough to give an elephant a sugar rush.

"Nanna, you talk a big game for someone who doesn't hit the gym. You wanna take this outside?"

"Oh please." She scoffs. "I don't need two hips to deal with you." She shuffles around the table and playfully jabs me with her walking stick.

"Nanna, stop, what you doing?" I laugh. She only just started using that walking stick because of the pain in her side, and she's already turned it into a weapon to poke me with. Even though she's off-balance, she keeps going, and at one point she hits me in the rib, on a nerve. I stop laughing abruptly and angrily say, "Nanna, stop." We hear keys jingling from the front, and Mum walks into the scene.

"Hey, everyone," she greets us brightly. Even though her hair is messy and the makeup around her nose is all worn off, she seems to be in a good mood. "What's going on here?" She gestures at us, where I'm still rubbing the sore part of my ribs.

"Nanna's been into the sugar again," I say. Nanna gasps at the betrayal. As I walk away to the sound of Mum berating her, I can't help thinking to myself, *Good!* Less than an hour later, when I'm dragging my backpack to the front door while she watches, Nanna gets the last laugh.

We get to the hall early. Mum's going shopping from here, so she decided to drive me there instead of walking. We've been sitting here for a minute, parked up behind the bus, but I still haven't taken my seat belt off. With my forehead pressed up against the window, I watch parents say goodbye to their kids, while the driver throws the bags into the lower compartment of the bus with all the care of an Amazon delivery.

"Anton," Mum says, turning off the engine,

"I know you don't want to be here, but just make the most of it, OK?"

"Mum, how am I gonna make the most of it?" This is my last chance to plead my case. Maybe if I come at it sad, instead of angry, she might change her mind. "Mum, you know me. You know I don't camp; that's for rich people who want to feel poor. We can go camping at home, just turn off the hot water and make me sleep in the garden." I'm only half joking. It's a communal garden for the whole block; the ground is uneven, and the grass is all patchy. Nobody really goes out there anymore, but even that's better than this trip.

"Listen, when I see that you can be trusted, I won't feel the need to micromanage. But the fact is, you were getting in trouble, your grades were slipping, you were up all night texting, and don't get me started on that little gang of yours." Oh, here we go. She always manages to bring it back to Kehinde and the others. I roll my eyes and reach for the door handle. "I'm serious, Anton; that boy's bad news." Yeah, I'm not listening to this again. "He's going to get you in serious trouble one of these days."

"Whatever, Mum." That's my polite way of telling her that I'm done talking. "I'll help you out with St. Luke's to get my internet back, but I don't need to be here. This wasn't part of the agreement. This is so long."

"Well, I don't expect you to agree with my decisions. However, I do expect you to respect them." Fascist, bruv. I start climbing out; there's nothing more satisfying than slamming a car door in an argument. "Anton, it's not easy being your mum," she says quietly. "I promise you that I'm trying." I hesitate, not fully in or out of the vehicle. "I want you to live the best life that you possibly can, to be happy, and prepared, for all of it. And when I'm long dead and gone, I picture you leaving the world a better place than you found it. There's more important things right now than you liking me." I remember the discussion that her and Nanna had the other night. I finally climb out the car and carefully close the door softly behind me.

Once I've got my backpack from the trunk, I

notice Mum's got out to hug me goodbye. I lean in, letting her wrap her arms around me. Cheek to cheek, I tell her that if a badger eats my sneakers, she's buying me a new pair. She pulls me in for one more big squeeze and says, "You can have your data and the Wi-Fi password back as soon as you get home on Sunday." Then she releases me, and Rob appears. He's wearing stupid cargo shorts that expose his weak knees, and a giant fluffy V-neck over a polo shirt. Man looking like a divorced dad at a speed dating event.

"Bye, Miss Charles." He waves at Mum. "We'll have him back to you in no time." Then he beckons me over. "Come on, Anton, pip-pip, bus awaiting and whatnot." He gives me a ridiculous salute as I climb on.

I do a deep sigh, shaking my head. Mum's holding back a smile as she waves to me. I think I can see a tiny bit of pity in her eyes.

Once inside, I realize I'm the last person to board. I barely have to scan to see there's only one space available. Of course. Matthew's big brown eyes catch mine, and he starts waving frantically. Maybe it's not too late to get off…

The hiss of the doors closing behind me are like nails in a coffin.

OK, I can do this. I start making my way over to the empty seat next to Matthew, shuffling past the geeky, sweaty, excited babble of misfits on either side of me.

I slump into the seat, and Matthew does the same little shoulder wiggle that Nanna does when she's content.

"Hello, friend."

"I told you not to call me that." It's bad enough I have to sit next to the guy.

"It's just that we're not in school. I thought that maybe—"

"You thought wrong," I cut him off. "It doesn't matter where we are, I am not your friend. Don't call me that. Actually, don't speak to me for the rest of the journey. I'm tired; I need to sleep." I lean back in my seat, closing my eyes. Maybe he'll get the hint. I try not to notice him anymore, but even when I'm pretending to sleep, I can feel him looking at me. I open one eye. Yep. He's staring at me. Why is this my life?

"Can I sleep, too?" he says.

"Why you asking me? I don't care what you do."

He keeps looking at me, raising his eyebrows, waiting for permission. I ignore him again; this isn't happening. Except now he's breathing through his mouth proper loud. He sounds like a gust of wind in an alleyway.

"Hey, like, for real, I really wanna just sit in silence. I'm asking you nicely, and if I have to ask again, it might get violent."

"How violent? On a scale of one to two." He doesn't even look scared.

"Why is that your scale? Two. Obviously, it's a two." This is a lot.

Eventually, he does sit back, and when I quickly open one eye, I see that he's taken out a book to start reading. Finally, a bit of peace and quiet.

It only lasts about thirty seconds, though, because now Rob and Jess are standing up at the front of the bus, and, even worse, Jess is holding a guitar. What fresh hell is this? This is my own fault for forgetting that Matthew's not the only annoying person on this bus.

"Toot-toot, everyone!" Rob shouts enthusiastically.

"Hoot-hoot!" The owl noises come back to him. Matthew's slammed his book shut and is bouncing up and down in his seat. Oh God. I pull my hood low over my eyes.

"Who's ready to go camping?" They all cheer, but apparently not loud enough for Rob. "I can't hear you. I said, who's ready to go camping?" The next cheer is louder. Rob turns to Jess, and says, "Hit it."

She starts to strum on her guitar. The timing's off because she has to clear her throat and shuffle in front of him to start playing. This is a shambles. When she sings, I'm internally apologizing to my ears for what they're going through in this moment.

"Today is gonna be the day that we're going on a camping trip. Right now, we'll be explaining how our activities will make you flip." It goes on for what seems like forever. I feel like Tupac walked so these people could crawl.

Once the song is finally over and I've started

recovering from the trauma, Rob and Jess go through some safety guidelines.

"Now, the person you're sitting next to will be your buddy throughout this weekend. We'll be hiking, foraging, climbing, eating meals together, and we'd like to be one hundred and ten percent confident that you'll be responsible for each other." Why say "one hundred and ten percent" when we know that 100 percent is the maximum, at least, I'm 105 percent sure of that. "Mother Nature can be kind and nurturing, but she can also be dangerous and unforgiving." I thought we were going to Devon, not the Australian outback. Bear Grylls ain't exactly shaking in his boots. "Always carry a bottle of water each. Dehydration is one of the leading causes of death among explorers." Funny, I thought it was Jess's singing. "Never go anywhere without telling your buddy or a camp leader where you're going. If you wander off and break both your legs, don't come running back to me." He's the only one to laugh at his joke. Someone coughs. Even the driver shoots him some side-eye.

The rest of the journey is dominated by Jess's terrible singing. I text Mum and Nanna.

> They're singing songs on the bus rn

> I'm not joking

> And tomorrow we're going berry picking

> Try and enjoy yourself, and be sure to stay safe. See you Sunday x.

Nanna tacks on:

> lol.

The campsite is a big, empty field with a few facilities dotted about. The last twenty minutes driving was through woods, with branches scraping the roof and windows on some of the narrow roads. Once we're off the bus, I stretch my back and shake my legs to get the circulation going. Check my phone, and only four calls from Kehinde. He messaged a few times telling me to pick up, but there's no way I'm calling him this weekend. If he hears Matthew's voice in the background, it's curtains.

Rob and Jess have brought about a dozen tents that people have donated. Some of the girls want to have a race with the boys to see who can put up their tents faster. Hard pass. I have enough trouble with duvet covers, climbing inside, finding the corners, and wriggling backward like a worm. Messing around with tent poles and canvas sheets isn't my thing. Obviously, I'm sharing a tent with Matthew; we live in the real world where good things don't really happen to people. I leave it to him to sort it out while I scroll through my old videos.

All of a sudden, a loud, shrill sound scares me so hard I almost drop my phone. Matthew's blowing a whistle that's hanging around his neck and pointing at something I can't make out. My entire body tenses up as he keeps doing it, pointing frantically, and only stops when I hold up my hands to acknowledge I've heard him. Jess has come sprinting over to make sure everything's OK. He explains to her that everything's fine, that it was a precautionary blast of the whistle to warn me of potential danger. He feels safer knowing she's on hand in case of emergencies, and they share a sickening secret handshake before she goes off to help some of the others. My ears are still ringing as he tucks the whistle back into his shirt.

"Why did you do that?" My tone is so calm it's almost like someone else's voice is coming out my mouth. If I had dropped my phone and damaged it, even the tiniest scratch, he'd be buying me a new one.

"You almost stepped in stinging nettles; I felt obliged to warn you." He points over at a small cluster of plants on the ground. Several yards away. "They can leave a dastardly rash, and I don't carry dock leaves in my first aid kit." I don't pretend to know what that means. I do know that was the most dramatic overreaction I've ever witnessed.

"You mean those nettles all the way over there?"

"Depth perception is no joke, Anton. My great-uncle Gregory once got hit in the temple by a Frisbee because he couldn't judge the distance. He tried to duck, but it was too late. He died twelve years later," Matthew says, bowing his head, all somber.

"Why did a Frisbee injury take twelve years to kill him?" I'm caught off guard.

"It didn't. He died of a chest infection when he was ninety-three. But that's neither here nor there. The fact is he was loved. And he had poor depth perception, like I said."

I almost respond but ultimately decide against it. That's what he wants, a back and forth. I ignore him and go back to my phone.

Once he's finished building the tent, I look up and am able to take in the true devastation of where I've found myself. The sun is setting now, and the trees that surround us are getting darker and harder to see through. The grass is matted and clumpy, and everything is so boring to look at. Like quinoa.

This is worse than my worst nightmare. The tent we're sleeping in is a two-man tent, apparently, but it looks like someone draped an anorak over a plastic chair. I feel around for the entrance and unzip it to throw my backpack inside. There's two sleeping bags on top of separate yoga mats. Prison beds look more comfortable.

Suddenly, Matthew's face pops up from inside the tent and scares me. "Hey, roomie. Glad you found my tent flap." Ugh. I don't know why that sounds so disturbing. "You want to tell ghost stories later?"

"No." I zip the tent back up and walk over to the main site. Apparently, this is where we'll eat. There's fold-up tables and benches inside, and another two camp captains or leaders or whatever they're called cooking a meal. One's called Steve; he's bald with a beard. I think the other one's his son, and they work here on the campsite. Part of me wants to introduce them to city life, where they can have Ben & Jerry's whenever they want, and eat authentic Chinese takeout. I wonder if they have contactless cards or if they're still on the iPhone 5. Either way, I don't respect their life choices.

There's only one toilet here, and it's one of those portable ones that you find on a construction site. The inside of it smells like years of discrimination and concentrated sulfur. RIP taking a dump for the weekend. I'm standing by the food tent, silently cursing my mum for sending me here, when that geeky Sebastian kid comes over to make chitchat. He closes his eyes and takes a big sniff of the air.

"Ah, the great outdoors. Is there anywhere you'd rather be?" he says.

"Trapped in a coffin with bees," I reply. He studies my face to see if I'm joking or not and then waddles off toward the camp leaders.

Dinner is a giant pasta dish. I'm more of a rice guy.

Apparently, they're gonna do a bonding exercise after we eat, something about doing impressions of celebrities. Hard pass.

I'm sitting far away from everyone, my pasta bowl untouched in front of me and my jacket on the chair next to me to stop people from sitting down. Apparently, the message isn't clear enough for one person.

"You mind if I sit?" Matthew's holding his bowl of slimy pasta in his hands.

"Yes."

"Yes, you mind, or yes, I can sit?"

I look over to the scout leaders, wondering how long it would take for them to intervene if I threw my pasta in this guy's face.

"Bruh, it's been a long day. Can't you just go and sit with your friends?" I'm running on low battery; my patience meter is wiped. When he starts trying to move my jacket, I jump to my feet. I been too nice so far; Anton, king of the school, needs to come out.

As I'm towering behind him, Matthew's distracted by something over the treetops. I think I hear him whisper, "Barn owl," before he leaps up, takes out his whistle, and starts blowing it, over and over again, waving his arms around to get people's attention. The adults all arrive almost immediately; Rob and Jess see me standing there looking as though I'm about to swing at him. Which maybe I was. I'm not sure.

Before I can say anything, Matthew's gone running off to chase this owl and I'm left with Rob and Jess, who are both fuming. I've never seen them without that permagrin on their faces, and it looks as if it's my fault they've both switched.

"Anton, that's not how we conduct ourselves in the great outdoors," Rob starts having a go at me. I try to tell them it's not what it looks like, but without Matthew here to argue my case, this is all pretty pointless. They tell me I'm not allowed dessert privileges tonight. After another minute of telling me off, Rob and Jess go back to their dinner, and Matthew comes wandering back.

"Anton," he says, red-faced and out of breath, "did you see that barn owl?"

"No, but I did see Rob and Jess come over and blast me because of your stupid whistle; they thought I was attacking you or something. Why'd you go running off like that?" I'm vexed how he's getting me in trouble on the first night.

He looks surprised, his mouth turning into a lit O shape. I kiss my teeth and turn away; I don't wanna see his face right now.

"I'll just explain to them that I saw a majestic creature of the night and I thought we could all share the moment," he explains. "We shall clear your name. I know you'd never do anything to cause me harm." Funny that. Every fiber of my being disagrees with that statement right now.

"Just drop it. Please. I wanna live my life in peace." This guy won't let me be a lone wolf. Lone wolves aren't besties with fuzzy koala bears; they eat their dinner in peace and pretend they're not on some dead camping trip.

After dinner, I'm making my way over to the food tent to get a can of soda. It's too early to nab an ice cream; all the adults are still awake. As I'm passing, I see the others are sitting around a campfire, doing their impressions. If I don't make eye contact, maybe they won't notice me. Jess is reaching for her guitar again, and they're starting to sing along to some whack nineties song. I shudder; I still haven't got over that bus journey. Matthew looks like he's having the time of his life, singing loudly and out of rhythm with the others.

"Anton, come join us," they call over to me. "Anton, over here." No thanks; I'd rather chew broken glass.

I go back to the tent to check my phone. No reception. Not even Kehinde's persistency is enough in these circumstances. I sigh and watch them all through the tent flap. They do look happy, I guess, laughing together. We never laugh like that with the crew, or when we do, it's usually at one another.

After a while, the music dies down. Rob and Steve go to bed, so only Jess and the other one are left. I think I can hear them telling ghost stories to the campers, bunch of babies. I'm living my own horror story right now.

But this is a good time to sneak out. Using my phone flashlight, I carefully step over tent wires pegged into the ground everywhere I look. As I get closer to the food tent, I turn the flashlight off; don't wanna attract attention.

I slip inside, confident that I know where I'm going in the dark. Tiptoeing over, I quietly open the freezer with a gentle pull and grab two ice cream bars. Only when I turn around, I'm face-to-face with Matthew. Oh God, no, not this. Who needs horror stories when you've got Matthew walking among us? I got my worst nightmare right here, fam, nonfiction.

"Bro, what you doing here? Duck out my way, fam."

"I just came to apologize for running off at dinner. I've explained the misunderstanding to Rob and Jess, and they are mortified."

"Yeah, that's great. Anyway, take it easy, I'm going to bed." I'm sweating, tryna hide the ice cream. I try to sidestep him, but he steps as well, blocking my escape path.

"Listen, Anton, I feel like we got off on the wrong foot."

"No, we didn't, because there is no right foot. I need you to get out my way." Too late. He's clocked it. Through the dark he's noticed the ice cream in my hand. He slowly reaches down his shirt, not breaking eye contact as he pulls out that stupid whistle again. "Matthew, don't you dare. Swear on my life, don't you dare blow that whistle." He puts the whistle in his mouth. "Matthew, please, I'm begging you, don't grass me up like that." I'm scrambling now. "Look, you can have one. I'll share; it ain't a biggie."

Matthew stares at the ice cream and then looks me in the eye. He reaches up to his face, and for a split second, I think he's gonna start blowing. Instead, he slowly removes the whistle from his mouth.

"Are you trying to tempt me into mischief and villainy?" he asks.

"Yeah. Sure." OK. I mean. Yeah.

He takes another moment to think. "Well, my birthday is three days before Miley Cyrus's; that can't be a coincidence." He clocks my confused expression. "We're both Sagittarius," he says, like it explains something.

I hold the ice cream out for him to take. He hesitates but then accepts and follows me out to the food tables. We eat silently, occasionally checking over our shoulders to make sure we don't get rumbled. He's got a little smile on his face while he eats. Bless, I think he's excited to be breaking one of the rules.

When we're done, he digs a hole in the ground and buries the wrappers. Not exactly Don Corleone *Godfather Part II* vibes, but it'll do.

After he's "gotten rid of the evidence" (sigh), we join the procession of campers now being sent to bed. Tomorrow's going to be a long day of fun and adventure, Jess says. I agree with exactly half of that sentence.

In the tent, Matthew curls up. I can't explain it, but he even sleeps annoyingly. Hands folded across his chest and that.

"Good night, roomie." He yawns. When I don't respond, he says it again. Now it's getting awkward. Just hanging there like a fart in the silence. I'm worried he's gonna keep saying it until the sun comes up.

"Yeah. Night," I respond. A few minutes later, I can hear him softly snoring. And then I nod off, too.

MAN, I HATE sleeping in a tent; I can't believe people do this on purpose. The birds chirping are so loud I just wanna hit the mute button and go back to sleep. And the ground is so hard and lumpy it's like sleeping on cement. It's only been one night, and I miss my bed more than I could ever miss a human being. I'll never take it for granted again, I swear.

Matthew's sleeping bag is empty when I get up. I guess he has to get an early start if he wants to annoy the whole planet.

When I step out the tent, the sun is blinding and uncomfortable. Looks like everyone's already awake, so I drag myself over to the main tent for breakfast, feeling bare sorry for myself. Steve is ladling food into bowls again. My stomach's rumbling like thunder, and I remember that I barely touched my pasta yesterday.

"Morning, Anton, would you like some porridge?" I know he's tryna be kind, but that's the worst question you could ever ask someone. Porridge is for people who do crossword puzzles in their spare time. I am starving, though, so I'll just have to suck it up.

The only space available is on the end of a bench next to a couple of younger kids. I notice the two closest to me shuffle and turn away from me slightly. Is this because of the incident at dinner last night? They're talking about some card game they play, involving wizards and potions and stuff. They're getting so animated about it, so passionate about their nerdy magic world, that I almost want to try it. But even the thought of playing would get me canceled by the crew. They'd be so disappointed in me right now. Mum and Nanna would be OK with it, though.

Rochelle and her brainy friends would probably find it cool, too....

No, Anton, why you thinking about that nobody? Concentrate on your porridge. First, I slept on dry cement, and now I've got a wet bowl of it in front of me. I shovel the sludge into my mouth, eating solo like an old lion. I'm used to the playground, where people respect me, where kids hurry past when they see me approaching. When I'm with Kehinde and that, I like that people try to avoid me. But when they do it here, it feels more personal, as if they don't like me *or* respect me. It don't feel good. When Matthew walks past and says, "Hey, roomie, have you tried the porridge? It's delightful," I almost miss his company. Almost. At least he treats me like a human being.

I barely look up when Rob calls for our attention.

"OK, peeps, after breakfast, let's get cleaned up, walking shoes on, and meet over by the campfire to start our first adventure." How does he have so much energy in the morning?

Standing there with his hiking boots; the terrain ain't calling for that. "Remember to bring your water bottles, and any essentials for a morning of very merry berry-picking. We'll be back around one PM, so pack accordingly. Any questions?"

Nobody has any; they all just look eager to get started. Rob tells us to regather in ten minutes to head off. As we disperse, he calls me back. "Wait, Anton, can I have a minute?"

Oh geez, what did I do now? I stroll over to him with my hands in my pockets. "I just wanted to apologize for yesterday's incident at dinner; Matthew explained everything. I shouldn't have got so riled up without hearing your side of the story, and it's important to admit when you're wrong. So, I'm sorry." He holds out his hand for me to shake it. Can't lie; I'm actually confused. I didn't know adults were allowed to apologize to children.

"It's cool," I say as we shake hands. Weirdly, I do respect him more for that, even when he straightens up and says, "Right, off you pop. Berries wait for no man."

I still have time to go brush my teeth back at

the tent, where I find Matthew already doing his. We have to rinse our mouths with bottled water from a feeble tap in the field. Everywhere you look, there's little puddles of toothpaste, water, and spit in the grass; it's nasty. When we head back to the group, I notice Rob's gotten changed for our death-defying berry-picking adventure. His colorful windbreaker makes him look like a Rubik's Cube, and those cargo shorts need to get canceled.

"Does anyone have any experience berry-picking?" Jess asks. Matthew's hand shoots into the air. "Great, Matthew. How did it go?"

"I ate the wrong berry and had to go to hospital." He says it like he's proud.

"Right. Matthew brings up an important point," Jess tells the rest of us. "Don't eat anything you find without showing us first." Who would just eat random berries they find in the forest? Matthew, of course.

"They said I was lucky that my only symptom was projectile diarrhea," he tells me. "It was like an upside-down volcano." I did not need that information.

And so off we go into the forest. This place is so dead. I keep stumbling over tree roots and there's noises in every bush, like rustling sounds from animals you can't see. Rob and Jess keep stopping, telling us useless facts about this tree and that flower, garbage I'll never need to know. Very soon I start to hang back. As long as I can still see them, I'm fine.

After about half an hour, Matthew starts looking around, noticing I'm not with them. He comes bounding over to me.

"Berry-picking not your thing, huh?"

"It is not." I can't even pretend to be enthusiastic. We carry on walking for a bit, and I can see him eyeing the branches overhead.

"Bird nest, bird nest, in the tree, keep the songbird safe for me," he says solemnly, and it proper weirds me out.

"Come on, bro. See this is why I don't rate you. Life isn't all unicorns and rainbows." If it was, he'd probably be even more annoying than he is now.

"Anton?"

"What, fam?"

"If you *did* rate me, would the rating be numerical or alphabetical?"

"Nah, you're on a time-out; I've had enough." He always feels the need to talk; I'm sick of it. Maybe now that we're more or less alone, I should nip this in the bud, once and for all. "Listen, Matthew, I don't think you're a bad guy. But you don't need to do this, coming over to talk to me all the time." I say it very seriously so he understands.

He stops in his tracks and furrows his brows. "Sorry, I just thought we could be friends." His voice squeaks.

"Why?" I ask, genuinely confused. "Why are you so intent on us being friends? It's weird." I have to be mean; it's the only way to get through to him.

He bites his lip before responding, and I can see that he's hurt. Good. When he replies, he's looking straight ahead. His voice doesn't have that annoying playfulness to it anymore. "We've been in the same class since primary school, I've known you longer than some of the Happy Campers, and they're my best friends in the world."

That's it? Some tenuous link, boy, and I don't

have fond memories of back then. "But I ain't ever spoken to you like that," I tell him. "My life started in secondary school, and you've seen who my friends are; they actively dislike you. I'm not saying it's right; I'm just saying that's how it is."

"Exactly, and you're the only popular guy who's never been mean to me. Even when the others are being terrible, you've never stooped that low. At least not to me," he says. I mean, yeah, that part is true. True that, Matthew was always chill back in the day; he never made fun of me like all the other kids when my dad got taken in. I ain't gonna say that to him, though; that's soft vibes, and it don't change the present. Our time in primary school is irrelevant. He puts his hands in his pockets as we carry on walking. "Look, I know I don't have many friends at school, but it's different at Happy Campers; it's easier. I thought now that you're here, too, things with us could be different." He looks up at me, all hopeful.

Geez. I need to redirect him before this gets worse. "Well, I don't need any more friends, thanks. I'm good. Why don't you try someone else? There must be someone at school you can chill with?"

He swallows. "I do have people I'd like to be friends with. Like Fernanda, she's so cool. I wish I could chat to her one-on-one." He goes red like a sun-blushed tomato, shaking his head like he's just told me his grandma's secret recipe for cupcakes. Fernanda—I know the name. She hangs out with Ramiro and Santi, part of a harmless Latino crew.

He starts going on and on about how smart and kind and funny she is. And it hits me that the Matthew I see here, chatting away, confident, smiling, is so different compared with the quiet kid in the corner of the classroom at school. Like, it's night and day. Don't get me wrong; he has zero chance of ever getting with a human girl with eyesight or good hearing, even if he does open up to her. He's entertaining, though; I'll give him that. I'm starting to see that he's not a loser; he's just a loner. I never knew there was a difference until now. Still, there's no way I'm gonna sacrifice my rep just because this loner wants to be my friend.

"Sorry, my guy, I'm not the person to help you out. We're too different; it just wouldn't work. You probably will make other friends; they just won't be me." He flinches when I say that, as if I actually hit him. "I told you, I'm here to do my time. Once the St. Luke's project is done, I can have my life back, my mum will be off my case, and me and you can go back to being two random kids in the same class."

He nods quietly, and I can feel myself relaxing now that's out the way. But when he stays silent for the next ten minutes, it starts to feel a bit weird. Somehow I got used to him always talking.

When he stops to do his laces, he's taking a minute, looping and starting again. The temptation to keep going without Matthew is almost too strong for me, but it ain't worth the smoke I'd get from Rob and Jess if I ditch him. I tell him to hurry up.

"Come on, man. Why you taking so long? And why are you tying your shoelaces like that?"

"Like what?" he says, his first words in ages.

"Like a five-year-old."

"This technique is called 'bunny ears.' Whenever I look at my shoes, it feels like two bunnies are smiling up at me." He looks down at his shoes and smiles, and suddenly things feel a bit more normal again. I start going ahead to catch up to the group, who are now out of sight, until behind me I hear a feeble, "Oh no."

When I turn around, Matthew's staring at a small cut on his knee from where he was just kneeling. "I hate the sight of blood; I pass out whenever I see it."

"Then stop looking at it." I can't believe he's the same age as me.

"Too late," he replies, and starts rolling his sweater into a ball.

"Bruv, we need to go. We need to catch up to the others," I say, starting to panic because I can't even hear them anymore, let alone see them. And he's looking pale, like, super pale.

"Sorry, Anton, I can't go on. In case I don't come to, tell my mum I love her."

What?

Matthew places his balled-up sweater on the ground and slowly lies down. He strategically positions his head and, when he's a couple of inches above it, faints onto the sweater.

I'm desperately looking around now; how is this guy unconscious all of a sudden? They're gonna think I killed him. My hands are literally shaking when I pull out my phone. No bars. Of course, we're in the middle of the armpit of nowhere. I'm about to cry; I don't know CPR. Come on, Matthew; pull through. The world needs kids like you. Don't do this to me.

Barely two seconds later, Matthew's finger starts moving. His eyes flutter open. And I'm so happy I actually scream out loud.

"Bro! Don't scare me like that." I reach into his backpack and pull out a bottle of water to give him.

"Thanks. How long was I out?" He starts sitting up.

"Only a few seconds. Now get up; we have to go." I'm jerking my head around, hoping someone will come back for us, but Matthew's got Band-Aids in his bag, and he wants me to help him out. "I ain't bandaging your little paper cut, bruv; you're not a toddler." Now that he's sitting up, he's looking around, too. "I think they all went that way." I point in some random direction that I'm only 50 percent sure of. Less than fifty. Actually, I have no idea. We have no idea. Great. I'm stuck in a forest with Matthew, and we are completely and utterly lost.

I'm breathing proper heavy. The rustling in the bushes got me on edge still. We've been walking for ages, and that's the second time we've passed that tree stump; I'm sure of it. Worst part is I'm getting hungry, and all we have is a bottle of water each. I don't get why Matthew's so calm. He thinks that being a Happy Camper makes him invincible in the wild. He's got confidence; I'll give him that. He decides to sit on the stump, preserve our energy, and wait for Jess and Rob to come and rescue us.

"We're gonna starve out here," I say to myself.

"Fear not, Anton." Geez, why's he talking like one of the three musketeers? Man's not taking our imminent danger seriously enough. "They don't call me a master hunter for nothing." Bruh. Only the beginning part of that statement is true. I'm pretty sure he couldn't hunt a moth.

"Have you ever caught an animal?" I'm trying to stay hopeful.

"Caught? Yes. Killed? No. That would be inhumane." He lowers his voice like he's narrating a nature documentary. "The real trick is patience. You find a squirrel, then follow it around until it dies of natural causes. And if we're lucky, we get to see it in its natural habitat, interacting with other squirrels. Now isn't that one of life's greatest gifts?"

"No, life's greatest gift would be for us not to be lost in the woods right now." I think *I'm* about to die from natural causes. I don't know why I bother. The idea of sleeping out here is almost as bad as starving to death. The fear in my chest becomes low-key rage whenever I look at him. Why did he have to faint like that? Getting me rattled. I thought he was gonna die on my watch. Over the tiniest graze.

"Bro, you're actually so moist it's unreal."

"Thanks." He smiles to himself. "Some of my

favorite things are moist. Lemon drizzle, the nose of a puppy, the condensation on a fresh carton of chilled orange juice."

"Bruv, it's not a compliment. Stop taking it as a compliment," I snap. Won't even let me insult him properly. I tell him I want to carry on walking. In my mind, the longer we sit around, the more chance an animal has of tracking us. I can't believe this is how I die. With flipping Matthew, in the woods, unshowered and scared.

When we get to a small patch of forest that's got fewer trees, I notice him looking up at the sky. He smiles and tells me he has an idea. "We're saved."

"Yeah?" I come running over to see what he's looking at. It's just blue sky.

"We can wait for the sun to go down, and I'll try to locate the northern star to navigate us back to the tent." Fam. He does the shoulder wiggle. I'm looking at him with the same dirty look I gave my bowl of porridge this morning.

"We ain't waiting for nighttime; that's a stupid idea. And stop wiggling your shoulders like the Shaq GIF." I don't know whether to laugh or cry at this point. I'm rubbing the corners of my eyes.

"Anton?"

"Yeah."

"When you called me moist earlier, you said it in reference to me losing consciousness. You said it was an insult." Oh, here we go. I'm not even addressing the way he said "losing consciousness," like a maiden in a tight corset, bruv. My guy hurt his knee and fainted. And why does he want to talk about everything? He's too into his feelings; we don't need to talk about emotions. "I just wanted to know what it means to be moist, that's all."

I frown while I think about the right answer; this could be a turning point.

"There's levels to this," I tell him. I feel like some old granddad imparting wisdom under a lemon tree. "The lowest level of being moist is, like, guys who wear flip-flops in the city or people who wear a helmet when they cycle."

"But helmets keep you safe."

I roll my eyes. "Yeah, and so does that whistle you wear around your neck; it's still moist." He's leaning in, concentrating on every word. I carry on, "Mid-level moist is for grown adults who still say mummy and daddy or people who take dance-offs seriously."

He's nodding, his mouth a tiny bit open. "Wow. And what would the top levels of moist include?" Bare fascinated.

"Good question, Matthew. Let me ask you, what were the first three things you did this morning?"

"Let's see, I had my morning tinkle, singing ABBA, of course."

I roll my eyes. "Of course."

"Then I walked around the tent, barefoot, because I like how the fresh grass feels beneath my tootsies. It makes me feel closer to nature."

"Shout-out nature."

"Yeah, and then I asked Camp Leader Steve for a hot chocolate with marshmallows, but he didn't have any, so I made a promise in my heart to be passive aggressive to him for the rest of the day. I'm not proud of that one, but a promise is a promise." When he balls his stubby hand into a fist, it's like looking at an angry toddler.

"Matthew, everything you just said is among the highest levels of moistness anyone's ever heard. Everything."

He nods, and I can see his face is still thinking. His little frown is getting heavier and heavier. "Surely my moisture is relative." Pause. "Therefore, it must be subjective. So who decides the definitions?"

"I don't know. Cool people, or society, it don't matter." This guy's always questioning stuff. Sometimes I don't wanna think about the answer.

We slow down, still carrying on in the same vague direction, mostly in silence. The shade is definitely welcome, and in the heat, I wrap my T-shirt around my shoulders. OK, I think I need a water break. I take out my hoodie and lay it on the ground to sit on. Matthew goes to join me but catches my eye and decides to sit on his own sweater instead.

After a couple of gulps of water, I feel more lively. Still angry and lost, sure, but I'm not super thirsty like before. Although something is tickling the back of my neck. I whip around at Matthew, thinking maybe he's pulling a prank or something, but he's still sitting a few feet away, inspecting a ladybug that's landed on his arm. The tickling starts again, so I slap it. Immediately, there's a sharp pain where I just hit. I scream out loud, making Matthew yell and duck.

"Argh, stupid nature!"

"Oh, my goody gosh, Anton, are you OK?" He comes running over to check my neck. "It's a beesting. Here, let me take the stinger out."

"Hell no, don't come near me." I shrug him off. The last thing I want are his soft hands touching me.

"But you could be allergic, or it could get infected. That looked like a carpenter bee; I could tell by the wings. Please, let me just take a peek." He tries to step behind me, but I shuffle around to face him.

"I said no. I don't want your help, fam; real men have to tough it out sometimes."

"Real men accept help," Matthew mutters under his breath, but he doesn't say anything else after that. What does he know about being a real man? I've seen him sing into a hairbrush with his eyes closed.

I get up and carry on walking, but the pain is throbbing, making it hard to concentrate on stuff. I feel myself getting out of breath very quickly. Then my heart starts beating weird; it's too fast. When I try to mention it to Matthew, my tongue isn't working properly, either. He startles when he sees my face, bare analyzing it and that.

"Anton, are you OK?" His genuine concern is getting me more panicky. "Anton?" Now my throat is getting tighter. It's happening so quick I don't even have time to think about my death. My knees crumple underneath me. I'm gasping for air like a fish, colorful spots in my vision. I love you, Mum. The last thing I see before things go dark is Matthew frantically reaching into his backpack.

"ANTON?" HE'S STANDING over me looking nervous. My heart is still quick, and my arms and legs feel totally weak. But I'm alive. I pinch myself to make sure. Damn, I'm actually alive. I'd punch the air if I could. The relief makes me want to pass out again.

"What happened?" I say, my voice groggy like I just been to a football match.

"I think you had an allergic reaction to the beesting." Matthew's still worried, biting his lip, and I can see sweat patches on his shirt that weren't there before. "I had my EpiPen with my first aid kit." He gestures to a little green box lying open, with bandages scattered around. "I hope you don't mind; I had to inject it into your thigh." My hand gropes around, and yeah, the top of my thigh feels badly bruised where he jabbed me. I should be dead, but he saved me.

I'm honestly speechless. I get to see Mum again. Bruv, I'm gonna hug her so tight. And Nanna. Then Rochelle's face pops into my mind, and I force it down. Again. Think about how I'll be able to chill with the guys at school on Monday instead.

After a few gulps of water, I let Matthew pull me to my feet. I still can't fully articulate how grateful I am to be alive. I keep opening my mouth to tell him, but the emotion's too much.

"Who would've thought that berry-picking would be so perilous, eh?" Matthew says as we shuffle along. "I can't believe we both fainted. Hashtag twinning."

"No," I correct him, "*you* fainted. I almost died." How is he tryna compare the levels of urgency?

My legs go still when we suddenly hear voices in the distance.

"Matthew, you hear that?" My heart is

electric right now, hammering away inside me. He squeals with delight. Where are the voices coming from? In front of us? Behind us? Matthew's shouting back, and I try to shout, too, but my throat is still scratchy and painful. But the people don't sound like they're getting any closer, if anything they're getting farther away. *Think, Anton, think.* We need to be louder. And that's when it hits me. Tied around Matthew's neck.

"Dude, your whistle. Blow your whistle."

"Why, where's the danger?" He ducks down.

I almost laugh, but this is urgent. There's absolutely no way I'm spending the night in the forest after that ordeal. "No, you fool, so they can hear us!"

Matthew starts blowing then, and the shrill noise echoes through the trees. The voices get louder and louder, and then I see it. A pop of color in the distance. Rob's stupid, geeky windbreaker.

Back at the campsite, people are just finishing their lunch. Apparently, we were lost in the wilderness for only an hour, but that can't be right. After Rob and Jess have checked us both over, me and Matthew sit together and wolf down Steve's spaghetti. And I can't even lie; it's the best thing I've eaten in my whole life.

After lunch, Rob starts reading aloud from his clipboard like a medieval jester making an announcement. All he's missing is the silly hat. The shorts can stay the same. He says we've got two choices for our afternoon activity. "One group will go climbing, while the other group will visit Steve's petting zoo," he says. My hand goes straight up for the petting zoo.

"You scared of heights?" Matthew teases next to me.

"Nah. I just like petting zoos. Me and animals go way back." Not strictly true. There aren't many things I dislike more than heights, but I ain't about to let that slip. "Why aren't *you* going climbing?" I ask when I see his hand is up for the zoo, too.

"Well, I *am* scared of heights." He says it just like that, almost proud. This guy, man. "And plus, you're my camping buddy." Technically true. If he went off climbing, I'd be doing this all alone. It's not like me and Sebastian have a lot to talk about.

Jess takes the climbers off, while Rob and Steve lead us down a little path behind the food tent. I'm looking out for a farm or something, but instead it's just a little hut. Horror films have warned me not to go inside places like this.

"All right, you lot, a few rules. The snakes aren't venomous, but you do need to be very careful when handling them," Steve says as we all gather outside.

Hehe, say what now?

"And no sudden movements when you're holding the tarantulas; they don't respond well to that kind of fear. If one bites, it probably won't kill you; however, it can cause a nasty swelling. Is that all clear?" He starts leading everyone in, except my feet are glued to the ground. On a list of things I'm more scared of than heights? Yeah, spiders is top. So thank you, next, nuh-uh, you man are trippin'.

"What's up?" Matthew and Sebastian come over.

"Bruh, when they said 'petting zoo,' I was

thinking more llamas and goats and stuff. Man said tarantulas. I ain't going in there, fam."

"You're scared of spiders?" Matthew asks.

I think about denying it, but really what's the point? Besides it's only Matthew—not like he's gonna taunt me for it.

"Yeah, have been my whole life." I look at the ground.

"Since before you were born?" Sebastian asks.

I immediately look back up. "What? No. What's wrong with you? Get out of here, man." Sebastian toddles off toward the death hut, and then it's just me and Matthew outside.

"I didn't know you had an irrational fear of spiders," Matthew says. He smiles slyly. "I thought you and animals go way back."

"Bruh, a fear of things that can hurt you ain't irrational. It's very rational," I tell him.

"You're right. You're absolutely right; I'm sorry." Matthew holds his hands up. It feels weird to have someone apologize like that when you disagree. Kehinde never reacts that way when people call him out. He just goes round and round in circles, getting louder and louder until you drop the subject. "How about we conquer our fears together?" Matthew suggests. I must be pulling a face, because he quickly says, "Hear me out. I help you with the spiders, and in return you can help me get over my phobia of heights."

I mean, I'm still not convinced, but Matthew's so ready to confront his fears I can't not do it. I don't want him to look braver than me.

"It's a deal." I reach out and shake his hand.

"Great. And if all goes well, you can help me with other things that scare me," he says.

"Oh yeah? Like what?" I ask.

"Well, I can't stand the sight of blood—that you already know—and I'm terrified of people who blow bubbles. I don't like airplanes, either; flying freaks me out, but that's probably linked to my vertigo." Pause, rewind it back.

"Did you say blowing bubbles? That's literally the most harmless thing."

"You've clearly never got soapy water in your eye. Let me tell you, it's no picnic. In fact, it ruins picnics."

"OK." I can't tell if he's being serious or not. "That's low-key kinda funny."

"What's funny about splashing soap in your eye and stepping in a bowl of pudding and farting in front of your grandparents?"

"Lol. Why did you fart, though?"

"I was spooked!"

OK, we're proper laughing now. I feel a bit better.

Matthew looks between me and the hut. "I believe in you. You literally almost died this morning, and you got right back up like a lion." He makes it sound way more heroic than it actually was. Especially as he was the one who saved me. I suppose he has a point, though. "I'm going in," he says. "See you in there?" And then he joins Sebastian inside.

OK, Anton, it's a bug. Just a little bug.

It's not, though.

One of my only memories of my dad is from before he went inside, when I was seven or eight. We were in a friend's garden and a spider crawled across my hand. I was screaming, thinking it was gonna bite me, and my dad got vexed. He caught it in a cup and made me stand still as he dashed it on me. He said it would make me man up. I've hated spiders ever since, and I'm still not a fan of barbecues.

I shake my head to get rid of the memory. Whatever, I got this. Matthew's in there, and I'm braver than him. Sebastian, too. I'm definitely not gonna be shown up by this brudda; that kid's not just moist, he's drenched. Deep breath. I tiptoe toward the door. I don't hear no screaming, just excited chatter. Cool. Let's go.

Inside the hut is pretty dark, and the place smells damp. One camper is holding a little snake in her fingers, her mouth open as the thing twists itself around her hand. I shudder. Not a huge fan of snakes, either. I turn away and watch other campers crowd around glass boxes and tanks, full of creatures that belong in a horror film.

Then I notice Steve. He's standing in the corner, a group of kids huddled around him, holding the dirtiest, hairiest, thickest spider I've ever seen. My eyes are fixed on it as a shiver runs down my back. The way its individual legs move, like the thing is only half rendered or something, adds to the creepiness of it. He starts to pass it around the group and they take it in turns, carefully holding it in cupped hands, not moving, like they're holding a bomb. When it gets to Matthew, I watch him lift the thing up to look more closely. His funeral.

He spots me and gestures me to come over.

I shake my head; there's no way I'm going over there. Then he gently holds it up to one of the younger campers, and she timidly pokes out a finger to stroke it. Imagine, the spider's so big she can stroke it. Like a cat.

Fine, I'm not gonna be shown up like that. My knees feel heavy as I make my way over. Matthew smiles at me as I approach, like a mother introducing her newborn baby to its older sibling. I close my eyes tight and hold out my hands as if I'm some Dickensian orphan. Matthew chuckles because I'm so far away, and he literally has to walk over to me.

"Matthew, I beg you don't play about with that thing," I tell him, my entire body seizing up. "I knew I should have gone climbing."

"Nah, you got this." His voice is soft, trying to encourage me.

I grit my teeth hard when I feel the tickles in my palm; my jaw is completely stuck. Then I'm holding the weight of it; this spider is so jacked. Opening one eye, I see the monster in my cupped hands. I start breathing in little bursts like I'm giving birth, and Matthew nods in encouragement.

"That's it; you're doing fine. Just breathe." I'm nodding back to him, and after ten seconds, I tell him to take it back. He scoops it up immediately, and all the campers standing around start clapping for me, congratulating me and that. I'm beaming, bruv; I can't help it. These kids are so wholesome, like, so safe.

After the adrenaline calms down a bit, and Steve has put the tarantula safely away, I'm able to walk around and look in some of the other enclosures. There are two boas, thick things that could eat a car; the tarantula; three lizards; and a rabbit cage. The snakes probably eye up that rabbit cage every night, boy, some beta animals. Sebastian's favorite, of course.

Once we're back at the camp, Rob comes over to me and Matthew holding a clipboard and a pen. He looks like a real adult for once; he's got his serious face on, not moving like some overgrown kid who may or may not be obsessed with dolphins.

"Ah, there you two are," he says, like he's only just seen us. I look around. We're in an open tent, ain't exactly a dozen places where we could be hiding. "I wanted to talk to you two about St. Luke's." He pulls up a chair but turns it backward and straddles it like a horse. It's a chair, bro; why sit on it like that? The engineering is tried and tested. "Now, Anton, I know how important this is to your mum, and I promised her all the Happy Campers would help out every Saturday until it's completed."

"Thanks, I guess," I mutter, although I still don't know that much about the project.

"We're going to be helping with the decorating, and Jess and I would like the two of you to have a more specific role on the project. We want to give you your own room to assist on; it'll be like a quiet zone for families, and we think you'd be perfect. You've shown great teamwork and problem-solving skills together today." Matthew blushes and does a pouty smile. "How does that sound?"

I don't know what to say; Mum's gonna be so gassed when I tell her. I know she's been stressing about this project for some time; she's always going on about how personal it is to her, even if I don't really get why. It's pretty cool of the Happy Campers to volunteer their time; I'm starting to see them a bit differently. Still weird, but they're being selfless; I won't forget that. Mum already knows I'll be helping out every week, but this feels extra special. And it's kinda cool Rob and Jess are trusting me with this. Although my veins go a bit cold when I think about telling Kehinde that all my Saturdays will be taken. Maybe I can just tell him that Mum's making me do it. Which is kind of true.

I CAN HEAR the clanging bowls and chitchat that means dinner's been served. I slowly retreat from my tent, where I've been napping, like a groggy bear coming out its cave. As I'm walking up to the group, Rob and Matthew come over, asking me how I'm feeling after my eventful day.

"Yeah, I'm all right, you know," I tell them. The food is some kinda boiled cubes of potato and minced meat, which would usually be scraped straight into the bin, like corned beef. Hasn't the cow been through enough, bruv? But right now it tastes so good, despite a criminal lack of seasoning. I'm sitting next to Matthew and Sebastian, who are going on and on about that game they play, something about goblins and wizards. How this guy saved my life, I'll never understand; he can't even save a girl's number into his phone.

After food, everyone starts heading over to the campfire for the last night of lame singing and childish ghost stories. I pull Matthew aside.

"Look, about today," I tell him, "I never got to thank you."

He looks hella awkward, rubbing the back of his head as he blushes. "I'm sure you would've done the same for me in a life-or-death situation."

Questionable. But I can't ignore what he did. Nanna always told me there's a lot to be said about doing the honorable thing. Can't lie; I wasn't super helpful when he passed out, especially as he saved my life just after, but it's not too late for me to do the honorable thing now. "Well, if there's any way I can pay you back, I literally owe you my life." Maybe I can buy him a Lego set or something, or a new whistle.

"You can be my best friend at school?" he says hopefully.

"Nah, it has to be something realistic," I tell

him. He can't save my life just for me to throw it all away the second I'm back with Kehinde and them man. Matthew's head drops, but I can see him trying to think of something else. "Sleep on it, and let me know tomorrow."

The rest of the night is bearable. I don't join in with the singing, and Jess's guitar playing still makes my eyes water. Even though she definitely doesn't have Drake in her arsenal, I decide to sit with them for a bit. During the ghost stories, mostly about haunted museums or something dumb, Matthew leans in next to me and whispers, "Anton, this is moist, isn't it?" I smile to myself and nod. "Medium- level?" he asks. I tell him that it's only low-level because they're children.

When we all trudge off back to our tents, I can feel emotion radiating out of me. My bed, my house, Mum, and Nanna are all waiting for me, and I guess despite everything, this trip hasn't been that bad. I fall asleep within minutes, despite Matthew's light snoring and the hard ground I'm sleeping on.

The bus is running late the next day, which gives us a bit longer to do the morning activities. Jess is organizing climbing again, for anyone who wants to do it, and I remind Matthew about our deal from yesterday to face our fears. I'm not doing it, obviously—the mammoth-size spider was enough for me—but he gulps and bravely nods, as if he's Kanye's PR agent gearing up for a new day.

It's actually not that deep. The wall isn't super high; it's only three of me stacked upward, and you're proper harnessed in. That doesn't stop Matthew from screaming the entire way down, his face contorted under his helmet like he's genuinely convinced he's gonna die. I'm tryna be supportive, telling him it's OK. I do have to turn away to hide my laughter when he cries, "Oh Mother, my mother, do not forsake me."

Once he's back on the ground, legs trembling and tears in his eyes, I rush over.

"You good, bro?"

"Yeah," he gasps. "That was exhilarating." Behind him, the little girl from the petting zoo calmly rappels down the wall, her expression almost bored as she nears the bottom. "Let's go back to camp; I could do with a chamomile tea."

Matthew's still shuddering as we head back. As highly ridiculous as that was, he did go through with it. Fair play to him.

Some of the youngers are playing cards as we wait for the bus to arrive. One of them asks if I want to join in, and I politely tell him I'll watch. I don't really know any card games other than blackjack.

When the driver eventually pulls up, I'm ready to get back to civilization. Saying that, this trip was pretty eventful; I ain't mad at it.

After we've packed everything down and said thanks to Steve and his son, I'm waiting with my bag by the bus when Rob comes around the corner.

"Good job this weekend, Anton," he says. I catch myself smiling at him and rein it in. Before I go to step onto the bus, he gestures for me to wait a sec. "I wanted to let you know that

Matthew saved you a seat on the journey here. He's friends with everyone in the troop, and lots of kids wanted to sit with him, but he's very selective about who he opens up to, who he can be himself around. You must be doing something right if he's chosen you as that person."

I nod, not really getting why he's telling me this, and he lets me go. As I store my bag and board the bus, I'm still thinking about what Rob just said. For whatever reason, Matthew trusts me. I don't want that weight on my shoulders, but maybe I could help him find someone else to open up to instead. Pause. That gives me an idea on how I can pay him back for yesterday.

I take an empty two-seater near the back, deep in thought. Sebastian comes down the aisle and starts eyeing up the space next to me.

"Not on your life," I tell him. I've already got one Matthew; I'm not in the market for two. He does a little whimper and waddles off somewhere else, looking like a mother goose. When Matthew comes over, I move my jacket aside so he can sit down. We have unfinished business.

"I've thought of what I can do for you.

Something to pay you back for saving my life. Something realistic that I think can help you out," I tell him as we finally start driving.

"Really?" His eyes light up like I've just promised him Taylor Swift tickets.

"Yeah, I've been thinking about you and that girl you like."

"Sweet Fernanda?"

"Yeah. Chill." I shake my head. Where was I? "I can't force her to like you, but I can teach you how to be more likable. I can make you cool."

He starts contemplating the offer. "Well, cool is subjective. Like, I think it's cool that I can identify several types of bees." It's not. "I mean, thank you for your offer," he says quickly when he sees my face. "How will you go about sculpting me in your image?"

"I was thinking maybe I could coach you after school hours, just one day a week. And we have to see each other at Happy Campers and when we're doing the St. Luke's project anyway, so I can coach you then, too."

Now he's nodding along, stroking his chin. "Well, she is funny, and lovely, and smart, and I do need help talking to her. My mouth dries up whenever I try, and my top lip goes all sweaty." Yeah, I get it. She's just too cool for him.

"That's exactly my point. So it's a deal?"

Matthew looks out the window, all somber, like I'm about to turn him into a vampire. "Don't you think it's better to be your true, authentic self rather than trying to be someone else?"

"No. At least not in your case," I say. He looks sort of disappointed in my answer, but I don't really know what he was expecting. "So, you in?"

"Well, if it's something we get to do together, I guess so," he finally agrees. "What a hoot this is going to be...." Then he whispers, "Secret friend," and shoots me these stupid puppy-dog eyes, batting his lashes like a cartoon deer.

"Oh God," I sigh. "Lessons start now. Lesson number one: Never flutter your eyelashes at her like that. It makes you look like a haunted doll."

He didn't even hear what I just said; he's too busy celebrating our little truce. "Oh, Anton, thank you; you won't regret this, I double-bubble promise." Then this fool opens his arms out and tries to hug me.

"What you doing?" I push him away and lean back. Guys don't hug. I'm regretting this already, and it's barely been a minute. Rob peers over his seat to see what the commotion is because Matthew's whooping and punching the air.

"All right, chill out, man." I try to calm him down and he claps his hands like an excited seal. "Stop grinning so hard; I can see all your baby teeth."

"They're not baby teeth," he says.

"Well, they're teeth and they're in your mouth, so that qualifies as the same thing."

"Heh, sick burn." He giggles and nudges my leg. I keep having to remind myself what he did for me.

As the bus pulls up, me and Matthew make a plan to meet up after school tomorrow. He puts his number in my phone and adds mine in his. His iPhone is five years behind, because of course it is, and he's put cupcake stickers on the back of it. High-level moist.

Rob and Jess are giving their "didn't we all have a great time?" speech, and I'm kinda here for it, as long as she doesn't bring out her guitar again. I'm not hooting out loud like the others, though; we don't have that kind of relationship yet.

"Thank you all for being your best selves on this trip and for always watching out for each other," Rob says. "A caring camper is a..."

"Happy Camper," they all shout together.

Not gonna lie; this trip wasn't as bad as I expected it to be.

"Starting next weekend, campers, we'll be commencing our work on St. Luke's, turning the abandoned hall into a fully fledged family refuge, and your help will be going a long, long way." Jess gives her parting announcements. My ears and cheeks are proper burning when she talks about Mum's project; I'm gassed and proud of us, and a bit embarrassed and silently grateful, all at the same time. "In the meantime, we'll see you all for our weekly meeting on Wednesday." Everyone gives a round of applause, and I even find myself clapping along.

Out the window, I see Mum's already here to pick me up and Nanna's come, too. Buzzing. They look kinda stressed, probably because we're twenty minutes late. I'm fighting back tears at how happy I am to see them, cause guys aren't allowed to cry like that. I have to play it cool. But I missed them, for real. Before I even grab my bag, I walk over to them and give Mum the biggest hug I've ever given in my whole life. Then I pull Nanna into the same hug, and she does a little nervous laugh.

"Mum, you won't believe the weekend I just had." It all comes spilling out. "They were singing on the bus, and the food was horrible, but then I got lost in the forest and I almost died, and I held a tarantula and..." Something's wrong. Mum and Nanna are looking at each other worried, and Nanna turns her head like she's the one who's about to cry.

"Anton, it's your father. He was released from prison this morning."

12

EVERYONE IS PRETTY quiet on the car ride home. I think Mum asks if I want to talk about it, but I can't really remember what I say. Her and Nanna keep giving each other that worried look, and I ain't here for that.

The minute we're back, Nanna heads off to the living room to watch reruns of *Murder, She Wrote*. It's funny, because it makes me want to literally murder the TV.

"You wanna talk about it?" Mum says as she starts prepping dinner.

"I don't even know what to say." My mum always says, "If you don't have anything nice to say about someone, don't say anything at all," and I think because of that, we never talk about him. I've built my whole rep on this guy, I've had scraps to protect his name, but I don't know anything about him except he threw a spider on me once.

"Does he... Did he like me?" I don't have a whole load of memories to draw from. Surely there would've been other times, better times, maybe. Mum thinks about it for too long, so I ask another question before she can answer. "Did he ever call me?"

"Twice," she answers immediately. "The first time was just after he got arrested. But he was not in a good way, and you were having a tough time—some nosy parent at school circulated an article and everyone was talking about it. Me and Nanna deemed it too soon to talk to you."

"And the other time?"

"Christmas a year later. Your cousins were over and you didn't want to talk to him; you were too busy playing. He got upset that I didn't force you onto the phone, and that was the last we spoke. He sent a couple of texts over the years, asking how you were. After you got your first phone, I gave him your number." She looks at me as if she wants to ask if he ever reached out, but she can probably tell the answer from my face. "It's up to you if you want a relationship with him, as long as you know you can talk to me about anything."

This all kinda hit me like a ton of bricks, so I take my time thinking about what I want from this convo.

"You still got his number?" I ask eventually. I don't know what I'll do with it. I'll probably never need it, but part of me might feel more at ease having it. I keep picturing some guy I don't know, walking the streets, passing me in the shops, and neither of us knows he's my dad. Mum's jaws are clenched when she texts me the number, but she don't say anything further. The more I think about it, the more I think it's right for me to have it. If he messages or calls me, I think I'll wanna see straightaway that it's him.

I'm probably kidding myself; the man ain't called me in all these years, so why would he start now? I always thought the reason he never reached out to me was cuz he was in high max or something and couldn't. But turns out it's cuz he was angry at Mum for not making me chat one time? Bruh, I was a child. SMH. No further questions, Your Honor. For now, at least.

"Well, think about it," Mum says. "If there's anything you want to ask, within reason, we can discuss it. I'm here."

Something inside me feels like I'm being pulled in different directions.

"Yeah." I turn to leave, a bit dazed and confused.

"Hold up, Anton." Mum stops me, her voice a bit more chipper. "You're back from the camping trip, so you know what that means?" She's really grinning at me like a crocodile. Is this a trick question, like the time she asked if I thought her earrings looked cheap? When I don't answer, she goes on, "It's a big day...."

It's Sunday today, I know that. I don't think it's anyone's birthday; Nanna's is in winter and Mum had hers recently. I got her black hair dye to hide her grays, as a joke, and she hid my favorite Jordans behind the couch "as a joke." Nanna watched her do it, that serpent.

"It's time for...," Mum says. Again, I'm not getting it. She's confused that I'm confused. "The camping trip is done; you can have the Wi-Fi password back!" She raises her eyebrow. "I thought you were counting down the days until you got your internet back. And I'll take the data blocker off your phone this evening."

No way, of course. I just been so busy with thinking about my dad and Matthew and school, I completely forgot about all that.

She's looking at me like I'm unwell. "I thought you'd be more excited."

"No, I am. Yeah, I am, thanks, Mum." But actually I'm getting all jittery. "What's the password?"

"Antonloveshismummy, all one word." When I type it down and tell her it didn't work, Mum throws her head back and cackles like a witch. "That's not really it, I just wanted you to write it." She wipes a tear from her eye; honestly, she's actually proud of herself. Nanna comes limping in shaking her head, looking very amused at the whole thing. I swear, this family sometimes. "The real password's Badface123 with a capital *B*."

"With your corny-ass jokes," I mutter, finally

connecting to the online world after a week in isolation. Yeah, I thought about going to McDonald's or Starbucks to use their free Wi-Fi, but it's been impossible to find the time under Mum's curfew. I thank them for picking me up and give Nanna a kiss on the head as I go to my room.

Being very careful not to accidentally call or send anything, I'm looking at my dad's profile picture on WhatsApp, trying to remember a time when we were happy. None come to mind. Staring at his photo, I don't know how to explain it; he's got a criminal face. Gaunt in the cheeks, with dark eyes like a shark. The phone starts buzzing in my hand, making me jump. It's only Kehinde.

"Bro, where you been?" His voice is immediately aggressive. I don't reply with "Hello to you, too," because that's low-level moist, and in fairness, I have been gone for a minute.

"I just been about, man." I forget what my excuse was for being away this weekend, if I even gave one.

"About where? I called you and you didn't pick up." Why does it matter? He doesn't really wanna know where I've been; he's just upset that I didn't call him back straight away.

"I was busy. But I'm here now, aren't I?" Before he can reply, I ask, "How was the thing yesterday?" It works, kinda.

"You would know if you were there." He takes a breath. "The thing is, yeah, Jen is some average gal, anyway. Who is she that she thinks she can ignore me? We didn't even stay that long, dead vibes. And I took her brother's minifridge." That last part throws me off, so I ask him to repeat it. Stole. Her brother's. Minifridge? "Yeah, she thinks she can take me for a mug, so I took her stuff." That's so wild I do a slow laugh.

"You didn't take her stuff, though, you took her brother's stuff. Not exactly heist of the year." The more I think about it, the dumber I'm finding this. "So you walked home with the thing under your arm. Are you even gonna use it?"

"Well, nah. What do I need a minifridge for?"

"That's what I'm sayin'; you basically inconvenienced yourself. You carried something home that you don't need. You're like one of those moving men, except super inept at the job." I'm trying so hard not to laugh right now. "Why her brother? And why a fridge? You could've stolen her lampshade, or her mum's dehumidifier, or something just as random." If I was gonna be super petty, I'd steal someone's TV remote. That would be so aggravating; the hours wasted looking for it, and having to get up and cross the room just to change the channel. I'd be devastated. I don't tell Kehinde that, though; it might give him ideas. He once told me that his sister grassed him up for coming home late, so he cut her phone charger with a knife. Not even scissors, a knife. Like a pirate. Of course he was gonna be petty when Jen rejected him, low key she dodged a bullet.

"Whatever, fam, now she's gonna have to contact me if she wants it back." His voice gets growly when he's upset. I wonder if that was the ulterior motive all along: force her into speaking to him.

I can't believe he spent his weekend thieving from a girl who doesn't like him while I was out making memories, handling tarantulas and that. I'm thinking I had the better weekend. He's sick of me not taking him seriously, though, and calls the convo to an end. "I'll message you in the morning, so make sure you pick up your phone this time." When he hangs up, my dad's picture comes back again. I tap out of it. I don't want to think about that right now.

Out of sheer curiosity, I find Matthew's profile picture, figure I should see what I'm working with here. If this Fernanda girl does ever take his number, the first thing she's gonna do is find this photo and show it to all her friends. He's wearing a kind of *Star Trek* cosplay or something, holding up a colorful sword and taking himself way too seriously for someone who chose to wear a robe. My heart just sinks a little. Making this guy cool is gonna be virtually impossible. Although turning him into someone who's not a total weirdo might be doable. Difficult, but doable.

I spend the rest of the evening watching TV. I can't really concentrate, though; the thought of my dad being out is like a giant question mark hovering above me. Where's he living? Should I message him? I've got his number now. Do I even want to see him? I don't want to think about it, let alone talk about it. But I know the only two people who can truly understand me are sitting in the kitchen a few feet away. Even then, I wait for them to move to the living room, and that's when I sneak to the kitchen to get dinner.

Having Matthew's number in my phone feels like carrying this guilty secret with me, like I'm walking around with a really crusty, smelly sock in my pocket. Outside of that, knowing that my dad is walking the streets don't feel great, either. It was better when he was more of a myth, someone I could chat about but never really have to think about in any serious way.

Part of my mission for today is to keep an eye on Fernanda; I'm interested to see how difficult it's gonna be to get Matthew on her radar, and it's a good distraction from everything else. At lunch, I notice her chilling with a little group outside the science block at break time. She's pretty,

I guess, like she should be driving around in a Malibu convertible. Thick, wavy dark hair, eyebrows threaded to perfection, proper tanned like she's just been on vacation even though she probably hasn't. You can see she's liked; when she's talking, her friends are listening and reacting.

"Is that you, yeah?" Marcus has caught my sight of vision. "Anton's out here checking out Fernanda. Let's just cut to the part where she finds out your mum cuts your internet when you're naughty. You ain't sliding into no DMs, boy." He grins. Obviously, that isn't the case, but I'm not exactly gonna take it from Marcus, of all people.

"This coming from the guy who spells *automatic* with an *O-R* at the front. I'm surprised you can even spell *DM*, let alone slide into one." I'm smiling; this is our normal kinda banter, but I do feel guilty straight after. It's a bit of a low blow; the others don't know that he gets extra support sessions after school on Thursdays. Thankfully, he just laughs it off. If I go in deep sometimes, it's only because I respect him, like he's one of us. Yeah, Marcus is a good sport; I should chill.

"He's right, though, Anton; you've been slacking recently," Kehinde says, not being playful at all.

"You ain't exactly Captain Charisma yourself," I reply. "Coming at me after what happened with Jen." As soon as I say it, the mood changes. Caleb leans back to catch my attention and shakes his head with his bottom lip stretched. Marcus literally mutters "bruh" under his breath. And I can see it before it happens, Kehinde baring his teeth and shaking his head, his face boiling like a kettle.

"Don't mention that wench, that slug, that nobody." He's using all the terms an Arsenal fan uses to describe Tottenham. He needs to chill with that "women are the real problem" podcast. It's a bit much. "How is she gonna kick me out her house, for doing nothing, and then block me? Nah, I'm taking a baseball bat to that minifridge. Her brother don't deserve convenient hydration." Yo, Kehinde's on one, acting like a five-year-old having a tantrum.

"Fam, you called her nine times," Marcus says, just loud enough to hear.

"So what? That means she had nine opportunities to answer the phone." My man's spewing. It's almost like people don't enjoy being called that many times. He's getting more and more worked up. "She thinks she can ghost me? Well, I'm the ghostbuster." Ironically, the one ghostbuster who doesn't get a call. I give him mad side-eye while he isn't looking.

Just then a little Year Seven runs past. He clips my elbow by accident, and a bit of my drink spills onto my hand. Kehinde calls out to the boy to come back and straightens up as the kid shuffles over to us. He nods at Caleb, who reaches out and grabs the kid by the collar.

"What you think you're doing, bruv?" Kehinde snarls in the boy's face. Two more baby faces come over to apologize and help their friend. The one struggling to get out of Caleb's grip locks eyes with me, terrified. He's shaking, his mouth is gaping open and closed like a goldfish. I think he thinks I'm gonna bang him in his face or something. If it was anyone else, maybe. This guy's tiny, though.

"It's cool, little man, just watch where you're going, all right?" I tell him.

Kehinde turns to me, confused, and Caleb loosens his grip. The boy takes the opportunity to wriggle free, and his friends drag him away as they all apologize in their little voices. I hear one of them say, "We just saved your life. Do you know who that was? You know who his dad is?"

I've heard that a hundred times at school. It's part of the reason everyone on the playground respects me. It's also why Caleb, Marcus, and Kehinde rate me so highly. But I can't lie; for some reason, when I hear it this time, it stays with me, like a grease stain. I mean, I know my dad's not perfect, but I've always been proud of my rep at school. It's the one good thing that comes from him. But now I'm not so sure. That definitely didn't feel like respect.

I'm distracted when Marcus reaches into his backpack and tries to slyly pull out a silver can. I see Kehinde's eyes clock it, and I brace myself for what's coming.

"Bruv. Are you drinking a Diet Coke?"

"Yeah, fam, allow me. I'm tryna cut weight."

Marcus tries to hide the can in his sleeve, looking proper sheepish, but it's too late. I feel for him; I know his size has been playing on his mind this year—he wants the girls in our class to look at him differently. I don't bother saying the reason they stay away probably has nothing to do with what he looks like. Kehinde ain't letting it drop, though.

"By drinking women's drinks? Bro, just hit the gym."

"I'm already banging gym; my mum even bought me a weighted skipping rope. How you getting so triggered by a drink?" Marcus protests. He starts slurping it down while Kehinde looks on in disgust.

"Marcus, I'm feeling to slap that drink right out your hand. Why you gotta drink it so loudly, all slobbering over it like that?" He scoffs. "Diet Coke. You, man, are a joke. See, this is why nobody respects us. You got Anton getting shoved in the playground like it's nothing, and next man drinking female drinks in public. What next, cranberry juice? Nah, we need to step up."

I chuckle at how triggered he is by one drink.

And I do wanna take the attention off Marcus; he's done nothing wrong. "Yo, say what you want, but don't be coming for cranberry juice. With ice on a hot day, that stuff is elite," I say.

"Yeah, shout-out cranberry juice," Caleb joins in. "You see them antioxidants there, cuz you ain't getting them from no Mountain Dew." He grins and starts nudging me. "See, Anton knows."

"Lol, bruh, stop nudging me with your ashy elbows, looking the aftermath of a forest fire," I say to him, and we all laugh. Tension defused.

We start heading to class when the bell goes. Kehinde takes a bit longer than everyone to swap his kicks back to his shoes. He's got his serious face on again.

"Marcus, if you ever drink Diet Coke in front of me again, me and you are gonna scrap. Swear down, I'm just saying." Sigh. Why's he always got to bring the mood down? Marcus pretends not to hear at first and eventually grunts some sort of acknowledgment when Kehinde keeps prodding him.

I split off from the others to use the can. I can

barely concentrate on Kehinde's rants; that scared kid keeps popping up in my memory. Passing an open classroom, I spot Matthew sitting inside by himself. He's painting a little figurine with the world's thinnest paintbrush, and I'm both sorry for him and appalled that this is how he spends his time. He's coming to my house after school to start training, and having a quick convo now wouldn't hurt, I suppose. Although I make sure the coast is clear. Twice. But the second I step in, instant regret. Out of view of the door, sitting at the front of the class, are Rochelle and two of her nerdy math friends. I can't be talking to Matthew, not in front of live witnesses, so I have to pretend I'm there to chat to Rochelle instead.

"Hey."

"Hey," she replies. Good, that means she's not blanking me. Wait, why is that good? We actively hate each other.

Matthew's staring at me with his mouth open. This was too risky. I shouldn't be here; I'm not supposed to be seen with him at school. And now I've been standing in front of Rochelle for far too long. I haven't moved or said anything else. "Is there a reason you're just standing in front of me?" she asks.

"Nope." I'm tryna think on my feet, which is something I'm usually good at, but right now I'm hella flustered.

"Right. It's just that you never come to classrooms at break time. You and your stupid gang run out of kids to terrorize?"

"They're not a gang; they're my friends."

"Yeah, keep telling yourself that."

"You know what, I don't like your tone." It sounds more threatening than it's supposed to.

"Well then, it's a good thing I don't care about anything you have to say about anything." She stands up, and her friends stand up with her. It's like a nature documentary where one lion gets brave and all the others band together. I'm not looking for smoke, though; I need to dip. This was a terrible, terrible idea. But Rochelle chooses that moment to turn to Matthew. "Is he bullying you? Did he come in here to pick on you? Tell me now."

Matthew, who's been staring at us the whole time, is like a deer in the headlights when she addresses him. He lets out the longest, "Uuuuuuuum," and then squints at the ceiling. He pulls out his calculator and pretends to answer it like a mobile phone. "I need an extraction from an awkie-sitch, pronto." I guess he's just doing what he's told; we said he can't speak on our agreement, so I can't be angry at that. But this one time I wouldn't mind him breaking our little rule.

"I'm telling you now to stay away from him. On my life, you best not come for him again." Rochelle jabs her finger into my chest. She's not like Kehinde. Even without her little squad, I know she'd be just as brave.

When I leave, Rochelle has gone over to talk to Matthew. I slump against the wall outside the classroom. Everyone at this school, including my crew, thinks I'm some kinda thug because of who my dad is. I'm supposed to be king of the school, but this crown is heavy; and I just got verbally destroyed by Rochelle. The worst part is I actually rate her for that.

AFTER SCHOOL, I don't wait around. Marcus and Caleb are so used to me bouncing early we just fist-bump and it's cool for me to leave. With Kehinde, it's never that easy. He ignores my hand and just says, "Bye," really loudly without looking at me. Or if I'm still there thirty seconds later, he'll say, "I thought you were leaving," and then bell up my phone an hour later to chat.

I need to remind myself that he has been there for me since day one. When I started secondary school, I thought it'd be different from primary, where everyone knew who my dad was and what he did. I thought secondary school would be a fresh start, but people still found out, and they made jokes about how my dad would have to break out of jail to come to parents' evening. Or they'd sing "Locked Up" by Akon at me. When I met Kehinde, though, and he found out my dad was in prison for a violent offense, he made friends with me immediately. He thought I was cool, not despite that but because of it. After that, if kids made jokes, he'd tell them my dad was a murderer who taught me everything he knew, and they'd back right off.

I ain't never forgotten what he did for me, and I know I can still rely on him for a lot of things. So why haven't I told Kehinde about my dad's release? I guess we didn't have time to go through all that today; I'll tell him later.

I texted Matthew my address earlier, and he replied with a thumbs-up and a heart emoji. I need to tell him not to do that again. When I get home, I tell Mum and Nanna that a friend's coming over. I shudder at the word *friend*, but I'm not about to get into our whole arrangement with them. Mum rubs the corners of her eyes. She's working at the table again.

"Fine. But I'm not cooking for him. And if you two take drinks into your bedroom, I don't want to see any mugs or glasses in there tomorrow, you hear me?" Lol, she thinks it's Kehinde. So does Nanna. She's scuttled off into her bedroom; she hates when I bring people over. And she's been complaining about headaches again. I know how she feels.

When Matthew does turn up, at 5:30 PM on the dot, I take a deep breath for a few seconds before opening the front door. He's rooted to the spot and gives me a little wave.

"Don't do that," I tell him. He drops his hand to his side immediately.

I lead him into the kitchen to get a drink. Mum's face is priceless when he walks in. She stares at him. And then looks at me. And then looks at him again. She's almost scowling, like it's a practical joke I haven't revealed yet.

"Hello, Miss Charles. I'm Matthew." He offers his hand for a handshake. Mum shakes it, still frowning in confusion at me. "You have a lovely home," he says brightly.

"Thank you, Matthew, what a lovely thing to

say." She cracks a tiny smile at his stupid shoulder wiggle. "So is Matthew here to tutor you, or . . . ?" she says to me.

"Nah, Matthew's a Happy Camper, remember, Mum? We're gonna be working on St. Luke's together. He's the one who's helping me with the quiet zone. I took your advice to be open-minded and that." Mum's nodding along, and I can tell from her face that she's deeply impressed. Then Nanna pokes her head around the corner. She must've heard a voice she didn't recognize as Kehinde's and has come out to investigate. Mum does the introductions, doing a bad job of hiding her joyful surprise.

"Mum, this is Matthew. They met at the Happy Campers," she says, clearly searching for a reaction. Nanna's checking him out, her eyes lingering on his ridiculous hair and the formalness of his uniform.

"Hello, dear." If Nanna's shocked, she's hiding it better than Mum. "How much is Anton paying you to hang out with him?"

"Oh, I'm just using Anton to get closer to you," Matthew jokes back. Fair, maybe he's got some game after all. Although I'd rather he didn't use it on my nanna. The two women giggle like a pair of Miguel fans, and he's lapping it up. I roll my eyes and then nod for Matthew to follow me to my room to begin our training. I hear Mum and Nanna whispering excitedly as soon as we leave.

"Your grandma's pretty awesome," Matthew says. No agenda, just being nice. I remember when Kehinde called Nanna "dusty."

"Yeah, well, you can save the flirting for your own grandmother." I try joking with him.

"No, I can't. Mine died two years ago. She choked to death on a brioche." I don't know if that's true or not, let alone funny. I decide to ignore it.

In my room, he goes over to sit on the edge of the bed, feet together, legs together, hands placed firmly on his lap. I stand there looking at him. I knew this was going to be hard work, but I've clearly got a mountain to climb. Though I guess everyone who reached the top of Everest started at the bottom.

"OK, lesson one. You're sitting wrong."

"Am I?" He's like a statue, all straight and rigid.

"You look like you're riding shotgun on the back of a broomstick. You need to slouch a little." He slouches, but only his head and neck. "Your legs need to be farther apart, and take your hands off your lap. You look like Queen Victoria posing for a photo." He knocks his legs apart and awkwardly crosses his arms.

"Better," I tell him. And it is true, technically, in the same way that a Harry Styles concert is better than falling down an open manhole.

"Lesson number two." Now this is where I get to shine. "We need to fix up your image."

"How so?" He pulls a little notebook out of his pocket to write in. Good, at least he's taking this seriously.

"How can I put this? You look like a puppet made a wish to be an accountant, and that accountant had a son he wasn't proud of."

"Am I the puppet or the son?" He shrugs. "Either way, it's a win-win."

"What? How? You know what, forget it. Come to the mirror." He stands up and comes over to the full-length mirror in the corner that Mum got for free on some website. "Look, you need to stop tucking in your shirt. That ain't the way; it makes you a target." And I know from my time with the boys, if you're a target, sooner or later you'll become a victim. He cringes as he untucks his shirt, like it physically discomforts him. "And undo your top button; it's not cool." When he does that, he stands back to get a better look.

"Wow, I look like a rock star."

"Yeah, OK." I guess Tom Jones is technically a rock star; it's a very wide bracket.

"What next?" He's posing side to side, feeling his reflection.

"You need a trim. Your hair looks like a wig that was run over by a car." He looks disappointed, but he jots it down in his notebook. We make a plan for our next session. On Saturday, the St. Luke's renovation starts, so we'll stop off at the barber on the way there. I can't risk taking him to my usual, too many eyes, but there's one next to the car wash on Copeland Road that'll do. Matthew nods bravely, as if I just told him we're going skydiving. I don't feel guilty, though; it needs to be done.

When I walk him to the front door a bit later, Matthew insists on saying goodbye to Mum and Nanna first. He pops his head around the living room door and thanks them for having him over.

"You're not staying for dinner?" Mum asks. Five words she's never said to Kehinde. Speaking of which, I have a couple of missed calls from him. He's definitely gonna feel a type of way. I practically have to push Matthew out the door; I don't care how disappointed my mum is that he's not sticking around. When I ring Kehinde back, all he wants to talk about is the latest episode of his anti-modern-women podcast. Usually I'm up for the discussion, but this time only half of it goes in.

I'M DRAGGING MY feet on my way to the Happy Campers meeting on Wednesday. My dad still hasn't reached out, which I'm kinda relieved about. Although a part of me asks why he hasn't.

"You OK? You look like you've got a lot on your mind," Matthew says to me as soon as I walk in. I thought I was hiding it well; none of the crew have clocked anything different.

"The only thing on my mind is that I'm spending my night in a stuffy hall with a bunch of losers," I tell him. He looks stung, but there is truth to it. Two kids said, "Toot-toot," to me when I walked in; these people are getting too comfortable. I guess I can ignore them, focus on something that can take my mind off it.

Luckily, Rob and Jess have the perfect distraction. Scratch that, they have a distraction. Nothing here is perfect. Ever.

There's a new adult with them today, some guy who looks kinda out of place standing next to Rob and Jess. He's wearing a hoodie and Timbs, and judging by his skin fade, he could be some random dude from the hood. I try blinking at him in Morse code, warning him to get out.

"OK, everyone, we've got a special guest speaker in today, who'll be talking to us about developing healthy identities and behaviors," Rob says. "This will be especially helpful for our work with St. Luke's, as our guest is a specialist in gender equality."

I don't know what I expected a gender expert to look like, but this wasn't it. Whenever Kehinde moans about gender equality, he makes out like it's only women who care about it.

"So please welcome Joshua Nikos from Safe Havens. This is for everyone, so I want you all to pay close attention."

Matthew sits up in his seat, poised to take notes on whatever this is gonna be. True story, I ain't never been poised, or perched, or parched, or any of the bird descriptions you could use to describe Matthew.

"Thanks, Rob." Joshua Nikos speaks with all the calmness of someone out for a stroll. "So, yeah, I work for Safe Havens, and we provide safe spaces for vulnerable women and families by developing and supporting projects like St. Luke's." Geez, they've got more outsiders coming in for this refuge—Mum's council, Happy Campers, and now Safe Havens. So many people for such a small building. Must be kinda important.

"A huge part of our work is education," Joshua continues. "Our goal isn't just providing a safe space to those who need it; our aim is to make sure that fewer women need to rely on our services in the first place. That's why you've got the pleasure of this talk today." A few nervous laughs as he straightens up a little and pulls his hands out his pockets. "Now, let's start with an easy one. Have you all heard about gender equality?" A few nods and a chorus of shy yeses come back at him. "Great. And who can tell me what it means?" Now there's silence. People look like they're thinking about the answer, like they're trying to solve a math equation. One of the girls looks like she's about to put her hand up, but then she decides to sit on it instead. Geez, I just want this to be over, so I shout the answer out.

"It's about men and women being the same as each other," I tell Joshua. Finally, we can move on.

He smiles at me. "Thanks..."

"Anton," I fill in for him.

"Thanks, Anton. You're on the right path, for sure, but not exactly right. It's not so much about *being* the same as it is about being treated with the same level of fairness and respect." Joshua gestures between me and Matthew. "Are you and this guy the same?"

Lol, me and Matthew are different in every sense of the word. From the way we look and talk to the way we experience every second of the day. Also, I don't use the words *cutie patootie* as often as he does.

"We are not," I answer with confidence. He can't correct me on that one.

"So, if you two are different, should I treat you differently, or respect one of you more than the other?" Well, no. "Nobody disputes the fact that people are different: different genders, races, ages," Joshua continues. Cool, I'm following so far. "Difference is good. If we were all the same, that would be boring. But if someone treated you differently because you're a different race to them, what would you call that?"

"Racism," Matthew shouts out as his hand flies into the air.

"Right." Joshua nods. "And to treat someone differently because they're a different gender would be?" Now Joshua's asking me directly.

"Sexism," I murmur. I've heard Mum say it before, but I never really understood it. Suddenly, I'm thinking of all the videos I've watched with Kehinde, the ones where they say women shouldn't leave the house without makeup, or women need permission from their man to leave their home. Like, with Joshua's logic, that's hella sexist. If Mum was in a relationship where she *had* to wear makeup and get permission to leave the house, I'd take the guy's head off. Who is he to tell my mum if she's allowed to leave the yard? She's a boss; ain't no man gonna come tell her to put makeup on. Kehinde been wrong since day one. How's man gone unchallenged all this time?

The discussion moves on, and Joshua is talking about how we live in what's called a patriarchal society, which means women's needs aren't always considered equally to men's, and that's why something like St. Luke's is so important. I'm trying to listen, but I can't stop thinking about podcasts and the boys and the girls at school. I shake my head to refocus.

"Patriarchy is bad for men and boys, too. Can anyone tell me why?" Joshua is asking now.

The girl from earlier puts her hand up, more confident now. "It can make them think they have to be a certain way. Which is a kind of toxic masculinity." All these phrases I've heard before that I just shrugged at in the past are now starting to make sense.

Joshua gives her a thumbs-up. "That's right..."

"Evelyn."

"Thanks, Evelyn. And do you think you can give an example of toxic masculinity for anyone who doesn't know what it means? I've heard quite a few people challenge its existence and wanna get your thoughts on it."

She thinks about it before responding to his question. "Some boys at the bus stop are always making comments about me and other girls that they see, but they only do it when they're in a group. If one of the boys is by themselves, they stay silent, but around the other boys they egg each other on." Fam, I seen that, too, especially at the big bus stop near New Cross Station. It's weird to hear a girl say it, though, like it cuts deeper.

"That's a great example, and thank you for being brave enough to share it," Joshua says. "Masculinity isn't a dirty word, but the toxicity sometimes associated with it is a result of the patriarchy. It can put a lot of pressure on young boys and men to be a certain kind of 'masculine.'" He uses air quotes around that last word. "How would you all define masculinity?" he asks the group, and he seems pleased when loads of hands go up. He listens to each person individually and then explains why it's a good or bad definition.

When someone says that being masculine is

about never showing weakness or crying, Joshua counters it with a question. "Why? Why is it masculine not to cry?" Nobody can come up with a clear answer.

When someone else says that masculinity is about physical strength, Joshua says, "I know lots of people—men and women—who can beat me in an arm wrestle, that doesn't mean they're more of a man than me." And that pretty much ends that train of thought.

"A boy at school says being masculine is when you grow up and provide for your family. He said that's what being a man is," one kid says.

"And if a man's unemployed?" Joshua asks. "If he's not able to earn money or provide for his family, he's still a man, isn't he? And women can provide for their families, too; that doesn't make them 'masculine,' does it?"

Yeah, can't lie; Mum does that and she's definitely not a man. I see what he's saying—loads of this stuff is just plain wrong. But I like being thought of as strong and masculine; it's what gets me respect at school, and now I'm hearing it's meaningless.

I put my hand up and Joshua gestures for me to speak. "But what's wrong with being an alpha male? I get that not every guy has to be one, but what if you want to?" Kehinde loves using that phrase to describe himself. He says it means the strongest male in the group.

"I hear you, Anton. Of course, women and men should be allowed to be whoever they wanna be, and to express themselves however they want—as long as it doesn't harm other people. But I would steer clear of words like *alpha male*—we aren't wolves, we're human beings. Which is just as well, because I'm not a fan of raw meat." He gets a couple of giggles. "Also, the idea of an alpha male being the biggest and strongest, even in a wolf pack, has been unanimously debunked by science. Wolves follow the smartest in the pack, the one who is more likely to lead a successful hunt, the problem solver. Leadership isn't all about physical strength, it's about showing empathy and critical thinking."

Yo, this is gonna blow some minds. If Kehinde ever calls himself an alpha again, I'll know he lyin' because it doesn't exist. Science says so. I won't tell him that, though; he might ask where I got my information from.

The rest of the workshop with Joshua Nikos goes by pretty quick in the end. It's kinda fun, like he calls out examples of scenarios and we have to say whether it's sexist or not. Like, a lady who gets a job as a scientist isn't sexist, but if she gets paid less for the same work and hours than her male colleagues, then that's a problem.

"Before I go, if there's anything I want you all to take away from this, it's to remember this: People are people." He looks at all of us. "What we all have in common is so much easier to find than any differences. And for the boys in this group, I want you to be kind, not just to each other, to the girls, to *everyone* you meet, but also to yourselves. Kindness is never a weakness." There's a round of applause as he thanks us for listening. And can't lie; I'm joining in, too. Shout-out Joshua Nikos; he's a real one.

Once he's gone, Rob checks the clock and confirms we have some free social time before today's meeting ends. Me and Matthew go off to a private table to discuss Operation Fernanda.

After that talk, Matthew's got some renewed energy in him, like he's extra galvanized.

"You got your notebook ready?" I ask him. He nods enthusiastically and puts it on the table. "Good. So we already spoke about fixing your image, finding ways to make sure you don't look like a Care Bear mixed with the kid on the Haribo packets."

He smiles to himself, probably because he knows all the Care Bears and he's got one in mind. "Yeah, I told Rochelle at school that I'm thinking about cutting my hair, and she said if it's my idea and it brings me joy, she'll support my decision."

"Rochelle? You spoke to Rochelle?" My entire body immediately perks up for some reason.

"Don't worry; I didn't mention you," he's quick to reassure me. "But yes, she and I are friends now." Man loves to talk Shakespearean, so unnecessary.

"What? Since when did this happen?"

"Since that day you burst into the science class. She did say you can be a bit aggressive sometimes.

And why the sudden interest in Rochelle? Huh? Huh?" Sigh, he's so dramatic.

"Bruv, I didn't burst into anywhere. Stop describing me like I'm a firework. And how am I aggressive? I never even said one word to you that day." I decide to ignore the other stuff.

"I guess you didn't have to say anything, maybe your stance was aggressive. Did you know that ninety-three percent of communication is nonverbal?"

"Sometimes I wish it was a hundred percent."

"Oh, that would be amazing; we could communicate in sign language and purring noises."

That's not the message I wanted him to take home from that comment. I hate it when my insults don't land. Actually, you know what, I'm gonna try to be more kind. Joshua's speech is still fresh in my mind. Plus, it's good for Matthew to chat to someone at school, even if it is that smarty-pants and her squad of geeks. This could be good for him. It could be great for me.

"Hey, have you seen *Wicked* the musical?" he asks out of nowhere. I let the pause sink in, giving him time to truly reflect on whether I've watched *Wicked* the musical.

"No," I eventually reply when he doesn't seem to be getting it. "I'd rather skip barefoot on a cactus."

"That would be an easier feat if you defied gravity." He chuckles to himself. Sometimes I literally feel like we're talking a different language; he should come with his own subtitles. Which reminds me...

"If I'm gonna keep training you, we need to talk about your speech."

"My speech? As in my articulation?" He slaps his hand against his cheek and moans to himself. "I knew I should've accepted those elocution lessons last summer." Elocution lessons? How monied is this kid? I should start charging for these sessions. No, I remind myself, he saved my life. That's why I'm doing this.

"I'm talking about your speech as in chat-up lines," I tell him. "Girls are good listeners, that's how they're programmed. And if they're listeners, then we're the talkers, which means your speech has to be on point."

He does a little frown. "Programmed?" He holds his pen in the air above the notebook, not writing down what I've just said.

"Yeah, like, through nature, because... I don't know, I just heard it on a podcast." A podcast that I'm questioning more and more.

"Did the podcast provide verifiable numbers and stats?" Matthew asks. Clearly not; they never do. I gotta stop quoting those videos from now on.

"OK, maybe the podcast got it wrong, but let me tell you what *I* know from my own experience," I tell him. "If you can't talk to girls like a human being, you'll never get a girlfriend. You want numbers? I count one Matthew. Zero girls. Now, are you gonna trust the process or you wanna keep interrupting me?"

He wipes his forehead with the back of his hand as he scribbles down the notes.

"I'm gonna get you to practice talking to girls, ones you don't like. That way, when you finally do chat to Fernanda, you won't be so nervous. And if she sees and gets jealous, that will only make her like you even more," I say, pleased with my plan. He finishes writing and puts his hand in the air to ask a question. "You don't need to raise your hand, Matthew; there's only two of us in this discussion."

"It's just, I don't want to make her jealous," he says. "I want to be kind to her and that doesn't sound very kind. I always thought I could make her laugh by just being myself."

"You're not being mean by making her jealous; she might like it that other people are into you. The way I see it, it would be *un*kind for you to just walk in without a plan and risk upsetting her with some of the wild stuff that you say. This is about trial and error." I'm expecting lots of error, but that's my job, my burden to carry. I chose this. He doesn't look super convinced, and we agree that if he feels like he's being shady or unkind, we'll abort the mission on making her jealous. I still think that practice makes perfect, and I do want this to go perfectly for him. "Pretend I'm Fernanda; hit me with your best line."

"OK, how about this?" He clears his throat and straightens up. "I want to collect my loose eyelashes and blow them in your face, like a defensive tarantula rubbing its back legs together."

I take a beat to digest the colossal stupidity. "Why the hell do you think that would make her like you?"

"It's visual, and it shows I'm knowledgeable about the natural world."

"It shows you're some troubled guy." I take a deep breath. Maybe I need to give him examples, show him how it's done. "Make it witty, something like, 'Our relationship won't be rocky, so give me your number ASAP.'" He looks at me with a blank face. "A$AP Rocky is a rapper," I tell him.

"Right." He jots down that A$AP Rocky is a rapper. "Oh, how about this?" he says and clears his throat again. "Are you a postal worker? Because you deliver everything my heart needs, and I support you going on strike if you feel like it's something you must do." Better. Not objectively good, but better. "And then I could do an interpretive dance of our potential love. I'm very nimble on my feet, you know." I spoke too soon.

"Probably best not to do that."

"Don't believe me?" He goes to stand up, and I stop him before he does something I won't be able to ever unsee.

"Matthew, just because something *can* be done doesn't mean you should do it." I feel like a wise owl.

"Like picking your nose and flicking it out the window?"

"That's oddly specific, but yeah, sure."

We're interrupted by Rob coming over then. He wants to know if we're interested in hot cross buns. Pause. Matthew's licking his lips, but I tell Rob thanks, but no thanks. Hot crossed buns are not the one; I ain't never seen a thug eating baked treats in public. If you're from the street, only banana bread and cookie dough are acceptable. Matthew says, "More for me," and takes mine for himself. I'll have one on the way out if there's any left.

Rob calls us to attention, and Jess comes over to join him. They want to tell us what's what before work begins on St. Luke's this weekend.

"OK, everyone, just a note for Saturday. We'll

be convening around ten AM for an initial tour. It's a decommissioned church, so lots of structural work has already taken place to get it ready for its new purpose, but there's still work to be done, like painting and decorating. The main hall will need the most work, as that's where the bulk of activities, support groups, legal advice meetings, children's play, and the like will happen."

Whoa, how big is this thing? No wonder Mum's been stressing for some time; this is a lot of responsibility.

"Jess and I will be there with the equipment and paint that a lot of you have donated, and Safe Havens are coming with their own team of volunteers. Anton and Matthew will be in charge of the quiet zone, the part of the refuge where people can go to take a breather, relax, and maybe get one-to-one therapy sessions. No pressure, boys." He nods at me and Matthew. Geez.

Rob and Jess go on to explain the health and safety stuff, saying there needs to be an adult present at all times. For once these toot-tooting psychos will actually come in handy. As long as Matthew can keep up the act of not knowing me at school, hopefully everything will be fine. Can't lie, though; the stakes are high. My reputation at school, this project, my friendship with Kehinde and the guys, there's a lot to lose. And for some reason again, Rochelle's stupid face pops up in my mind.

School on Friday is a weird one. Miss Lilly makes me read out loud in class, and Kehinde and Caleb are clowning around. Last time she asked one of them to read, they pretended to snore halfway through it. It's only half a page, though; I ain't got a problem with that. Matthew perks his head up when I read, but thankfully he doesn't turn around. Seeing him alone in his corner, it's weird that not more people chat to him. Don't get me wrong; he's annoying as hell, but he can also be kinda funny sometimes. I do notice that he's one seat closer to Rochelle, his one friend, apparently, and that's probably not a coincidence.

At lunchtime, the guys are talking about the

podcast again, more stuff about why women should concentrate on pleasing their man instead of their career or whatever. Can't lie; I'm getting a bit defensive. Mum's always had a good job, and she's always been a good mum; she ain't never failed at either of those. When you really think about it, half our teachers are women, and I'm pretty sure most of them have families. How did Joshua Nikos undo all the podcast's logic in a single evening? I zone out of the conversation and make an excuse to go to the vending machine.

"I'll come with," Kehinde says. I can't tell him I just wanna be by myself; that's not how we do things. Barely halfway across the football pitch, all the questions come flying out.

"Why you ain't been answering your phone no more?" His tone's immediately hostile.

"What you talking 'bout; I do answer. We chatted the other day." True, but we both know I'm only taking about 50 percent of his calls these days. In my defense, he does call around twenty times a day. And then messages me to pick up the phone.

"Nah, but you been different somehow. Even at school, you're being bare distant and that. The others have said it, too; you moving kinda shady."

"Fam, what do you want from me? I told you, I been busy helping my mum out. And now I have to go help her with this stupid project on Saturdays, like she's taking up all my time." Slyly drop it in there that I won't be about. But the guy's still worked up.

"I'm not having that," he responds. "She's just some little woman; you could put her in her place if you wanted to."

"Careful how you speak about my mum." My blood is getting itchy; he can chat about me all he wants, but not Mum.

"Big man out here, you still get bossed around."

The anger is heating me up from the inside out like microwaved food. I take my hands out my pockets. Fighting Kehinde wouldn't be ideal, although I'd probably win. I can't remember the last time I saw Kehinde scrap, which is weird considering this guy's always on smoke. He knows it, too, so he plays it safe, curls the corner of his mouth into a little smile. Good choice.

"I'm just saying, there's something you ain't telling me. You're moving different, and we can all see it."

"Chill," I reply. "I've said what I've had to say, all right? If the guys wanna talk, they talk to me." Judas moves out here.

He smiles again, a more genuine one this time. "You think Caleb would ever say anything to your face? The way he ran when he had that beef with Aaron Mullins, my guy was out like a light." Rah, I swear it was Kehinde who ran from Aaron that time. Caleb stayed, and got floored, even though it was Kehinde that started the beef. He laughed at Aaron's skinny legs in PE and said he was built like an upside-down fraction. My guy's rewriting history like the reality stone, Thanos, and that. But I can tell he's tryna defuse the tension from before, so I smile and nod to be polite.

When the bell goes, I realize I never made it to the vending machine. One thing I know is that me and Matthew are gonna have to be extra careful about our arrangement. Kehinde's suspicious, and I have no idea what he'd be capable of if he found out. Or maybe I do, and that's what scares me.

I'M WEARING MY hood down very low on my way to meet Matthew on Saturday morning. This is the least gangster reason anyone on my block has ever looked this shady. Outside the barber, I look left and right, making sure I'm not being followed, and casually slip inside. They're busy; it's a ten- to fifteen-minute wait. Matthew walks in a couple of minutes later and joins me on the couch to wait his turn. I clock the barber glance at Matthew's feet for some reason, so I lean forward to inspect.

"Are...Are you wearing frilly socks?" I'm

surprised that I still get surprised. They're ridiculous, covered in bright pink and white ruffles.

"They give my ankles character, and they're comfortable to boot. Safe beneath these shoes of mine, you don't think they're cute?"

"Fam, I told you to stop rhyming; I wanted to headbutt you just now." This guy gets me so vex sometimes. "And never ever wear those again. How am I supposed to make you cool when your feet look like cupcakes?"

"Don't worry; they're not mine. I was in a hurry this morning, and I picked up my little sister's socks by accident." Good. I'm glad we got that cleared up. I relax a bit.

"I never knew you had a sister," I tell him.

"You never asked."

"Fair. You got both parents?"

"Yes, they basically leave me to do whatever I want," he says.

So it's like that, yeah? "Bruh, that sounds like a dream, not having someone breathing down your neck every minute of the day. You wanna swap?"

But Matthew's not hyped for once; his voice

is a bit subdued. "The grass isn't always greener. I would swap some of the material things they give me for the banter you have with your mum and nanna. But generally, yes, they both love me and, although lonely sometimes, my life is pretty easy." He shrugs. "Hey ho."

I'm wondering whether I should ask him a bit more, but then the barber is calling him up for the haircut. Right. This is where I shine. I tell the barber to give him a skin fade into a 0.5 millimeter, blend it high, and go in with the trim on top. Then I sit back and watch as the boss man carefully creates part one of my Frankenstein's monster. Although in this case, Matthew is more of a forest nymph than a monster. He's got his eyes closed the whole time, buzz clippers gliding up the back of his neck. When they spray the top of his head with water, he closes his eyes and juts out his chin like he's in a shampoo commercial. OK, I'm slightly icked out by that, but the trim is fire.

Matthew finally opens his eyes, and his jaw drops as he looks at his reflection. He turns his face, pouts, smiles, touches the back of his head, rubbing his hands up and down his new trim. I'm grinning and shaking my head as he squints into the mirror, gently touching the underside of his chin with the top of his fingers. He's so busy goofing about he hasn't noticed the barber waiting impatiently at the register.

"Yo, come pay the man." I half laugh. He walks over and thanks the barber, shaking his hand and giving him a tip. Seriously, this trim looks cool. The borders are on point, the top is clean, and I ain't never seen Matthew's face so clearly. It's like he's finally got features.

When we leave, Matthew's checking his reflection in all the shops and car windows.

"What do you think?" I ask him.

"Whenever I see myself, it's like there's a stranger looking back at me." He seems unsure, but I take it as a super win.

"That's the point, cuz." I smile. He smiles, too. The rest of the walk to St. Luke's, he keeps stopping in the middle of the street and voguing. People are chuckling as they go past, and one couple across the road literally shouts, "Go on, son." It's so entertaining I actually forget to put my hood up.

When we get to St. Luke's, Mum's already standing there with Rob, Jess, and Joshua Nikos. A couple of other people from Safe Havens are there, too, and a few of Mum's colleagues are arriving now. It's always strange seeing her outside the house, out in the real world. Like seeing nurses on the bus when they're still wearing their blue scrubs, or a teacher doing their weekly shop in the supermarket. She looks a little nervous, but happy to see me.

"Ah, Anton, there you are," she says as I walk over. "Good grief, is that Matthew?" Oh right, last time she saw him, his stupid shaggy hair covered half his face. Matthew's beaming, so proud of his new trim. And he should be.

When all the Happy Campers have arrived, we follow Mum inside so she can show us around the site, pointing out what needs to be done. This wall needs to be painted white, that space needs clearing, these floors need waxing, all that stuff. We see the big meeting room, a play area, and the main hall for events and that. Mum calls this place a "sanctuary" for women in need, and I can actually see it from how she describes it.

"I do wish we didn't need places like this," Mum says, "but the rates of poverty and domestic violence in the borough have spiked again, and they don't look like they're slowing down. Thank God we've got the funding to convert it." There's so much desperation in her voice; I ain't never seen her this emotionally attached to a work project.

"What was it before?" Jess asks, and Mum takes a deep breath to compose herself.

"It belonged to the church next door, which is now a block of modern apartments," she replies. "They turned the hall into a pharmacy, kept the St. Luke's name, but that closed down years ago. There was even talk of knocking it all down and building a parking lot that nobody needs. We've been refurbishing for a few months now, doing the big structural stuff, but the painting and decorating phase is always so exciting; it means we've only got a few weeks before opening."

We carry on following her around as she talks to Joshua about the color schemes, what makes people feel safe, and where's the best place for furniture.

When we're done with the main hall, the kitchen, and the bathrooms, and the campers are getting to work, she and Joshua lead me and Matthew to this small room around the back.

"Rob tells me you boys have been tasked with the most important room. Vulnerable women, and sometimes their children and families, will use this as their quiet zone. Group therapy, one-to-one support, maybe even a reading nook." Geez, Mum's going in. I didn't know this place was gonna be such a big deal.

"The door's a bit temperamental; you have to jiggle the handle sideways and give it a bit of a kick. Best to use a doorstop," she says as she leads us inside.

Thankfully, Matthew's been taking notes, because I have not been paying attention, boy.

"I'll go and get some equipment and overalls

so you can get started," says Joshua, and he ducks out.

Mum gives me a quick shoulder squeeze. "Thank you, bubba," she whispers, and then heads back out to carry on with her own work.

While we wait, I'm taking a minute to analyze the room. The place is dusty and the plastic sheet on the floor crinkles when you step on it. The cobwebs on the ceiling and windowsill make me shudder.

Matthew notices. "Don't worry; I'll get rid of them."

"Yeah, cool." Tbh, it's not that bad after the petting zoo. I'm still grateful, though. When Kehinde found out I was scared of spiders, he put one in my hood as a joke. I was shook, but I guess it was funny. Sort of.

Matthew brushes the webs away with a broom, his little tongue sticking out. "Did you ever get scared of Spider-Man, too? Because you knew he could just climb into your window while you sleep?"

"No. What?"

"Me neither. I was just asking."

Joshua comes back in then with all the painting equipment. He gives us a few pointers on how to get the best coverage but pretty much leaves us to it. I can think of worse ways to spend an afternoon.

Painting the wall actually feels kinda nice. Starting in the corners and working your way across the room, rolling the paint up and down, seeing the progress, it's proper therapeutic. I'm standing on a stepladder, concentrating extra hard. It takes time, though, and we would be going faster if Matthew was taking it more seriously. He keeps dabbing bits of paint on my leg and running away giggling.

"Bruv, can you stop? I wanna get this wall done today." At least the first coat.

"Come on, Anton; we can have fun and do some painting at the same time. You ever heard of multitasking?" This guy's so annoying, for real.

"I can multitask; I'm doing it right now."

"You are?"

"Of course. You see how I'm using both hands to hold the roller and brush? I'm also stopping an idiot kid from getting his head dunked in a paint bucket."

"Really? How?"

"Self-control," I say in my serious voice.

Matthew chuckles, unsure if I'm joking or not. He decides not to mess about for a bit. I feel bad, though, so after he goes back to painting, to show him it's not that deep, I flick a bit of paint at him. Most of it goes on his overalls, but a couple of tiny flecks hit the side of his face.

"Waaah, you cheeky bean!" Lol, how is he squealing like that? His voice just went supersonic; I think I just saw a moth explode. Man called me a "cheeky bean," that's too funny. We go back and forth for a while, laughing but also getting on with it.

Mum comes in around 2:00 PM with lunch. Two cans of Coke; she knows me so well. She gives me a quick pinch on the cheek and goes off, busy again. We get back to it, into the rhythm of painting, when Matthew looks up at me.

"Hey, Anton. Do you ever think about the future?" He's tilting his head.

My insides shift uncomfortably. "What are you, my student counselor? Why you asking me that?" I don't know what it is about that question that makes me switch so quickly, and why is Matthew asking me? I thought we were getting along.

"Oh, no, sorry." He's shocked, eyes wide at my response. "We don't have to talk about it. I know it's ages away yet." My heart rate calms down immediately, but I can feel shame burning through my face. I don't know why I took that so personally. He doesn't bring it up again, so I decide to break the silence and redirect the conversation.

"Tell me about Fernanda. What are the three things you like most about her?" It's better to keep stuff lighthearted if we are gonna chat. Good for the work environment.

His eyes light up at the question.

"And you're not allowed to say generic stuff like, 'She's pretty,' or 'She's nice.'"

He makes me laugh because I can actually

see the uncontrollable outburst of emotion from him before it happens, like a water balloon in the seconds before it bursts. He swivels on the spot, throwing his arms out like he's in *The Sound of Music*.

"But, Anton, she *is* pretty, and she *is* nice, and so much more," he almost shouts. Swear, if he were a cartoon character, he'd have hearts in his eyes. "She's so passionate when she talks about stuff, especially things she likes; I could listen to her all day. And she's funny and witty, which makes me laugh out loud, so I have to pretend like I'm coughing up snotsicles." Nah. Gross. "And she cares about people; she's always on the school committees for charities and stuff, so I know she's got a good heart. Last year, she did a sponsored silence where she didn't talk for two days and raised over two hundred pounds." Lol, I would pay double that for Matthew to do a sponsored silence for half the time. Nah, for real, though, I didn't even know the school did charity stuff like that. Damn. When I look down at Matthew, he's blushing a bit and making sure nobody's about to walk in.

"Anton, can you keep a secret?"

"Yeah." Technically true if I don't care that much.

"I've never been kissed on the lips," he says. Oh. It's like that, yeah; I was definitely not prepared for this conversation. That doesn't stop Matthew, though. "I'm like Snow White before she went into a coma. Or Sleeping Beauty, you know, before she went into a coma." There's a second where we're both thinking the same thing: Those films were a problem. I'm not even gonna ask why he's the princess in both these scenarios, and I tell him it's not that deep, or surprising, that he's never kissed anyone. Fact, I'd be more surprised if the opposite was true. But I'm sure it will happen eventually. Some day.

"You think?" he asks, proper hopeful.

"Well, yeah, you can't talk if you're kissing. Someone's gonna want to use it as a last resort. Or second to last resort." I forgot about violence.

"I hope that someone's Fernanda." He blushes again.

"That's what we're training for," I tell him. I ain't gonna tell him that none of the guys have kissed anyone, either. Kehinde says he has, but we all know it's fake news.

"Yeah," Matthew says. "I just wish there was a way you could control me." Pause. "As in, if I had your voice in my head telling me what to do, and I could learn that way."

And he's right. He's totally right. A discreet way for me to be in his ear and literally tell him what to say...that's exactly what Matthew needs. We make a plan: At school on Monday, Matthew's gonna chat someone up for the first time. Let's go.

Me and Mum get home from St. Luke's quite late. Can't lie; my arms are aching from a hard day's work. Nanna's already had her dinner and gone to lie down for a bit. As a way of thanking me, Mum orders pizza and wings for us both. And the surprises don't end there.

After dinner, I wash my plate and head to my room. Only when I pick up my PlayStation controller, I'm thinking about the day I just had.

For real, it was mad productive, and I didn't hate chilling with Matthew. It's easy, like, I don't have to try to impress. And Mum's chilled out quite a lot in the last few days, even though she's never been busier. Good vibes, man, I'm here for it.

Then it happens. My phone buzzes on the bed next to me. Geez, almost forgot I had a phone. I glance over, ready to ignore, but it's not Kehinde.

He's changed his profile picture to him hooded up with a balaclava in his bedroom. My hands are trembling as I pause the game and reach for my phone. There's a single short message.

> Hey, son. I'd like to meet.

PUTTING ON MY uniform on Monday, it's like there are two clouds hanging over me, a light one and a dark one. The light cloud is the excitement and uncertainty of how today's gonna go when I'm coaching Matthew. The dark cloud is that stupid message from my dad. I haven't mentioned it to Mum or Nanna yet. Mum's still in a good mood about the St. Luke's project getting up and running, and Nanna might try to talk me out of it. I don't really know who else to talk to about it. If I told Kehinde that my dad's out and messaging, his eyes would probably light up.

On the way to school, I text Matthew. We're gonna meet in the library at lunch. It's risky, but nobody will ever think to look for me there. Fact, I've only been to the school library once in the last three years. Matthew knows the place well; he spends his lunch hours hanging out with the librarian. Poor kid. Apparently, Fernanda's started chilling there, too, so it's a "double-bubble-gum bonus." Cold shivers when I quote him; the guy's so ridiculous.

From there, I'll give him one of my AirPods and put the other one in my ear. I'll follow him at a distance, tell him who to chat to, what to say, and I'll be sure to do it far away from where we usually chill with the guys. What could go wrong?

It's a bit awkward when I get to homeroom. I take my usual seat between Kehinde and Caleb, and we literally have nothing to talk about. I haven't been watching any of their podcasts, and I can't exactly tell them about my weekend. Beyond the initial greet of, "Yo. What you saying? . . . Yeah, nah, all good, bro. . . . Cool," there's nowhere for the convo to go. It's even worse in actual lessons. Like, in English, Miss Lilly is trying to control the class, but she gets no respect from the back row. Kehinde is literally playing music out loud from his phone and Caleb is filming it like some sidekick. I can't believe that used to be me.

Some people are entertained, but Rochelle keeps shaking her head and tutting at them. My stomach tightens when I see that. I get it. Like, I haven't changed my mind about how boring English class is, but it don't feel right that Rochelle and the others have to suffer. Matthew's sitting even closer to them now, and I get a little feeling of pride that his shirt's untucked, his top button undone, and I think I heard Rochelle compliment his trim. Part of me fantasizes about telling her it was my idea. But that can never happen.

When lunchtime finally rolls round, I go to meet Matthew in the library. My excuse for leaving the others is that my nanna's unwell and Mum wanted me to call the doctors for her. Half true, Nanna's always unwell. Sometimes it's her ankles, sometimes it's her diabetes; the woman's got the fitness levels of Homer Simpson. And we're still waiting to hear about that MRI.

I wait for the corridor to clear out before ducking into the library. Matthew's bobbing around behind the shelves in the fiction section, waiting for me.

"Fernanda's just arrived," he whispers, actually trembling. I peer between the books and see her, long dark hair with reddish highlights, handing a book back to the librarian.

"Quick, make her jealous. Talk to another girl in front of her." I nudge him out into the open. He does this wheezy little sound, like a vacuum cleaner that's got something stuck in it. He's desperately looking around, but there's no other girls nearby.

Instead, he grabs a book from the closest shelf, opens it, and loudly shouts, "Oh my, that Katniss Everdeen is a hoot." Then he puts on a tragic American accent and says, "My, my, I've never read such a hero; she must be mighty perdy."

Luckily, Fernanda's already on her way out the door, although everyone else in the library is just sitting there staring at him.

"Psst." I hastily beckon him back to our hiding spot. "That was an epic fail. Why did you do that voice?"

"I panicked." His voice is full of despair. I tell him we're going back to the original plan. I should never have deviated from it. Boy needs proper instructions. No more accents. Ever. He nods silently. Then his lips purse into a little smile. "Looks like I'll have to make do with an Anton special, chef's delight." I go to shove him.

"Never say those words in that order ever again." I'm trying to be quiet, but he gets me so angry. We're drawing attention, too many heads in here. "Remember, this is practice, but we're also trying to make her jealous. So it has to be public—let's go outside."

As we go through the plan one last time, I notice he's shaking again.

"Hey, come on, man; you'll be fine. Just repeat what I say," I tell him, slipping one of the earbuds into his sweaty palm. He nods bravely. I call him to see if it works. "Testing. Testing." OK, we're good to go. I watch him leave the library, and I wait twenty seconds before following.

"Anton, I'm not sure about this." His voice is loud and clear in my ear.

"Bruh, you got this." He's at the end of the corridor, walking oddly stiff like he's got a plank of wood down the back of his shirt. "Loosen up. And be confident; people respond to that." I trail him out and around the side of the school, away from the football pitch. "Right, there's a group of girls. Go over and introduce yourself."

"I can't go straight up to a group; that wasn't the plan," he starts screeching. I have to calm him down and encourage him to find a girl standing by herself. "But what if a girl doesn't want me approaching her? I don't want anyone to feel uncomfortable."

He stumps me with that. It's a good point. But he needs to get on with it. "Well, that's how couples met before online dating. How did your parents get together?"

"They danced the night away at a summer solstice." I don't know what that is, maybe some kinda outdoor event for rich people. "Yeah, my dad stood no chance. Mother can be pretty rhythmic when she's close to nature." He's got a dreamy smile on his face. Yep, I been doing the math, and one in ten things out of Matthew's mouth makes my soul deeply uncomfortable.

"Trust me, girls prefer it when you approach them in person. Dating apps are for guys with no chat. You got this; just pretend you're at a summer soul search."

"Solstice," he corrects me. He takes a deep breath and we carry on with the plan.

Sitting down on a bench outside the assembly hall, I get full view of his actions. I'm pretending to scroll through my phone, secretly keeping an eye on him. "What about that girl over there?" he says.

"Yeah, go for it. Be confident."

Matthew marches right up to her, elbows swinging like a UFC fighter. "Walk properly," I tell him. He slows his pace and stops dead in front of her. But then he just stands there. She seems totally confused.

"Erm, hi?" she says. Matthew doesn't respond. Geez, he's waiting for me to tell him exactly what to say. I quickly tell him to say hi and introduce himself.

"Hi, I'm Matthew." He holds out his hand for her to shake it.

"Don't shake her hand," I whisper. He puts his hand in his pocket, but only after she reaches out. Now it looks like he's just aired her. "Pay her a compliment," I urge him.

"Erm, I like your eyebrows," he says. Me and her both react in the same way.

"Eyebrows?" she says. Bruv, what is this guy doing?

"Preventable," I mutter under my breath. The girl's baffled. And she should be.

"Did you just come all the way over here to tell me that?" she asks.

"Yes, they're a great shape, freshly plucked, I see. Did you know, they also stop sweat from going in your eyes; that's their main purpose."

"Right..." She looks around as if she's waiting for someone to pop up and tell her it's a prank.

It's time for me to take over. I tell Matthew to repeat exactly what I say, which he does, but it's on a two-second lag so it sounds a bit off.

"I'm just saying, your eyebrows, lips, lashes, I'm liking all of it," he copies me. "I can tell you take pride in how you look; I like that. Anyway, I thought you deserved to know how pretty you look on this glorious day, and I needed to tell you that you made me smile from over there." He says it all, word for word. And from here I can see her posture change; she gets less defensive.

"Well, that's very nice of you to say." I hear her voice is lighter, too. I tell Matthew that we saved the situation, and there's a sigh of relief. I get him to move in for the kill, ask for her number. When he does, she says, "Aw, sorry, I would, but I've got a boyfriend."

"Yeah, me too," Matthew replies, waving his hand. We didn't practice for rejection.

"You have a boyfriend?" she asks, obviously confused about why he'd be asking her out if he's already taken. I'm in shock; I don't know what to say at this point.

"Well, I have a boy who's a friend." Nice save. I'm racking my brains, but he's talking faster than I can think. "We're not together in that way, although maybe one day—who knows what the future holds?"

I have to jump in. "Stop saying the things you

are saying!" I hiss at him, my jaw clenched. "Pay her another compliment."

"I think I love you," Matthew says to the girl. Immediate facepalm.

I tell him, "No, anything but that," trying hard not to shout. Then out of nowhere, Rochelle comes over. The girl turns to face her, and I almost fall off my bench. He's been talking to Rochelle's cousin this whole time, the one from the bus.

"Matthew? How do you know Grace?" I hear Rochelle's voice so clear in my ear.

Matthew squeals in fear, proper panicking now. "Argh, Rochelle. Rochelle's here, what do I do?"

"Stop talking to me; you're making it obvious." This time I can't lower my voice; everything's falling apart.

"Matthew, is that a headphone? Are you on the phone right now?" Rochelle's noticed his ear. The operation's over. She looks around, clocks me, and scowls. I hang up the phone, put it in my pocket, and pretend to look at the sky with fascination. This flipping guy, man, he's a one-man army against subtlety. I glance over quickly.

Matthew's bowing to them for some reason, like a Chinese diplomat. Then he turns and runs away toward the library. I can feel Rochelle's eyes on me as I walk off, but I don't dare look back. This was an absolute fail.

I'm resting up against the wall, catching my breath a little bit. Nobody's noticed me here; I can think for a minute. He chatted up her cousin. Badly. And we got rumbled. You have to laugh; otherwise, you'd cry. I think I can just hide out here for the rest of lunchtime, there's only—

"Hi," Rochelle's voice says behind me. I do a scream and duck, but I straighten myself up quickly like it never happened. She's alone; that's good. And she leans up against the wall next to me.

"Hey." My voice gives me away. How can one word make me sound so guilty?

Rochelle's half smiling, half scowling, as she stares straight into my soul. "I don't know what's going on," she says, "but if you hurt him, I will kill you."

"What you talking about, fam? I don't know what you're tryna say." It's not true if I don't admit it.

She ignores the obvious lie. "Anton, if this is some game, where you and your crew get him to do weird stuff for you, I swear I'll hunt you down myself." When she says that, I'm starting to feel kinda triggered, you know.

"Is that what you think of me? That I'm just some sheep who can't think for himself, that I just follow the crowd? That I'm some bully?" She sounds like my mum. I take a deep breath. "I don't even know what you're referring to anyway."

"Right," she answers, nodding slowly. And as she turns to leave, she says, "You've only got one headphone in your ear, by the way. Did you lose the other one?" And I'm just left staring at her. Damn, this girl's good.

In math after lunch, we're sitting at the back in our usual place. Mr. Benjamin already told the guys to be quiet four times, but they always pipe up again a few minutes later. Halfway through the lesson, Kehinde leans over to me.

"Caleb said he saw you chatting to Rochelle at lunchtime," he says. My stomach drops, but my face doesn't give anything away. "Is it true? Why you chatting to that nobody?" Wow, if he thinks Rochelle's a nobody, imagine what he thinks of Matthew.

"She's not that bad," I say, tryna be chill.

"Not that bad? I did not just hear you right. Man, that girl's a problem, fam." I shift in my chair; I can feel myself getting defensive. "Anton, for real, bro, what is going on with you?"

"Don't worry about her, man; I got other stuff on my mind."

"What stuff?" He's not asking to be helpful; he's asking to be nosy.

"I told you, stuff at home, all right?" It seems to do the job. He grunts and sits back in his chair. He never cares about anything deep. Things are either funny or gangster to him. Nothing else is worth talking about.

When the lesson's over and we all start

heading out, Mr. Benjamin asks me to stay back. Oh God, here we go.

"Am in trouble?" Allow it, I just got my internet back. Last time I mouthed off about his shirt, I was just showing off in the moment. I been on my best behavior since then; if he's gonna blast me, then I have genuinely no idea what I've done.

He waits for the last people to trickle out. "No, Anton, quite the opposite." Come again? "I can see you trying to pay more attention in class. I just wanted to let you know you've been more focused recently, and it's not gone unnoticed."

"Yeah?"

"Yes. I don't want to jump the gun, but if we're at the beginnings of change, then I think your seating arrangement might hold you back going forward." Oh. This again. Am I actually smart or is he just trying to move me away from my friends?

"I'm trying to move you away from them because I can really see potential, and the next two years of your education are *so* important." It's like he's read my mind. And can't lie; I'm kinda psyched. But things are already tense between me and the boys; if I switch places now, things would just get heated.

"I can't do that, sir," I tell him.

Mr. Benjamin sighs. "I know, I know, unfortunately. But would you have any qualms if I did it for you?" Huh? "Hear me out. I'll make a song and dance about moving you publicly. I can make it seem like you don't have a choice. It'll only be to the second or third row, where you can actually concentrate. If you want, you can pretend to put up a fight. Your friends will have no idea, I promise." Bruh, this is all happening kinda fast. "Think about it, Anton; it's your education, not theirs."

I REPLIED TO my dad's message; I couldn't ignore it. Nervous as I am, it's about time I meet the guy I've been tryna imitate for years, see if he was worth it.

I swapped out one of the days with Matthew, who's coming over tomorrow before Happy Campers instead. School was fine today, I guess. Mr. Benjamin's plan worked perfectly. I pretended to answer back and eventually moved to the third row. Nobody questioned it, except I could see Rochelle staring at me from the corner of my eye. Whatever, she can't prove nothing. Passing Matthew in the hallway, I quietly told him to shave his unibrow; that thing's built like a cobra. The others didn't hear or see him nod, and the day went on as usual.

After school, I text Mum and tell her I'll be a little late getting home. She thinks I'm chilling with Matthew, and I'm not about to correct her. I know she gave me my dad's number, but I still feel like I'm low-key betraying her in some way.

We're meeting in Café Culture on Camberwell New Road, about a ten-minute walk from my house.

I'm there five minutes early and my dad turns up ten minutes late. Seeing him through the door, I recognize him from the profile picture on WhatsApp, and my nerves kick in. I'm tearing bits off the paper straw in my hand and rolling it between my fingers. Once he steps in, I realize he's taller than I imagined. I wonder if I'll grow to be as tall as him. He hovers for a second; I think he's expecting me to stand up. I almost do.

"You're looking strong," he tells me as he sits down. First time we've chatted in years, and that's his opening line. I guess he must be feeling as awkward as I am. I stare at him, noticing every detail, the specks of gray in his hair, and the gold tooth that makes him look menacing and welcoming at the same time.

What if he don't like me? The thought pops into my head. My guy didn't call or message for how long, and I wonder what he thinks of me now. I suppose if the only thing I get out of this is a free meal, then I'm up by a meal. I've ordered a full English with hash browns, and I've almost finished my orange juice already.

"How's your mum?"

"Yeah, she's cool." I cross my arms. I don't know if he genuinely cares or if he's just making chitchat because neither of us knows what to say. I down the rest of my orange juice, waiting for him to say something else.

"Listen, there's nothing I can say that'll change what I did." His voice is so deep and gravelly. We sit in more silence. I thought I'd have a ton of things to say, but the reality is the man sitting in front of me is a stranger. There ain't no warm, fuzzy feelings; this might as well be a job interview. My heart thinks it knows him really well, or at least the image I'd created of him over the years, but my head doesn't know him at all. He's kinda skinny but muscular; you can tell he'd do damage, although he's not built like he works out every day. Sitting in his light army jacket and jeans, this doesn't feel like the big man who shaped my whole identity for the last three years.

"What was it like? Inside." I can't think of anything else to ask. I should've wrote down some questions, like Matthew does in his little notebook.

"I'm not gonna lie to you, Anton; it was rough." He points to a thick purple scar on his neck. "Lots of wannabes in there trying to prove a point, that they're tougher than the lifers." He leans forward and clasps his hands together. "The only thing more dangerous than a real gangster is a fake one; remember that." I don't know why, but my brain immediately thinks of Kehinde. "You carry a knife with you?"

My shoulders tense up. "No."

"Good," he says, and I relax a bit, but then he continues. "It's the tool of a coward. A real man uses his fists to settle an argument; that's something your old lady could never understand."

I squirm a bit in my chair. I read all the news articles from when my dad went to prison. He KO'd a guy with one punch to the side of the head. The guy took nine weeks to recover; my dad got seven years in jail, although apparently reduced to five for good behavior. Kehinde always talked him up, loved that story—that he could take down someone just like that. I guess I did, too, but now I'm thinking of what Joshua Nikos told us, that being a good man is about problem-solving and empathy, not physical strength.

"Why did you do it?" Whenever I pictured us sitting down like this, my mind always circled around this one question. "What did the guy ever do to you? You were gone for all that time, and for what?" The first few birthdays without him did feel like there was something missing. I didn't know what, because I didn't really know *him*; I just know that things could've been different. I wasn't planning on actually going there, not today, but here we are.

He does a long sigh. I think maybe he's gonna say something profound, something to make up for his absence, but then he just waves his hand.

"You don't know what my life was like, providing for a little kid, living with someone constantly nagging. I shouldn't have done what I did, but the way the feds came for me, it was a madness. Total overreaction. From everyone."

"Overreaction? Fam, you almost killed someone. And you only got five years in the end. That's an underreaction." The lack of remorse, for the victim, for me and Mum, I wasn't expecting it. Like, at all. "Crying over spilled milk and screaming at a cow is an overreaction," I say. He tries to interrupt me, but I just talk louder. Five years, and that's what I get from him? "You can't do what you did and act surprised you got taken away. The way I see it, you abandoned us. Nanna had to move in because Mum couldn't do it alone." Now I've raised my voice. I never really thought about it from Mum's perspective before, but hearing this I know he ain't right.

"Your mum wasn't perfect, either, always changing the locks, lying about me to anyone who'd listen to her sob story. I was on these streets every day, putting food on the table; bet she never mentioned that part, did she?" His tone is so bitter, like everything that's happened to him in his life is my mum's fault.

"Those things don't make you a man, or a dad," I snap, thinking about that discussion we had on masculinity; Joshua Nikos knows what's up. "And you keep talking about my mum, I'm gonna leave." I push my chair out with the threat. "Ducking and diving like a politician—you're a grown man; why can't you just apologize?"

He shows a quick moment of weakness when his eyes react to me getting up, but then he shuts it down. People have always told me I look like him, but I don't see it myself.

"You're right, son," he says quickly. "She did deserve better; you both did. And I am sorry." It looks like real remorse, but I can't tell with this guy. I slowly pull my seat back in. "I was angry, Anton, so angry. But you can use me as a lesson. The world's not gonna hand everything to you on a silver plate; sometimes you have to take things by force. But choose your battles; don't do what I did. Be smart about it." I don't really know what to say to that. We sit in silence for a while again.

"You go to the gym?" he asks. I can see him inspecting my arms.

"No."

"Well, you look like you do. Whatever you're doing, keep it up." More silence. "You got a girlfriend?"

"Nah."

"But you like someone."

I don't understand how he noticed that from my expression. Rochelle's face pops into my head. It's unavoidable; I have to face the fact that I like her. But there's no way I'm having this conversation with my dad.

"You know what to do, yeah? Act confident, take the lead, make 'em jealous. Girls say they hate seeing you with someone else, but they secretly love it, trust me. Take it from me, as someone who's been inside for years, one woman is never enough anyway. Do McDonald's sell single chicken nuggets? No, they sell them in boxes of six, nine, or twenty."

I can see he's trying to make a joke, to lighten the mood, but it's kind of a gross analogy. I can't stop thinking about Joshua Nikos, telling us that people are people first and foremost, regardless of their gender. I think my dad needs to sit through one of those discussions. And besides, I don't want twenty girls. I just want the one. He's still going on. "Remember, dating is just a game that you have to play; females do it, too."

I keep a straight face, but inside I'm cringing at the word *females*. It's bare dehumanizing.

"And I'm serious about making them jealous if you can. That always works."

As he's saying all this, I know it's a load of rubbish. As if this would ever work on any girl—they're too smart for that, and they deserve better. I'd never try that with Rochelle. And I shouldn't have made Matthew do it to Fernanda, even if it did end up failing. Which means Matthew was kinda right about his own approach of being kind and honest. Damn. I guess I owe him an apology.

When my food arrives, I'm concentrating a lot on my plate. My dad just orders an orange juice, lots of ice. It's so weird; he's just proudly watching me eat, like one of those enthusiastic soccer moms. It's a bit awkward when we're finished and paid up.

"I'd like to see you again," he says, his eyes proper serious across the table.

"Yeah, we'll see."

"If I have to bribe you to come see me, then I will. That's how much I care. Speaking of which…" He pulls out a brand-new iPhone, still in its box, and puts it in front of me. "It can't make up for all your birthdays I missed, but hopefully it's a start." My hand is itching to reach out and take it. But I ain't about to get nabbed for handling stolen goods; only one of us is a criminal right now.

He can read my hesitancy. "I bought it with my own money; it's totally legit. If you don't believe me, here's the receipt." He brings that out, too.

I don't want anything from this guy; I'm not so fickle that he can bribe me with an iPhone.… But I could do with the money, and it'll help Mum and Nanna with the shopping this month.

"I'm gonna sell this online," I tell him as I grab it off the table.

He chuckles. "It's yours to sell."

I get up to leave, and there's no hugs or handshakes or nothing. And ten minutes later, I'm back home with Mum in the kitchen.

Sigh. I have to tell her, don't I? She'll clock when she sees the phone, or the money, so I might as well.

"How's Matthew?" she asks. She's got her glasses on and she doesn't look up from her paperwork. It looks like the floor plans of St. Luke's.

"Yeah, actually I didn't see Matthew today." Yikes.

"Oh? Kehinde?" She still can't say his name without a touch of venom.

"Nah, I went to see my dad." I'm trying hard to stop my face from scrunching up.

"Oh." She takes off her glasses and pulls out the chair next to her. I take it, and we sit for a bit.

"What was he like? Before he went down?"

When she speaks, it's slow and careful. She's choosing every word wisely. "Initially, your father was very charming. We were young, foolish and I thought I was in love."

"So what happened?"

"The things I found exciting, adventurous at first, the fact that he was streetwise, a bit rough around the edges, I thought I loved that about him. Once we were living together, the reality was very different. Sometimes I wouldn't see him for days, and he'd turn up asking me to hide things for him."

"What things?"

"Not important. Nanna never liked him, by the way, but I convinced myself that I could change him, make him a better man."

"So why didn't you break up?" Mum's so strong, I can't picture her in the relationship she's describing. This is the same woman who cut my internet and made me join the Happy Campers over a detention.

"I was thinking about it. But then I got pregnant, and we were so excited about you. I thought things would get better, that being a dad would finally make him grow up. And things did improve for a while, but he eventually went back to his old ways. And by then I was trapped."

"Trapped how?"

She takes a while to respond. "Financially," she finally says.

I'm not buying it; there's something she's not telling me, something she's missing out. She took way too long with that answer.

"And... physically?" I'm a bit embarrassed to ask, in case I got it wrong.

"Sometimes. That was probably the darkest time in my life. I wanted more for you, more for us. That's where somewhere like St. Luke's would've been helpful; it would've changed my life. Had he not been arrested, had we stayed in the relationship the way it was, a refuge might possibly have saved my life. That's how it is for so many people."

I wipe my eyes on my forearm. This is a lot.

"Mum, what exactly did he do?"

"No." She says it so firmly I almost jump. "I won't go into details. If you still want to know when you're older, we can discuss it more then. You're old enough to hear some stuff now, but way too young for the rest. I want you to enjoy your childhood, what's left of it, as much as you can, Anton."

I have to respect that. I wouldn't have thought I'd ever get this emotional hearing about Mum's struggle, so she probably has a point. And I almost don't wanna know more; I'm scared of how angry I'll get. Hearing about how he was, how Nanna moved in with us because Mum needed the childcare, busting a gut at work to put food on the table, I'm losing so much respect for the guy. The same people who think I'm cool because my dad went to prison didn't see how he treated her. She went through it, stayed in that dodgy relationship, all for her baby. For me. Strength comes in all different shapes and sizes, boy.

"It's not a sad ending to the story," Mum says as I wipe more tears away. "Things were difficult for a while, after he was taken into custody, but my life slowly became my own. Putting food on the table wasn't easy, especially when I went to university, and for that I owe your grandmother a lifetime of thanks. Over the years, I learned to forgive your father."

"You forgave him?" I'm shocked. After everything he did, everything he put her through? Yo, my mum's a saint, some superhuman.

She thinks long and hard before she continues. "I forgive him, in my heart. In many ways he was a product of his upbringing and his surroundings. But will I ever speak to him again, ever choose to be around him? That would be irresponsible on my behalf; I'd be doing myself a disservice."

"Why have you never said any of this before?" Real talk, why is this all news to me? I only saw the prison sentence; I had no idea what life was like before that.

"I was always careful not to say anything to turn you against him; that's not my role as a parent. Even if a small part of me wished you'd never see him again, that wouldn't be the way to go about it. I guess a big part of it was protecting you; children should never suffer because of their parents' mistakes."

We sit there for a bit. Mum's taking this so calmly. She has her hands wrapped around a cup of tea. I guess the big question that neither of us has gone near is if I'm going to see him again. Right now, the thought of it kinda icks me out. Saying that, a part of me doesn't know if I can just ignore him if he messages again.

And the tiniest voice in the back of my mind is saying, "What if he has finally changed?" and "What will our relationship look like in the future?" I tell Mum what I'm thinking.

"Anton, your relationship with him is your own, which is fine. As long as he never hurts you. But to me, he's just another one of the eight billion people on the planet. To forgive is to let go, and I did that years ago. For your sake, I won't speak ill of him. But as someone who knows him and cares about you, I'd advise you to be very careful."

"Careful of what?"

"Careful of remembering who you are, how kind you are, and how much me and Nanna love you."

MATTHEW'S BACK AT my house, sitting up in my bed, even though the chair was perfectly available. My meeting with my dad is still fresh in my head. And so is the convo with Mum, which got pretty deep, like, even though she was holding back in a way. I didn't know things were like that for her. It would have been easier if my dad was horrible to me; I could've just splashed my drink in his face and walked out. Instead, well, I don't know what to think about it all. I still have no idea what I'll do if he messages again.

"Are you OK?" Matthew can tell something's on my mind. Well, there's no point hiding it from him; I can tell from the puzzled look on his face he's not gonna drop it.

"Matthew, you know about my dad," I begin. "Everyone at school does." When that article circulated around the parents in elementary school, there was a few weeks when everyone at my lunch table moved away. Only Matthew stayed. We didn't chat, but I secretly appreciated it. That was a tough time, way before I was king of anything, and I've always pushed those memories down, like the time there was no toilet paper in the McDonald's bathroom and I had to use a receipt I found on the floor.

"I know what people *say*, but I'll only believe what you tell me," Matthew says.

I appreciate that, but it also creates a big swell of guilt in my stomach. Me and Kehinde treated this kid horribly for years. More Kehinde, sure, but I allowed it. Matthew's all right; he's wholesome. He didn't deserve none of that shade; man was just trying to live his happy little life. And we made it *un*happy.

"Well, he got out recently, and I met with him yesterday. And it's playing on my mind a lot."

"Did seeing him bring you joy?"

I chuckle at his choice of words. "Not really. It was weird. He was different to how I thought he'd be." My phone vibrates on the windowsill. I reject the call, message Kehinde that I'm busy. "I used to think it was cool, that people saw me and him in the same light. It helped me at school and that, made my life easier." I start fiddling with a pen at my desk. "It's just, now I've met him, and my mum's told me more about what he was like before, I don't think I do want to be like him anymore." Matthew just listens quietly. "When I think about the future, the idea of turning into him scares me. Fact, bro, it's terrifying. And the worst part is, I see people telling me I can be better." I tell him about my upcoming meeting with Mr. Wall and Mr. Benjamin's mastermind plot to get me to change seats. "I been trying so hard to be some parallel version of my dad I can't think of how else to be. I know I'm gonna let everyone down."

"No, you're wrong." Matthew says it so forcefully it catches me off guard. He never disagrees with me that strongly. "Your future is whatever you decide, Anton. You can use your dad as an example to follow, or you can use him as an example of how not to be." I tell him it's not that easy, but he shakes his head. "In a few years' time, you can go to university. And then you can get a job doing whatever you want. My dad didn't go to university until he was in his thirties, and now he owns his own investment company."

"You tight with your old man?" I ask Matthew.

In my head, his dad wears cardigans and plays catch with him on a grassy lawn. Can't lie; I'm kinda shocked when Matthew takes a long pause. Like, really long.

"My dad is... in my life, but he's not present." He shrugs. "It's all relative."

"What do you mean?"

"Well, he works a lot. And he comes home, and he pays the bills, and he does the things he has to do, I guess. But it's not like we really talk." He rubs the back of his neck. "It's obviously not as taxing as your situation," he says quickly.

"Nah, problems are problems, bro," I reassure him. "Nanna says that the size of someone else's leg brace won't cure your headache. You still need to deal with what's directly in front of you."

"Thanks, Anton." He smiles out the side of his mouth. I nod.

"Right, let's get down to business," I say, feeling a bit lighter but ready to move on from the feelings. Matthew sits up so we can talk about the failed attempt with Rochelle's cousin. "What went well? And what do you think we can improve on?" He opens his mouth to answer, but I interrupt him before he speaks. "Nothing went well. The whole thing was a mess. What's the opposite of success?"

"Niall Horan's solo career?" he suggests.

"Yes, sure, you were Niall's solo career." My voice flattens. "Stop agreeing with me when I insult you. You take the sting out of it."

"I thought I was oozing confidence," he says under his breath.

"You were definitely oozing something," I snap back, but then I remind myself to calm down. He didn't do it well, but he still did it. And my advice about trying to make her jealous wasn't right anyway. We need to focus on Fernanda only.

"So what do I do instead?" he asks.

I think about it. When my dad was giving me all that shoddy advice, I thought maybe Matthew was onto something about just being himself. It makes me a bit nervous, but it might just be worth a shot.

"You just do you. Don't overthink, just chat to her. Chat to her as if you're chatting to me right now, see if that works. Find your inner strength." This is by process of elimination; we've exhausted every other avenue. We're not gonna make her jealous; my dad completely threw me off that idea. The earpiece didn't work; I can't talk to her for him, because that was an absolute car crash. And it's clear he's never gonna be a thug on road. Unless *G* stands for "giggle."

"Oh, inner strength, flesh and bone, tooth and colon, how my soul pines for Fernanda." He starts twirling around the room like a dancing ghost.

"Oh, it's like that, yeah?" I'm encouraging him; I can't help it. He is low-key hilarious when he's like this.

"I want to hold hands with her."

"Yeah?"

"And kiss her. On the lips. While we hide under the sofa."

What the hell? "Yo, I'm just gonna say it; you lost me with the sofa thing. Like, completely." My encouragement turns into confusion.

Matthew stops twirling on the spot; I can see his eyes thinking. "Well, it's dark and dusty underneath there, like a bear's cave," he explains. "But it's still in a communal space, so not against house rules. Oh, Anton! It'll be a tight fit, but we can make it work."

"OK, firstly, I told you not to exclaim my name like that; we're not in a meadow. And secondly, that's so stupid, bruv. I shouldn't have to say this, but don't kiss her under your living room couch."

"Right, I get it." He nods seriously.

"Good."

"So can I hold hands with her under the couch?"

"Stay away from the flipping couch," I snap. This guy, man. I'm rethinking this new advice already. He flops back onto the bed, staring at the ceiling like he's deep in thought.

"Anton, you get loads of girls, right?"

"Oh. Er, I've been about. Yeah, I guess." I don't know where this is going.

"So if a girl holds my hand on a date, that's a good sign, right?"

"No. Holding hands is for children, otters, and elderly couples. You're supposed to put your arm around them. That way you can steer them wherever you wanna go." Wait, that doesn't sound right.

"Really? Is that how you're going to woo your future girlfriend?"

"I'm not gonna 'woo' anyone; I'm not a chambermaid in the 1600s."

"Oh, no, Anton, chambermaids were the ones to be wooed; they had all the advantages of being close to royalty, without the pressures of ruling." He thinks for a sec. "You'd make a good chambermaid. They were decisive thinkers. It would mean early mornings, though I'm sure you'd be up to the challenge."

"Thanks, I guess." It's definitely the weirdest compliment I've ever received, but I'll take it.

"Hey, Anton."

"Yeah, fam?"

"Do *you* fancy anyone?" Again my face must be giving me away. Whatever I did makes Matthew gasp, clap his hand to his mouth, and point at me. What the hell, man! I didn't even answer.

He lies flat on his stomach and crosses his ankles behind him like a teenage girl in one of those film posters from the nineties. "So who is it?" He's teasing me like a child, so immature.

"Yeah, we're not having this conversation," I dismiss him.

The guy doesn't stop; he's like a powder-puff Terminator. "Oh, please tell me. I'll tell you something embarrassing about me if you tell me who it is." Wow, he's desperate.

"Matthew, what on God's planet can you possibly be embarrassed about that I haven't already seen you do, or say, on a day-to-day basis?" The whistle, the frilly socks, the fainting in the forest, there's something worse than all that?

"Sometimes I sniff my own toenails after I cut them."

"..."

Yep. There it is. The new record for ugliest

sentence I've ever heard, a title held previously by Matthew. It's just gonna be his name on the leaderboard from now on.

"It's Rochelle," I tell him so we can move on from the haunting image of what he just told me.

Now he clasps his cheeks with both hands and shouts, "Rochelle? Oh. Em. Gee! I *knew* it!" He's rolling around the bed, and even I smile at his foolishness.

But then I clock the last thing he said and I'm just about to ask how he "knew" when I notice a figure in the doorway.

Standing there, open-mouthed, in his black hoodie and black joggers. Kehinde.

I'm racking my brains, trying to figure out how this is happening right now. Mum's been at work; she should still be on her way home, so she can't have let him in. And Nanna's at bingo. Wait, I left the door unlocked when I got home so Matthew could just come straight in when he arrived. He must have forgotten to lock it.

"You must be joking," Kehinde says, standing stock-still in my doorway. "Whoa, what is—nah, you're actually kidding me." He's rubbing his eyes in disbelief. "This. *This* is why you've been avoiding us, not answering your texts? Matthew? *Matthew*?" He starts pacing around the room, clapping the back of one hand into his other palm.

"Yo, chill," I say, holding my hands up in a calming manner.

"Don't tell me to chill, fam; don't ever tell me to chill. Are you dumb?" he shouts. My guy's moving aggressively. The room suddenly feels very tiny. "You're the king of the school, fam, and you're gonna throw it all away for this loser."

"Loner," I automatically correct him. "He's not a loser. He's a loner. And that's only because of us and how we treat him at school."

"Loner, loser, whatever, fam. This guy's a donkey. And you're choosing him over me? I made you what you are, bruv. Without me, you'd be a nobody. You wouldn't be king of anything."

Matthew says in his little-baby voice, "I think I'm going to go," but Kehinde pushes him back onto the bed.

"Yo, touch him again." I'm on my feet in a flash. "Touch him again, I dare you."

Instead of retreating, he takes a step toward me, his shoulders squared back. "What? What you goin' do? You gonna fight me? Over this clown?" He's frothing at the mouth like Colgate, screaming at me like he's in his own house. The disrespect.

Who's gonna make the first move? Both of us are ready. Nose and lips, that's where I'll aim first. Knowing Kehinde, he's probably thinking the same thing. But before either of us makes that decision, another voice from the door. Mum. She's standing there now, with shopping in her hand, which she carefully places on the floor.

"Go home, Kehinde." I've never heard her voice with so much authority. Yes, Mum, she ain't playing today. Me and Kehinde are still face-to-face, but he's side-eyeing her.

"This isn't over," he snarls at me.

"I said go home, Kehinde. *Now*." She pulls out her phone. "Don't make me call the police." She stands aside to let him out. If he even looks at her wrong, I will teleport over there. But Mum can handle herself; she's fearless, doesn't even flinch as he walks past her.

She stands in the corridor with her hands on

her hips and doesn't move a muscle until the door slams shut behind him. Soon as that happens, she immediately turns to Matthew, her face full of concern. "Oh my God, Matthew, are you OK? Did he hurt you?"

Geez, thanks, Mum. I'll be fine, too.

Matthew's suddenly a bit breathless, milking the moment like a prize cow. "I think I'm fine." He's breathing so deeply I can't help but chuckle and roll my eyes. Even Mum looks a tiny bit amused by the theatrics.

"Anton, have some sympathy." She's trying to sound stern, but the corners of her mouth are twitching slightly.

"Don't worry, Miss Charles; I knew I'd be OK." He pats his chest, and I know he's referring to his whistle. Sigh, this guy's not serious.

But I'm still feeling a bit on edge. I imagine an alternate reality where it's just Kehinde versus Matthew. How long would it take a team of doctors to surgically remove a whistle that's embedded in Matthew's forehead? And what's Kehinde going to do now? I ain't never spoken to him like that before.

The first text comes from Caleb.

> Yo, what were you thinking?

Then a missed call from Marcus, followed by a message.

> You ditched us for that little nerd?
>

My thumbs are shaking as I type back. I'm panicking. I thought I was doing the right thing sticking up for Matthew, but now I'm remembering what it was like to eat lunch alone, to have everyone mock it. I ain't going back to that, no way.

Kehinde's got a point; without my reputation, I'm nothing.

> You got no proof, fam

That's the best I got. I'll deny it if they say anything to anyone. Kehinde knows that no one would believe him anyway. It just means I now have to be extra careful not to be seen *anywhere* near Matthew, especially at school. And if anyone bothers to ask Matthew, he can just say our mums know each other, which is why he was spotted at my house. Nothing to do with me.

None of us make eye contact during homeroom the next morning, except I saw Kehinde lean over and whisper something to Caleb when I walked in. Lunchtime is even worse. I don't wanna hang with them after what Kehinde did last night, but I can't chill with Matthew even though I want to, because what if someone sees?

I know I shouldn't feel ashamed of Matthew, but I do. It's just the way these things work. I don't want anyone to be scared of me, but I can't let go of their respect, not yet at least. So I can't be seen by myself, just standing around, otherwise I'll look like a loner. I decide to walk around the school, not stopping for anyone. That way it seems like I'm going somewhere, doing something important.

The day gets a bit better when I pass Rochelle outside the geography block.

"Hey."

Apparently, we're on greeting terms now.

"Hey, you all right?" Why am I talking like that? I don't ask people if they're all right; it feels weird.

She looks past my shoulder and back behind her. "Not hanging with your boys today?" She frowns.

"Why would I do that when I got a chick right in front of me who's got my full attention?" In my head that was smooth, but based on her reaction, I can tell she doesn't agree.

"Wow. OK. Look, I can see you trying harder in class. And I think whatever weird deal you have with Matthew is commendable." So she's figured it out. She rolls her eyes at my surprise. "It's not a coincidence—the haircut and the way he dresses; I'm not an idiot. And I'm also not a 'chick.' That's derogatory language." Damn, if she thinks that's bad, she should hear my dad talking about chicken nuggets.

"OK, I won't say that no more. But if you're not a chick, then what are you?" I'm tryna be lighthearted, but I also kinda want to know for real. I wanna get these things right. And maybe I can be the one to teach Joshua Nikos something next time I see him.

"Friend, sister, cousin, math whiz, porridge enthusiast, you can pick any one of those. But a chick is an animal—do I look like an animal?"

Man, this girl's brilliant. Now's not the time to ask for her number, though. Her cousin comes lolloping down the corridor, wearing a stripy hat and round glasses, looking like if Where's Waldo? had a Jamaican sister that you didn't want to find. It's my cue to bounce.

As I'm walking away, I get a message from Matthew, and it almost makes me scream for joy. I'm walking past the big bins near the back entrance when I open it.

> Spoke to Fernanda in Spanish class. She's into Warcraft too! 🖤

He sends a GIF of a cartoon puppy celebrating. Cool. We need to work on his messaging;

but otherwise, that's great news. Genuinely, I'm happy for him. I reply with a , and he sends another heart. Because of course he does.

Mum lets Matthew and I carry on at St. Luke's after school because we missed yesterday's Happy Campers meeting after everything that went down. Her and Nanna both had a lot to say about Kehinde, and for once, I didn't bother trying to defend him.

Matthew's already waiting for me by the gate when I get to St. Luke's. It's just the two of us today, because everyone else has finished for the day, and the Happy Campers only help out on Saturdays. I brought my portable speakers with me, but Matthew's intent on talking over the music. He keeps asking me to turn down the volume. I'm reluctant, but eventually I lower it by a couple of notches.

I've already done the second coating of paint on my wall before he's even finished his first. He leans up against a dry patch.

"Hey, I've been meaning to ask all day, is everything OK with your friend? I feel bad; I know you didn't want to be seen…" He trails off. "I don't want to come in between you two." He looks down at his feet and I can tell he's in his feelings about this.

"Yeah, it is what it is, man," I reply. "Kehinde's some passionate guy. When he has your back, it's all good. He just doesn't always see the difference between right and wrong." Something I'm slowly coming to realize.

"Have you talked it through?" he asks.

"Nah, Kehinde's not someone you talk things through with. He takes stuff kinda personal." My mum told him off once for going through her fridge, and he's hated her ever since.

We carry on painting for a bit, when Matthew catches me completely off guard with another question.

"Did you ever think we'd find ourselves here, after that first time you came to the Happy Campers?"

"Can't lie; I really didn't." Me and Matthew, side by side, painting and decorating. Not to mention the million other things we've been through together in such a short time.

"Well, I'm glad it happened," he says, not looking up from the wall.

"Life is so random sometimes, but I'm here for it," I reply.

We continue painting, and I sneakily turn the volume back up. You know what, we're actually having a pretty chill evening. I've noticed Matthew has started experimenting on his wall, painting faces and Britney Spears lyrics. He has a sheepish grin when he sees me looking and says we're just gonna paint over it anyway. I do my own version, graphing my name in lines and swivels, only with a paintbrush instead of a spray can. Matthew copies me with his own name, and he's actually pretty good.

"What's that one?" He points to a graph of the tag name I'm trying out: "Venomz."

"It's like a stage name or nickname that people use on the streets," I tell him. "What would yours be?"

He thinks for a second. "Scarlet Moistcake." He's certain of his choice.

"Lol, you're actually not normal, you know that?"

"What's that in the corner?" He points down to where I've tried painting something. It's a woman helping another woman into a lifeboat. It's not great; these paintbrushes aren't right for the kind of detail I was going for, but I wanted to try to make the room feel a bit more special for the women who are going to be using it.

Matthew's gone and stood right up close now, inspecting it with his mouth hanging open. Pause. "Anton, it's brilliant."

"Thanks, man." Hopefully he's not exaggerating. I'm low-key psyched that it looks like what I want it to look like.

Around eight o'clock, Mum comes to pick us up. It's handy, because she can point out what needs doing next when we come through on Saturday. She laughs when she sees the graffiti, but she has the same reaction as Matthew when he shows her the little scene I painted.

She stares in silence.

"You did this?" Tears well up in her eyes, and now I just want to run for the door. But no, I need to own it. It's good. I hope. "You think you can do something like this in the main hall?" she asks.

"I guess so," I reply. "I'll need different brushes, though, and way more time. But I can do it." She pulls me in for a big, tight hug, while Matthew packs our stuff away, pretending not to notice.

I don't think she's comfortable having Matthew walk in this neighborhood on his own. Even with his fresh trim, the guy still floats like a butterfly and stings like a marshmallow. So we walk him to the bus stop and wait with him for the two minutes before the bus comes. It's light and breezy on the way home; we don't say much. Though, after walking in silence for a bit, Mum does say, "I like that boy."

"Me too."

I GOT A B for my English homework. An actual B, not a D that I had to draw over to make it look like a B. I can't wait to go home and show this to Mum and Nanna.

The guys are still giving me the silent treatment. It's awkward at school, but not having Kehinde calling and messaging me 24/7 is so refreshing. It's like I got space to think, or like I've been underwater for years and am just coming up for air.

Things seem to be looking up for Matthew, too. I just passed him on the benches chatting to Fernanda, Rochelle, and her horrible cousin.

Fernanda was laughing the most at whatever he was saying, and Rochelle seems to have really taken a shine to him.

"Proud," I say out loud before I can stop myself. I don't know where that came from.

I've got my meeting with Mr. Wall now, the first time I'm ever scheduled to see a teacher and it's not a detention. I have to go past the school reception to get to his office, and he opens the door to let me in when I knock, saying, "All right, you scallywag?" Yep, he still talks like a pirate. Probably a Chelsea fan in his youth. "I hear you've been keeping out of trouble."

"Yes, sir, I kinda have, still."

"Good lad." His office is smaller than I was expecting; there's just enough space for the desk and a couple of chairs. The walls are lined with school photos dating back to the midnineties.

"Rah, sir, I didn't know you had hair back in the day," I say before sitting down. Most teachers would take this as a dig, but he just chuckles and tells me to sit down and reminds me he has the power to expel me. The mood changes when we're sitting opposite each other.

"Now, I'm not going to ask you about your subject choices, not straightaway." If he does a Mr. Benjamin and asks where I see myself in five years, well, I won't be angry, just disappointed. "Tell me, Anton, what do you like? Right now, what are your hobbies and interests?"

Outside of my phone? Not a lot. I can't say chilling with the guys, that's not a hobby, and I don't really like it that much anymore anyway. I'm not much for football, either. Physical exercise makes me sweat too much, and my BO could wake a tranquilized rhino.

"Let me rephrase that," he says when I struggle to answer. "What do you do in your spare time?"

I wanna tell him that I'm a G on road, just to see what he says. Instead, St. Luke's pops into my head. At the moment, I'm spending most of my free time there or with Matthew, or both.

"I've been painting." I'm a bit relieved when Mr. Wall nods and smiles, like it's the type of answer he was hoping for.

"Tell me about that," he says.

"Er, well, it's just walls at this women's refuge

my mum is working on. But I wanna do more." I think about the mural Mum's asked me to do. I've already got some ideas for it.

"Ah, a regular Van Gogh." He grins.

"Yeah, except I have two ears. And I ain't Scottish."

"Dutch. Although I see why you might think he's Scottish." Mr. Wall strokes his chin. "Do you know any other artists?"

"Not really. I remember Van Gogh from a history book, not art." Mum would keep books in the bathroom, and before I had a phone, I would skim through them. She once got me an encyclopedia from a thrift shop, and I read through the whole thing instead of doing my homework. Mr. Wall asks if I've read any other history books, and I tell him Wikipedia's cheaper. The Romans, Victorians, the world wars, Rosa Parks, all that stuff is fascinating. He says the school library has some good options on those subjects. Maybe Matthew could show me around.

Wait, how does he know about me and Matthew? I guess he could show me around.

We talk a bit more about history and art, and

then when Mr. Wall does eventually turn the conversation to my subject exams, he looks a bit smug. He hands me a list of the subjects on offer and I skim through them.

Engineering. Lol, I can't even build a tent. Why would I want to build stuff when other people do it better?

Business studies. What if they don't want fries with that? I'd be lost.

Drama. Between Matthew, Kehinde, my mum and dad, I feel like I spend my whole life avoiding drama.

I don't need any more.

Digital technology. AI's gonna take over and destroy the world. Until then, I just be scrolling and snapping.

But the last two options make me raise my eyebrows. *History.* Where we came from. What happened in the past that led us up to this point?

And *art*. People get paid to draw. Album covers, anime, murals, animated videos. You think of how something looks, and then you make it appear on paper. Imagine, that's some people's jobs.

When I look up at Mr. Wall, he's pretending to check his nails, the corners of his mouth twitching. Pause.

"So am I to assume you might be taking art and history?" he asks. I nod and tell him yeah, thanks. "Well, wasn't that easy?" he says with a grin.

"Yeah, it sorta was, you know." All this time I been scared about this decision, or avoiding it, and now it's actually kinda exciting.

"I think you'll rather enjoy next year, Anton."

"Yeah, sir, I think I will."

"No, you will not. You *shall*." Sigh.

"What's the difference?"

"To will is just a simple want to do something. Churchill said we *shall* fight on the beaches, not we *will* fight on the beaches. There's a difference between desires and certainties."

"Oh, OK," I say, not really getting it. "I mean,

I was still right. I *shall* be doing art and history next year, and I *will* try to enjoy it."

He gives me a thumbs-up and sends me back to class. Luckily, it's history.

I'm so pumped at the end of the day that I message Matthew to hang out. It is Friday, after all. He replies immediately. Like, barely a split second after it left my phone. Apparently, he's got something important to tell me, and I'm not gonna believe it. I'm surprised there's no emojis in his message; maybe he's showing signs of improve—oh wait, no, here it is. A cheeky kitten, followed by a GIF of two friends high-fiving each other at the beach. Bleugh. I'm meeting him down one of the side roads out the back exit.

Five minutes later, he's already waiting for me at the end of the road.

"Hey, guess what?" He's positively buzzing. Look at him, bouncing up and down. This guy's like an excited puppy; he's always too hyped. I wanna tell him to chill, but I saw him chatting to Rochelle earlier, and I wonder if he put in a good word for me.

"What is it?"

"I got us a double date."

No way, he's lying. Get outta here. But he's got that smug smile that he does whenever my mum compliments him, radiating glows of annoyingness. I think he might be telling the truth....

I clear my throat and casually ask, "Oh yeah?" I don't wanna look too on it, even though my chest is tingling. "Is it with who I think it is?"

"You bet your bubble butt it is." He winks at me.

"Could've just said yes." I'm not even gonna get onto him about winking at me again. He got me a date with Rochelle. "When's the date?"

"Seven PM," he says cheerfully.

I stare at him. Seven? "As in seven PM tonight?"

"Yep." He's so proud of himself he's beaming.

"Er, that's soon." That's very soon. I haven't had time to work on my A game with Rochelle; this feels too sudden. Can't let him know that, though. "If Fernanda's there, she might accidentally let something slip and everyone at school will know that we're hanging out. Romance takes time."

"Oh." His face drops. "I didn't think about that." He shakes his head sadly, almost like he's telling himself off. "You want me to cancel?"

"Hell no," I say before thinking.

OK, let me think. Can we tell Fernanda and Rochelle that me and Matthew are related somehow? Cousins can be different races, if one of the parents marries someone different. Nah, that won't work; look at him. OK, we'll tell her that his mum and my mum are friends, and I'm only going on this date as a favor. I tell Matthew it would also explain why Kehinde saw him at my house, if word gets out and people start putting two and two together.

"Wow, you're really putting a lot of thought into this." He pulls a face like I've just insulted his favorite Disney film, but I look past it. I'm holding up my end of the bargain, and I've got bigger things to worry about than Matthew's feelings.

I drag us over to my house first so I can get changed, and then we leave immediately to go to Matthew's for him to do the same.

"What are you gonna wear?" I ask him once we're on the bus.

"I've got a great turtleneck."

"No. Just no. Turtlenecks are for guys who pose on Instagram while leaning against a car."

"I can lean against a car. I did it once when I got tired in the sun." Lord, save me.

"Look, do me a favor tonight—don't talk about leaning against cars because you're tired. Remember, we're trying to impress them."

"That's fine. I'll talk about balloon animals. I've been watching tutorials on YouTube."

"I'm gonna go with 'No, nay, never,'" I tell him.

"Why not, it's creative," he protests. "I can hang them up around my room like an art gallery."

"Bro, that sounds terrifying. Don't mention balloon animals in creepy galleries."

"Can I talk about anime?"

"No."

"But you told me to be myself!" He throws his arms up.

Ah, I did say that; he's using my own words against me.

"Fine, you can talk about anime, but don't blame me if she's not feeling it." For real, on a scale of one to holding a tarantula, this is probably the most nervous and excited I've been in a minute. At least me and Matthew have *that* in common.

We get off the bus near St. Mary's Road. Matthew's got one of those huge yards with space for two cars out front. Apparently, his mum and his sister are out. I rate that Matthew has this much freedom in his home life. When it comes to some things. Others not so much.

"Why does your room smell like that?" I say, looking around as we step inside. The scent is floral, all sickly sweet. Everything's made of old wood, even the floors, except the fluffy rug and silky bedsheets.

"My mum sometimes comes in in the morning and sprays the sheets with lavender." He says it like it's a good thing. It's probably the whackest thing I've ever heard. Sometimes I can't believe we're the same age. My mum hasn't been in my room for months, and even then, last time she came in was to collect mugs for the dishwasher.

"It helps me sleep," he protests. "Maybe if you had lavender spray on *your* sheets, you wouldn't be such a sourpuss all the time. It has very calming effects, you know."

I roll my eyes. I suppose it does smell kinda nice.

We have to leave in forty minutes. I'm looking fly for my first date with Rochelle. I dusted off my new Jordans that I've been saving for a special occasion, and I kept the mouthwash in my mouth for a whole minute before I spat it out. I'm tryna pick out an outfit for Matthew, going through his drawers looking for clothes, expecting him to help, but he just stands there. Oh no, why is he biting his lip like he's gonna say something that jars me?

"What is it? Why you just standing there like a lemon?" Clock's ticking, for real.

"I need your help." His entire mouth is trembling, and he's holding something behind his back. What is it this time? "I've got these two really long hairs on my shoulders, and I'm scared Fernanda's gonna notice them through my T-shirt." He's talking really fast and pulls out a pair of tweezers. Nope. Uh-uh. Not in this lifetime. "Please, I can't reach."

"Matthew." I sigh. "Listen…" How do I put this in a nice way? "I'd literally rather eat a bowl of fire. I can't even begin to tell you how much I'm not gonna do that."

"They're just hairs." He almost laughs at my reaction. But I'm not budging. I wouldn't do it for my own mum; I'm not doing it for Matthew.

"OK. You're right." He sits on the edge of the bed. My shoulders start to relax when he puts the tweezers down. "I'm just gonna have to call off the date."

"No!" I shout, jumping up. This is my chance with Rochelle. The mouthwash, my kicks, I'm ready for the date right now. "You can't call it off because of a couple of hairs. That's ridiculous." This guy would even jeopardize his own date with Fernanda.

"If they're just hairs, you shouldn't have any trouble helping me out." He does this little head-shake like he's just won the argument. The worst part is he kinda has.

"Gimme those stupid things." I grab the tweezers. I can't believe I'm doing this. "If you tell anyone, *anyone*, I'll shove these where the sun don't shine, and our deal's off."

"Fine by me." He pulls off his school shirt and I take a step toward him as he turns around. "I'm ready for my close-up, Mr. Exfoliator," he whispers over his shoulder.

"Nope." I throw the tweezers onto the bed. "I'm out." He takes it too far sometimes.

He laughs. "Please, please, no, please. Anton, I was kidding."

I look up to the heavens and beg my ancestors for strength. Why am I here? I take a deep breath. I'm not gonna let his stupid shoulder hairs ruin my date. With some superhuman courage, I pick the tweezers back up.

"Swear down, you're lucky we're friends, you know." I slowly go to pluck out the first one.

He's quiet for a minute while I concentrate. "Are we really friends, or are you just desperate for this date?" he asks without turning his head. His tone is different, and I think about stopping what I'm doing for a second. But I don't know what to say, so I choose to ignore him; we can get into it later.

I resume the dehumanizing task at hand. I'm frowning, and we're both silent as I gently grip the long, thin hair on the back of his shoulder. In my head, I'm screaming, "This is so weird, this is so weird!" but I don't give him the satisfaction of saying it out loud. I'm bare focused, like a surgeon in the operating theater. Matthew is very silent, letting me get to work without moving an inch. Nobody. Can ever. Know. Then all of a sudden…

"Ahem."

MY HAND IS frozen, midair. Matthew and I both whip our heads around at the same time. Rochelle is standing there, leaning in the doorway with her arms folded. There's a half smile on her face. I blink. And immediately throw the tweezers straight out the window. I take a giant leap away from Matthew and put my hands in the air like I'm being robbed.

"Yo, Rochelle, it's not what it looks like." Part of me is buzzing to see her. I can't help it; I'm crushing on her so much, and my body feels electric. But I'm also proper confused that she's here, like, I'm shocked. I can't look her in the eye after what she just witnessed.

"Hi, Ro-Ro." Matthew waves at her from across the room. Why's he not surprised to see her? What the... was he was expecting her?

"Yeah, I'll give you two a minute. I didn't mean to interrupt this." She lazily waves her hand at us. "Whatever this is." She goes downstairs.

The second she closes the door, I turn on Matthew. "What is Rochelle doing here? We're not supposed to meet until seven; you didn't tell me we were all going together." My voice is quiet, but it's all high-pitched and squeaky.

He just stares at me with a blank expression. "I messaged her about our double date; she came over to wish us good luck." When he talks, he sounds kinda confused, which makes me confused.

"What the hell you talking about? Why would she wish us good luck?" My stomach is starting to freeze over. "Matthew, who is the double date with?" I know the answer before he even says it.

"Fernanda and Grace," he says innocently.

"Her cousin?" My eyes are wide.

295

"Yeah. Why? Who did you think it was?" He raises an eyebrow and tilts his head. My fists squeeze into little balls; my arms, face, everything tenses up. My eyes are closed so tight I'm punching the air in pure frustration.

"No, no, God no, oh my days, no—arghhh!" I've lost all composure. How could he do this to me? "Bruv, you knew I like Rochelle, so why did you agree to double-date with Grace?!"

"You said it's a good idea to practice on a girl you don't like." He says it with this knowing smile. This guy's infuriating, using my own words against me when he knows I already know it was wrong. I guess it shows he's paying attention. Still, of all people, did he have to choose the one person who's about as joyful as a flickering light bulb in a horror film?

"She's just a person." Matthew laughs.

"Yeah, and a shark is just a giant fish," I snap back. Honestly, I'm fuming.

"Well, then it's a good thing I'm joking about Grace," he says, slapping his own thigh as he points at me. Man laughing like Santa.

"Are you kidding? Matthew, please tell me you're not joking now? Is it Grace or Rochelle?" I'm frantic.

He just taps the side of his nose, like what middle-class women do as a sign they won't tell you something. I think I'm going to lose it.

There's a little knock at the door before Rochelle comes back in again. I force myself to regain my composure.

"I hear you're my date for the night." Her voice is super deadpan. So hard to read.

"I am?" From the corner of my eye, I see Matthew smirking at the "joke" he just pulled. I'm biting my tongue so hard, trying to give him low-key evil eyes. Getting me all flustered. "Yeah, yes, I am," I say to Rochelle. For real, though, I do owe it to Matthew, he sorted me with this one. Even if I did expose the depth of my feelings for Rochelle with my little outburst, I'm proper grateful.

"So..." Rochelle raises her eyebrows, amusement flickering on her face. "Matthew asked me round to talk wardrobe choices." Oh, did he now? Matthew's standing there awkwardly, still shirtless, with his hand on the back of his head.

"We don't need you for that. I already got this." I march back over to his wardrobe and flick through, looking for something I wouldn't be super embarrassed to wear myself. I get to the end of his clothes and go back to the beginning. Most of this I wouldn't wear in the backyard, let alone in public. Rochelle comes over and nudges me out the way, pulling out two T-shirts. One is black with some anime characters on it, and the other one's a plain, washed-out pink.

"Oh, can I wear the pink one?" Matthew claps his hands like he's sat in the front row at a magic show.

I say, "No!" at the same time Rochelle says, "Yes." It's a tie, which means Matthew gets the final vote. He pulls a face at me with his bottom lip, visibly guilty as he picks up the pink shirt, staring me in the eye as he slowly puts it on.

"Why the eye contact, though?" I groan as Rochelle looks away to hide her laughter.

"How do I look?" He lifts his hand to his

chin, classic Matthew pose. The pink is a lot, all flesh-colored.

"You look like a brain," I tell him, "or one of those hairless cats."

Rochelle ignores me. She stands back, analyzing him as though she's a fashion designer checking out her creation. "I like it. It brings out your eyes." She pairs it with dark jeans and gives him her over-one-shoulder bag that's literally designed to look like a duck.

Nah, this is blasphemy. "I'm just saying, we should've got you better threads, maybe done a few push-ups here and there, instead of dressing you like a tongue and throwing a duck around your shoulder."

Matthew's been admiring his reflection, but when I say that, his smile drops. Now he's looking at himself in a different way, frowning at his T-shirt. "Is it too much? Maybe I should take it all off," he says.

Before I can agree, Rochelle tuts loudly and says, "Matthew, you're fine the way you are. Actually, you're more than fine; you're lovely. No clothes can ever change your true nature. If a rose by any other name is still a rose, then a Matthew with any other shirt is still Matthew." Whoa, go Ro-Ro. "If Fernanda likes you, it's because you're authentic and sweet, and not because you obsessively do push-ups."

"And if she doesn't?"

"If she doesn't like you for you? Well, it's a silly question because I know she does. She's emotionally intelligent and she can see your true nature."

Matthew grins and he and Rochelle head downstairs, chatting away. I race to catch up to them, still processing everything she just said. When you think about it, Matthew can never pretend to be someone he's not. In fact, he's incapable of it. If Fernanda likes him, at least it'll be genuine. If she doesn't, well, same logic applies. Either way, one-zero to Rochelle.

"You look good," I whisper to Matthew as we get on the bus. I know Rochelle heard, because she turns her head slightly, but she don't say nothing.

Fernanda's on her phone as we rock up to the bus stop Matthew arranged to meet her at. You can tell she's made an effort: Her hair's big and blow-dried, and she's got fake lashes we're not allowed to wear at school. She's even wearing Air Force 1s that don't have a single scuff.

"Hello, I'm Matthew from school." He reaches out and shakes her hand like he's at a job interview.

"Hello, Matthew from school; I am Fernanda, also from school." She giggles. Eughh. Rochelle's eyes catch mine and she bites her lip.

"Oh my gosh, Matthew, your T-shirt is so nice," Fernanda says. "It makes your eyes pop, qué guapo." He does a fake blush, telling her to "staaaawp." "And I love, love, love your bag." She turns to me and Rochelle, a devilish grin on her face. "He is *my* date; hands off." What. The. Heck. Is going on? Matthew looks like he's on cloud nine, like he's internally flying through the cosmos or in an A$AP Rocky video.

He says it's a nice evening and we should walk the rest of the way to Nando's to make the most of it. I have a sneaky feeling he's only saying that so he can walk and talk with his date, which fair play, is exactly what happens.

"Are you up to date on *One Piece*?" he asks. She puts her fingers in her ears.

"No, I'm not, so no spoilers. Have you finished *Dragon Ball*?" she asks.

"I'm still on season four. I really like you. That's not a TV show; it's just how I feel right now."

She blushes and shushes him, then looks around to see if me and Rochelle heard. We did. We also hear her say, "Me too." Seriously, the universe is broken right now.

"You heard that, right?" I turn to Rochelle.

"Leave them alone; it's sweet." She gives me side-eye, but she's smiling at the same time. My heart does a backflip. A little one, that doesn't stick the landing. 6/10.

"Do you even like Nando's?" I ask her.

"Nope." She pulls a face and clicks her tongue. "Nando's is like Drake. So overrated, but it was great ten years ago." Then the weirdest thing happens. Now we're firing off Drake songs at each other, listing them in order of best to worst, talking about our favorites, and singing along to the parts we know by heart. Once or twice, Fernanda even turns around and joins in. Thank God for overrated Nando's.

The thing about Nando's is you know what you're getting before you've even stepped in. There's always a family there for someone's birthday, or some guy with a date he's not talking to. The staff are borderline rude, but the wings are so awesome you don't mind the eye-rolling servers. We're in a four-seater by the window. Matthew is leading the conversation, Fernanda's lapping it all up, and Rochelle is nodding along like she's watching a sitcom.

"Hey, Anton, Fernanda's in the top class in math. Isn't that cool?"

"Oh. Yeah, sure, man, that is definitely subjectively cool," I tell him, trying to be supportive.

"I've got a math joke; you want to hear it?" Matthew says. "What shape makes curses disappear? A hex-a-gone." Fernanda finds it hilarious. She playfully pushes his arm, and he does the stupid shoulder wiggle. Again, I'm checking my heartbeat to see if this is really happening.

"So have you guys decided what subjects you're choosing for next year?" Fernanda asks the rest of us after we've ordered. I know Rochelle's probably thought about it. I used to think she was wound tight, but the more I get to know her, the more I see she's just some next responsible person. She's going places, you know.

"I wish I could do all of them," she says, "but I went with digital tech and business studies. They're the two most helpful subjects for what I want to do in the future. What about you, Matthew?"

"Drama and music," he says without missing a beat. OK, drama I get; this guy's always overreacting to stuff like he's on a bad episode of *Grey's Anatomy* or something, but music? He sings terribly, and he's got no sense of rhythm. Like, none. He must have tried serenading the girls at some point, too, because we all start laughing, and he sits up in his chair. "You can all laugh now, but when I'm playing the harp at my cat's funeral, we'll see who's laughing." Still us.

"What about you, Anton, what subjects?" Fernanda asks me.

"Yeah, well, I was thinking about maybe doing art and history." Why are my cheeks burning? I ain't never spoken to anyone about this kinda stuff before—apart from Mr. Wall, and that was only this morning.

I barely have to time to finish the sentence before Matthew practically shouts, "Oh, Anton, how wonderful!" He leans across to hug me, and I just let him. "You're so good at painting, and you're going to love history, I just know you will. Tap waters all around!" I can't help but laugh as we all cheers our glasses.

"Fernanda, how's your swimming stuff going?" Rochelle asks as Matthew finally calms down. Apparently, Fernanda's a very strong swimmer, like, future Olympic level.

"Other than my tired shoulders, I think it's going good," she says.

Our proper drinks come then, and Matthew says we should have a toast to Fernanda and her swimming for sports day, which is sweet. Then he says if we're having a toast, we should have butter, which is stupid.

"I'd do very well at sports day," he says next, which is way funnier than his toast-and-butter joke. This guy has all the physical prowess of a goth playing football.

"Naming unicorns by their virtues isn't a sport," I tell him.

"Actually, I'll have you know, I have the strength of a thousand baby antelopes."

"Why antelopes? You could have chosen literally any animal on the planet, and you went with antelopes. They're not even known for being that strong."

"Actually, I see where he's coming from," Fernanda chimes in.

"How, Fernanda? How do you see where he's coming from?" Even Rochelle is grinning at how riled up I'm getting. This guy's seriously *not* athletic. "He even specified baby antelopes, not even ones in peak physical condition. Literally, you went to the very bottom of the food chain." Fernanda's giggling at all the foolishness; she seems into it. It's perplexing me. "Rochelle, please tell 'em."

She pretends to think about it. "Actually, I think Matthew could be an Olympic gold-winner someday."

"In hopscotch?" he chimes in enthusiastically.

"In hopscotch," Rochelle confirms. I see what they're doing and it is pretty funny. Matthew has said so many wild things around me, I just know he's got more up his sleeve.

"I've even been doing leg workouts." He does a smoldering pose to Fernanda as he says it. She playfully fans herself with her hand. "And I've been working on my glutes. Last week, I dropped my chewing gum on the floor, so I squatted over the packet and picked it up with my butt cheeks." I'm done. I throw my paper towel on the plate and cover my face with my hands. I can feel Rochelle's leg shaking with laughter next to me.

We move on to playing a game where someone has to sing a song without using the lyrics, and the first person to guess it is the winner. Rochelle sings "Doo Wop" by Lauryn Hill, which we all guess immediately. I choose J. Cole's "Punchin' the Clock," and I have to sing it twice before Rochelle gets it. Fernanda chooses her favorite band, Aventura, and Rochelle gets that, too.

"Damn, you're good," I tell her, and she gives me this beautiful smile.

We're interrupted by the waiter coming over with our food. And even though I'm hungry, I kinda wish it had taken longer. Still, I demolish my wings within about two minutes. See, if this was a one-on-one date, I'd probably eat something less messy, but with four of us here, there's less need to impress. It's chill. Even with the hot sauce going up both sides of my face like the Joker.

"You've got a little something..." Rochelle points to my cheek. I lightly dab at the corner of my lip, acting like there isn't still a gallon of sauce around my mouth.

"All gone? How are my cleaning skills?" I don't know why, I put on a super-duper posh voice.

"Absolutely terrific. No notes." She copies my terrible accent.

Matthew's pouring with sweat from the lemon-and-herb spice, and Fernanda's fanning him with a menu, calling him a "poor niño." I'm rolling my eyes because he's totally milking it. Fernanda doesn't care, though. Once we've finished eating, they start some super boring chat about this manga or something they both read, real nerdy stuff. Me and Rochelle talk more about music, who we're listening to right now, who our parents listen to, shout-out Celine Dion, who deserves R & B album of the year this year, and honestly, it's a great vibe. I remember watching one of Kehinde's podcasts that listed annoying things girls do, and one of them was "when they talk about themselves too much." But seriously, I could talk to Rochelle all night about her taste in music, her family, where she's been, what her plans are. How else am I supposed to get to know someone? We've never spoken *this* much, and honestly, I've never liked her more.

When it's time to go, I take ages to put on my coat. It still feels so early in the night, and being around them, especially Rochelle, it all feels so easy. Natural, even. I really don't want to leave. But Fernanda's got curfew, so we kinda have to.

As we're walking out, we let Matthew do his

round of the singing game because he didn't get to do it earlier. Before he opens his mouth, I quickly ask, "Is it Britney Spears?" He shakes his head, saying he's not that predictable. Then he starts singing ABBA.

"Look at them," Rochelle says quietly on our way back to the bus stop. Matthew and Fernanda are holding hands, and once or twice, he's turned to us grinning and silently mouthed "Oh my God." I'm here for it, man. Like, I don't understand it. At all. But I am here for it.

"He deserves this." I meant to say it in my head, but it comes out my mouth instead. Rochelle smiles softly. "I mean, like, he's a good kid."

"And what are you then?" she asks.

Whoa, big question. I think about Kehinde and my dad, the two people I kinda looked up to, the way I moved at school, and how I treated kids like Matthew.

"I'm not good," I tell her.

"What are you basing that on?"

"I dunno; things I've done." I shrug. "I was such a jerk; I've upset so many people. Including you."

"I'm asking about present Anton, the Anton who's been helping Matthew, and volunteering, and tries harder in math class for some reason. I like who you are, and I don't really care about who you used to be."

She likes who I am! I scream in my head.

"People who want to change can change," she continues. "For what it's worth, I think you're pretty good."

"Tell that to your cousin, the one who hates me." I nudge her with my shoulder and she nudges me back softly.

"Hopefully, you'll have a different answer if I ask you again later." Hopefully. "And Anton?"

"Yeah, fam."

"If Matthew ever offers me a piece of chewing gum, please stop me from taking it."

WE'RE FINISHING PAINTING the quiet room. Our next task will be clearing out the main hall with all the other campers and washing the windows. It's only a couple of weeks until opening, and the place is buzzing with volunteers. It really feels like things are starting to come together. When Matthew comes strolling in, later than usual, it's because he was so happy after the date last night that he couldn't sleep.

"How did I do, Anton?"

"Can't lie; you did well. Fernanda's geekier than she looks. And she's definitely into you."

His face turns into a pouty smile. "For real? Are you sure?"

"Yeah, I'm sure. She likes you. It made me question the very fabric of reality, but it's clear as day." He drops his brush and runs over to hug me. "OK, OK." I laugh, trying to push him away.

"Oh, Anton. My bride, Fernanda, doth come hither." Yep. The very fabric of reality. "And what of your maiden, thy sweetest Ro-Ro?" He finally lets go.

"Yo, chill." I laugh. To be fair, I've been thinking a lot about her, especially our chat at the end of the date last night. All that stuff about not judging me for the past and how people can change. It makes me think of my dad. I wonder if it's possible he could change. What if I judged too early?

It's still on my mind when I go to get some water from the cooler. Joshua Nikos is standing there, cup in one hand as he scrolls on his phone.

"You good?" I ask when he looks up.

"Yeah, fine," he replies. "Anton, right?" He remembers me; that's a good start. "So your mum is the mastermind behind all this; you must be very proud."

Yeah, this guy's legit. I tell him I'm super proud, and we start chatting about a bunch of stuff, about my exams, and art, and football. And I appreciate it, an adult talking to me on a level. I'm so used to Mum and teachers. Maybe I can ask him about my dad; I do need an adult's perspective, and Joshua seems to know what's what.

"Uh, Joshua?" I ask just as he finishes his water.

"Yep?" I notice that his kicks are Off-White; I seen them online. They must've cost a bag. He's actually cool.

I start telling him about my predicament, how my dad was horrible to my mum but she's forgiven him and moved on, but I hadn't seen him in some time and he never called, and basically the entire story. It's a bit confusing because I zigzag all over the shop with my timeline, but I get the main points out. I finish with how now I'm second-guessing myself, and it's playing on my mind if I should see him again.

Joshua's super patient; he doesn't interrupt me, even when I lower my voice as two Happy

Campers walk past. He takes a minute to think about his answer, too, which I appreciate.

"I suppose if your dad's done his time, and he's received the repercussions for his actions, you can't tether him to the past," Joshua says. "If there's any uncertainty, it's important to stay open-minded. And I don't think one meeting is enough to know for sure whether or not you want him in your life going forward. Especially if you have your mum's support with that."

Yeah, all the arrows are pointing toward a round two. I tell Joshua as much, and he almost looks apologetic. He says it's a big responsibility for such a young man.

"You got any advice?" I ask.

"Don't mistake curiosity for expectation," he tells me. And because he said it, I know I won't.

I do like Matthew, but it is nice to get a break from him occasionally. Chilling with him is like watching films in the IMAX: Sometimes your senses need a rest.

I've been thinking about my chat with Joshua and how Rochelle said she won't judge me for the past. It's not like I'm betraying my mum by seeing my dad again; she's already forgiven him, and I am tryna look forward, not back. So I messaged him yesterday, and he took a few hours to reply, but here we are on Sunday afternoon, back in Café Culture. When I arrive, he's sitting in the same seat as last time. Creature of habit, I guess.

"You good?" he asks when I sit down.

"Yeah."

He orders us both a full breakfast this time. He quizzes me while we eat, asking me about "the girl that I like." It's a bit weird when he gets a call on his phone from some number he hasn't saved. He quickly cancels it and carries on chatting like it didn't happen.

It's not that bad, sitting with him. He's got loads of stories about prison, telling me about what he ate, where he slept, the things he saw. As we're finishing up, I finally pluck up the courage to ask him a question that's been on my mind for a minute. I already know how Mum sees it, and I'm curious to see what his answer would be.

"What went down between you and Mum back in the day? Like, what was it like before you got put away?" Based on his reaction, I can tell he's a bit taken aback. He opens his eyes wide and has a bit of a scowl when he finally responds.

"You got to understand; we were young. We had ups and downs like any relationship. But I do gotta say that your mum changed the older we got. She changed a lot even."

"Changed how?" Does he think they grew apart?

"Things were never enough for her. Always complaining about everything I did, who I was with." Oh. "I know I weren't perfect, but how was she talking about going to university and that, acting like her life weren't good enough?"

"That don't sound like change; it sounds like growth." I think about how incredible Mum is now, how important she is to St. Luke's and the community, and how she probably wouldn't be in this position if she hadn't gone on to study.

"Growth? You think I don't know what university's like? She wanted to be one of them social girls, surrounded by guys, drinking and partying. You think I'm gonna allow my woman to do that? Nah, I had to put my foot down. And it didn't help having your grandma in her ear, encouraging some fake dream."

I can't believe what I'm hearing. The mention of Nanna takes it a step too far, and did he just say "allow my woman"?

"Wait, so you stopped her going to school because you thought she'd meet other guys?" He acts like a big man out here, but the insecurities are shocking.

He tuts and turns his head, not taking me seriously. "You're too young to understand it. Parties and alcohol always lead to women cheating." His tone is so calm he obviously believes every word he's saying.

"What kind of wild statement is that? Women have birthday parties, Christmas parties, weddings, so many parties in their life, and you're accusing all of them for cheating?" I'm thinking about what it would be like to live with this guy, and my blood is boiling that he would've been like this with Mum.

"Imagine you're grown and your wife is out

partying with random dudes every night, how would you like it?" he asks.

"Fam, it's university, not *Love Island*. It's a bunch of nerds sitting in a library and sometimes playing pool. And by the way, it can't have been too much of a fake dream, because Mum did go to university, and she got a first-class degree, and she didn't go out partying every night. She came back to me and Nanna." For real, what are we talking about here?

He kisses his teeth, turning his head away like I just ate a slug in front of him. "Look, son, men and women are different; we have different standards," he says.

"I think you mean double standards. And that makes you a hypocrite," I snap.

He sits bolt upright and leans across the table. "Who you calling a hypocrite? Remember who you're talking to."

"Who I'm talking to? Fam, I don't know who I'm talking to. I don't even know you, and that's your fault. So Mum made the big-boy decision to go to university for a better life, and you couldn't handle it. You're some messed-up guy, bruv."

"She didn't need more school; I was already providing everything for us. Obviously, I'm not perfect, but nothing was ever good enough for her." That's the second time he's said that; it's so meaningless.

"Mum didn't need you to be perfect, she needed you to be better. *We* needed you to be better."

Hearing this guy talk about my mum like she's some any woman they're always discussing in one of Kehinde's videos, it makes me sick. I just wanna delete all those videos and all them podcasts from the internet, fam. No wonder she didn't want nothing to do with him all this time.

"When did you get so soft?" he says to me.

"If you were softer, maybe you wouldn't have been arrested." I'm raising my voice now. How did this become an attack on me?

"I knew this would happen; she's always coddled you. Anton, I can teach you how to be a man, a real man, not one of these 'yes ma'am, no ma'am' wet wipes. Roll with me for a week; it'll toughen you up. Living with those women is turning you into one."

I push myself up from the table. This time I don't lack the conviction. I'm not taking advice from someone who's too scared and insecure to let his partner go to university. I got enough people in my life to look up to: Mum, Nanna, Mr. Wall, Joshua Nikos, even Rob from Happy Campers, they've all taught me way more about being a man than this guy in front of me.

"This was a mistake," I tell him.

"Anton—" he says, and he literally reaches out to grab my hand. I sidestep it; we don't have that kind of relationship.

I walk out the café, taking a deep breath, stretching my arms out. Mr. Benjamin recently said he can sense the beginnings of change in me, and I'm starting to believe that he could be right.

Nanna's home when I walk in. She's stirring a glass of Coca-Cola to make it go flat, a Malagasy life hack that she says is good for the stomach. Probably not doctor recommended, but it means she must be hurting again. I wonder when we'll get those MRI results through. She can tell something's up when I flop into my chair with my head in my hands. Mum's out shopping, so I take the opportunity to offload onto Nanna, telling her all about this latest meeting with my dad.

"He kept saying stuff about Mum going to school and how she should have been grateful for what he gave her. He wanted to show me how to be like him, take me around and that. But then he got upset that I wasn't interested. And the scary part is a month ago I probably would've done it. What does that say about me, Nanna?"

She's a good listener, lets me rant, and waits patiently for me to finish before replying. We crack so many jokes that sometimes I forget she's been about, seen and done it all. Twice. The wrinkles on her face tell a hundred stories.

"Your dad is so lost right now, Anton," she says softly when I finish. "And you can choose to see him as a role model or you can choose a different path. But don't let *him* decide what kind of man you're gonna be. All these things he says and does, but he's missing the big picture, the most important thing."

"What?"

"It's that love matters, Anton. And I'm not saying that to win some kind of moral war, OK; it *truly* matters. It affects everything we say and do."

And she's right; of course she is. My dad doesn't operate with love, not for himself and not for others. How can he talk about being a man when he ain't even mastered the basics of how to be human. And what if I just wanna live my life not thinking about it, just be myself without all that weird pressure? Kinda like Matthew—he seems happy enough in his own skin. I'm glad Nanna doesn't expect me to be "manly," whatever that means anymore.

I sit there scrolling on my phone for the rest of the afternoon, and every now and then she comes over to stroke me behind the ear. Just like when I was a kid. It feels kinda nice.

Nobody's home when I get in from school the next day. It's been worse than most Mondays, which is saying something. The guys still aren't speaking to me, which I don't actually mind. But it means I still ain't got nobody to chill with. I wanna hang with Rochelle, but she's always with Matthew and Grace. And I do wanna hang out with Matthew, too, but I know that people are gonna chat. Part of me is holding on to what Kehinde said when he stormed out my house, how if I'm not king of the school, I'm a nobody. I don't wanna go back to being a nobody who's only known for having a criminal dad. It's bad enough not having the crew, allow diving straight into getting laughed at. I had to sneak into an empty classroom at lunchtime and scroll on my phone all alone.

There's nothing in the fridge except leftovers. There's tripe in the freezer; it smells like a belly button and the struggles of our people. I begged Mum never to serve it to me. She called me ungrateful and said people are starving back home while I'm sitting here being picky. I told her that tripe is an African dish, and the kids are still starving, so what does that tell you.

I barely have time to watch shorts when my phone starts buzzing in my hand. I missed two calls from Mum on the way home, and I forgot to call her back. When I answer, it's not good news.

"Anton, you need to listen to me carefully." She sounds out of breath; her voice is trembling like a fragile window. "Your grandmother's collapsed. I need you to go into my bedroom and get my phone charger; it's plugged in next to my bed." I jump to my feet and run into her bedroom. Charger, where's the charger? My hand is shaking as I find it and unplug it.

"Found it."

"Good, bring it with you. Now write this down. We're in the Leicester Ward in King's College Hospital, third floor." I type it into my phone notes. "Get here now."

"Mum?" I'm feeling properly shook; it's rising in me like a cold phoenix. "Is she gonna be all right?"

The deep breath she takes tells me everything I need to know.

"I don't know yet, Anton." So this is serious. Mum never lies to me, not even about the difficult things. I don't even put my jacket back on; I just sprint out the front door and make my way straight to the hospital.

Mum biting her nails is the first thing I see. On a little chair next to a hospital bed. The room is strangely quiet, considering the mayhem of all the nurses and doctors bustling around in the corridors of the ward. I stop in my tracks before I even get to the bed. It's the tubes. Nanna's already so frail; there shouldn't be tubes in her. She belongs at the kitchen table and on the couch watching her shows, not here.

When I come over, Mum thanks me for the charger.

"What happened?" The room is so silent I feel the need to whisper.

"The doctors think it happened weeks ago.

Internal bleeding in the abdomen, consistent with an accident." This doesn't make any sense. She's been fine; we would've noticed if she was bleeding internally. Then my mind skips to the other day. She was doubled over the kitchen counter. I just assumed she was hiding chocolate. How could I be so stupid? I was there at her hospital appointments for the pain in her stomach, and I know her MRI results are due back any day now.

"Oh, Mum," my mum says, stroking Nanna's hair.

When the doctor comes around, he asks if they can talk in private. My blood turns cold. If it's good news, he'd just say it. They step out into the corridor, so I take her seat by the bed.

"Nanna, I'm sorry, I'm sorry." I don't expect her to answer; she needs her rest. Hopefully she can hear me and knows I'm not just apologizing for the position she's in; I'm sorry about everything I've ever done. All those times I called her a snake. I swore at her once, a year ago; I was being petty about the TV or something. Oh my God, I can't believe I left her to get the bus on her own that time. Why wasn't I better?

"You've got nothing to apologize for. I'm proud of you, Anton." I didn't even clock she was awake, but she musters some kind of monumental strength and grasps my hand. I squeeze it right back. "I know you don't hear it enough. Your mum's proud of you, too; we all are." After everything I've done, all the grumbling and moaning, she's acting like I haven't been some loser, some ingrate kid at school and at home.

"*Why?* Why are you proud of me, Nanna? I haven't done anything to be proud of."

"I can see the glorious young man you're growing into."

I kiss her hand tight, my tears pooling around her knuckles. Where the hell is Mum?

"Nanna?" There's a shift, and I'm holding all the weight of her hand. I think she's fallen asleep again, but I continue anyway. "Remember what you said about your granddad, when you wore your white dress with the flowers on it? The way you loved him so much? That's who you are to me. That's how I feel about you." I can barely get the words out. "I'll keep trying to make you proud, Nanna; I promise. I am who I am because of you. So don't give up on me." Her eyes are closed, but her thin lips curl into a little smile.

It stays there while I hold her. Not too tight, but firm enough that she knows I'm here, that my life depends on it. She quietly leans into me. I remember her carrying me home when I was too tired to walk. And that time I scraped my knee on some gravel. She put me on the kitchen counter and pulled funny faces while she cleaned me up and put on a Band-Aid. Sometimes she'd sprinkle chocolate powder on my cornflakes when Mum wasn't looking. I don't deserve her. Her little hand comes up to tickle behind my earlobe. I close my eyes, desperate, intent that nothing will separate us. More tears; I'm trying not to move too much. She's my nanna. Her hand stops caressing me and I know she really has gone back to sleep this time. And for a while our hearts beat alongside each other, together as one.

NANNA DIES THE next day.

After that, the days blur into this weird muddle of time. I have to hug Mum a lot. She keeps cooking for three and then breaking down at the stove. Some of her friends came over one day, and she cried with them for a bit. On my side? I did a post on socials with a photo of Nanna with "RIP" as the caption. I didn't do it for sympathy or attention; I just want her on my grid forever.

There are no messages or phone calls from Kehinde, Marcus, or Caleb. I know the school knows because Mum phoned them. I did get a missed call from Matthew, but I ignored it.

Everything is too painful right now; my insides feel like a trapped nerve with tiny gusts of wind hitting it. He followed up with a message.

> Anton, please ignore my phone calls if you're not ready to talk. I'll try every morning at 11 am in case you change your mind. When I lost my grandma, it was a very lonely time and I felt like there was no one to talk to. But you can talk to me if you want to. Your nanna was awesome. And you're awesome. All the best, Matthew.

Even Rochelle sent me a message. Can't lie; I spent 99 percent of the week being miserable, but her message got me a tiny bit pumped.

> Sorry for your loss.
> Here if you wanna chat xx

I immediately saved the number and looked at her WhatsApp pic.

But my "friends," the ones who've known me for years? Nothing.

We had the funeral ten days after it happened, and we're already on day twelve. I still have a tiny panic whenever I go past Nanna's room. I make sure to close the door every time, but it's always a bit open when I pass it again. Mum must be going in there. But we don't talk about it. It's the scent coming out that gets me when her door's open, a mixture of minty VapoRub and flowery perfume. Maybe Matthew's right; it would be a relief to talk about this stuff to someone who knows what it's like. I haven't called him back, but I'm back to school on Monday morning. Totally unfair, considering Mum gets two whole weeks off work. I ain't gonna fight her on this one, though, not when we're both healing together. And I'm reminded about what Nanna said, about love being the most important thing. She was right. She was always right.

Washing the windows at St. Luke's feels good. It's been at a standstill for the last couple of weeks cuz we've been grieving hard, but Mum mentioned a reporter coming to cover the story of the renovation, so it felt like time to go back. The smell of new carpet and fresh paint, it's all proper welcoming. And with Nanna at the back of my mind in everything I do, the process of washing feels kinda therapeutic. Soap first, water straight after. But none of it feels as good as when I'm painting. I use the rest of the day to work on my mural in the main room. It feels soothing, like I get to take out my feelings about Nanna on these walls. And seeing the results at the end of the session is a bonus.

Matthew brings me an iced mocha, extra vanilla syrup. I turn my nose up at first, but it's actually gangster. He doesn't ask me how I'm doing; he's the only one. All the other Happy Campers give me that sad, pathetic look when they see me. Matthew didn't. He said that when

I'm ready to chat, he'll listen. And I appreciate that.

When he invites me for a sleepover that night, Mum thinks it's a good idea to take my mind off things. Once upon a time, the invitation would've been laughable, but now I'm kind of into it.

We go straight to his from St. Luke's and I meet his little sister, Anna, who looks like a mini version of Matthew. Same cartoon eyes and the physical integrity of wet toilet paper.

Matthew's sweet with her, doing little things like helping her take her shoes off. It's weird seeing him as the more responsible one in a relationship. When his mum lets us go upstairs to his bedroom, he's almost apologetic to Anna for leaving her alone.

"You wanna watch TV?" he asks when we get there.

"Yeah, what are you going to put on?" I guess a bit of screen time won't hurt.

"I've been watching *RuPaul's Drag Race*," he says, bare excited. "It's these guys with female alter egos, and they do tasks and stuff, and there's always arguments every week. It's so fun."

"Hard pass," I tell him.

"Why not? It's not so different to those wrestling shows people like. They're both silly entertainment about guys in sparkly costumes who have staged catfights for our amusement." I can see he's enjoying this. "Would you rather I put that on?" Well, not anymore, not when he describes it like that. Fine, I let him put on his show while I sit and scroll on my phone. Everybody wins. Two episodes later, and I'm the one reaching for the remote to skip the title intro. Stupid show, getting me hooked.

Matthew's dad joins us for dinner. He's soft-spoken, like a baby's fart, and he doesn't really join in the convo. I don't rate the guy; Matthew was desperate to show him a letter from Miss Lilly about an amazing essay he wrote on Martin Luther King, but his dad didn't even acknowledge it. He just said, "I've had a long day, Matthew, can you just let me enjoy my dinner?" After that, we mostly sit in silence and it's hella awks. Until Anna draws me a picture, which is pretty sweet.

"Do you like it?" she asks, all squeaky.

"It's passable," I tell her. "But thank you for drawing it for me, little one."

I feel bad for Matthew; there's no joy at his place. It's so different from my house, with Mum and Nanna. Nanna. I can hear her voice in my head, clear as day. Her laugh, the way she's always picking on me. *Was* picking on me. I quickly excuse myself from the table and run to the bathroom. This is the third time my eyes have cried without my permission today. After a bit, a soft knock at the door tells me Matthew's come to check on me. Again. This time he sits down on the other side of the door.

"I'll be here if you need to chat," he says. I don't want to chat. But I do go over and sit on the floor so we're basically back-to-back.

Later that night, when he's on a mattress on the floor, and I'm lying on my back in his silly lavender bed, I say to him, "Bro. You're not moist, you know. All that stuff I said to you on the camping trip, you can scratch that." Have to be real with it, fam. "You're all right, you know. And sorry, like, for how I used to be, way back when. I should've stood up for you more, with Kehinde and them man." I say all of this really quickly, not giving him time to answer. "And let me know if you want me to read that essay you wrote. I don't wanna dis your dad, but what he did was kinda cold."

His voice comes back at me through the dark. "Thanks, Anton."

"Yeah, bless." We lie in silence for a while longer. The darkness in here feels heavy; thoughts of Nanna are still in my heart. It pushes tears out the corners of my eyes and down the sides of my face. I hear Matthew shuffle around, which tells me he's still awake. "Hey, Matthew? When your nan died, how long were you sad for?"

"Honestly, it felt like forever, but it was only a few months. Or weeks. I don't know; it's difficult to remember."

"Right. Thanks, I guess." I think he can sense that that's not enough for me.

"Anton?"

"Yeah, fam."

"The sad tears eventually turn to happy ones. That part I'm sure about. I don't know how long it takes, but it'll happen."

"For real?"

"If your memories are happy, then yes, a million percent."

My eyes are streaming now, wetting my pillow. But I do believe him. As long as there's an end date for all this pain inside me, I guess it's OK for me to be sad right now.

Can't lie; the struggle is real. I've been in eleven fights, I've sat through the *Avatar* films, and I've opened baked beans with a penknife, but talking about Nanna is by far the hardest thing I've ever done. And yet I do feel better saying all this to Matthew. I've always thought emotional stuff was weak, that it's moist moves to cry like this, but sometimes you just gotta let it out. The truth is I don't have to suffer in silence; it's proper liberating. If I can talk stuff through with Matthew, or Rochelle, or whoever, in a way that I can't with the crew, it's safe to say I think I know who my true friends are. Or, more important, who they're not.

The second I get home the next day, I go to hug Mum in the kitchen, and she holds me tight, grateful. We break apart when my phone buzzes. I clock who it's from and then head to my room. Mum don't need this stress right now.

Sitting on the edge of the bed, I unlock the phone. Kehinde, Caleb, and Marcus have all messaged me. That cold phoenix in my chest is back. I open the first message. It's a bunch of screenshots from the Happy Campers website. That journalist from yesterday must've put up their article on the regeneration of St. Luke's, someone's seen my picture, and they've all gone straight online to find more. In the image, clear as day, you can see me sitting at the campfire next to a singing Jess and her terrible guitar. Me and the youngers eating that horrible porridge together. And a last one of me and Matthew, happily chatting while painting St. Luke's.

I swipe back to Kehinde's last message.

> We need to chat.

THEY'RE SITTING ON a bench in Myatt's Field Park, Kehinde, Caleb, and Marcus. From afar, it looks as if they're having a laugh, and it almost makes me miss the good old days. But then I remember that none of them reached out to me after Nanna died, that we never spoke about anything real. When Caleb clocks me in the distance, he nudges the other two. They put their phones away and fix up their postures, trying to look more threatening. It doesn't work. I know what it's like to be in this machine, and I'm glad I got out.

"Yo, here he is," Kehinde says. "Yogi Bear

finally turns up." Yogi Bear? I guess they don't have many camping references to draw from. Not exactly a devastating burn.

"Yo, what you got to say to me, man?" I'm on the front foot; let's just get this out the way so we can get on with our lives.

"How important is your reputation?" He starts waving the screenshots on his phone in my face.

"Bruv, my nan just died and you're pulling this on me?"

"How important, Anton?" He repeats the question more forcefully. I can't believe it; he's *met* my nan, and the whole thing means so little to him.

"You know what, do you? I don't care no more."

They exchange confused looks. They weren't expecting that. I should be putting up more of a fight. The whole school respects me because I'm the king; I know how to scrap, how to protect my name.

But that's not how everyone feels, is it? People at school don't respect me, or these man, not really. No, they're just scared of me, of us. That's not the same thing. And I'm over it. I don't want to be feared anymore; I want to be liked, thought of as a real friend, *be* a real friend. I want to spend my time with Matthew and Rochelle and whoever else I choose and not have to hide it. Because being king of the school will only last a few more years—then I got to get real, and I'd rather do it with true friends by my side, be King of Nothing, than be a tyrant with this court of jokers.

Caleb and Marcus stare at Kehinde, waiting for him to tell them what to do next.

"It's that stupid kid." He grits his teeth at me, seething. "I don't know what's happened, how he got to you so bad. His loserness is all over you like a bad smell. I can't believe you're choosing him over us."

"You made me make that choice," I shout. "None of you even messaged me when my nan died, none of you." They look at each other, almost with remorse. Except Kehinde. He just sneers at me.

"Anton, I'm gonna make this super easy for

you. We want you to come back and chill with us, pretend like none of this camping stuff ever happened. You're a thug, a soldier from the hood, not some camping makeover guru." Of course he sees me like that; we're all just loyal soldiers to him, blindly following orders that he's too weak to carry out himself. He used my dad's rep to turn me into a symbol, and I let him. But those days are done out here; I'm thinking for myself for once, and I love it.

"I ain't a thug, and I ain't a soldier," I tell him. Saying those words out loud, I think I just felt my life expectancy go up by thirty years.

"Well, whatever you think you are, you belong with us. We're your people, not that soft-chinned little Care Bear. If we see you with him again, he's finished."

"If you touch him, I don't care that it's three-one, I'm coming for all of you."

"Then we'll mess you up, too," Kehinde adds. "And after they've dragged him to the hospital, we'll wait for him to get back out and do it all over again. If we need to throw hands with you, then we will." Yeah, right.

"You know what," I tell Kehinde, "I've been racking my brains, thinking back to every beef and scuffle we've ever been in as a crew. And you know what I realized? You ain't never lifted a finger, never been in the firing line." I turn to the others. "He only jumps in when it's with someone he's one hundred percent sure he can take. You two should speak up, fam. You don't have to do his dirty work; this guy's got soft hands."

Kehinde glances at Marcus and Caleb, worried they might see sense. But they hardly react. I weren't expecting miracles from Caleb, although I'm disappointed that Marcus just stares at the ground. I thought we were tighter than that. Caleb's baring his teeth, rolling up his sleeves like the send-out, sidekick B-lister that he is. Kehinde's smirk is back; the odds are back to three against one. I could probably hold my own for a while, but Caleb and Marcus would eventually rearrange my face like Picasso. And I don't know how to protect Matthew from them, either.

"Bro, it's an easy decision. Hang with us or we get the tools out for your new friend," Caleb says. He's always been Kehinde's lapdog.

But I don't doubt they'll do it. Like my dad said, the only thing more dangerous than a real gangster is a fake one. And that's coming from a trusted source. Which means I've got no choice but to do what they say.

I texted Matthew to meet outside the library at Monday break time. Ironically, it'll be the first and last time I'll be seen chatting to him at school. I'm tryna justify the decision I've had to make. Matthew's going to be fine; he's got his life ahead of him. The world is open to him in a way he doesn't understand yet, in a way it's not fully open to me. His future's easier to see than mine is.

And technically, he doesn't need me anymore. I made him cool, for whatever it's worth, and he got the girl of his dreams. I held up my end of the bargain. But even that doesn't sound right. Like, it's incorrect. I haven't changed him at all; I just got him a fresh trim. He's still the same goofy guy from the first Happy Campers meeting. And

Fernanda seems to vibe with that, laughing at his silly jokes, and she don't even know the half of it. She's the lucky one. This whole time I've been trying to change him, and without even trying, he's the one who changed me. He's a cool little man. It's gonna make this hurt so much more.

"Anton, oh, Anton, I have so much to tell you." He comes bounding over. He's the only person I know who's always this happy to see me.

"Matthew," I say it forcefully, summoning all the hatred I have for Kehinde and channeling it into my voice. I need to get this over with quickly before I back out of it. "It's finished. I don't wanna chill with you no more. Not at school, not after school, not at the hall, not ever. Stop calling and texting me."

He looks bare confused. "But, Anton..."

I hold up a hand. "No buts. We're done."

He's trying so hard not to cry in front of me. He swallows back the tears. "But I make a mental note of everything that happens during the day so that I can tell you about it later." His big puppy eyes are threatening to well over. "You're my best friend."

I swallow. "I'm not your friend, Matthew." I've tried the soft approach, which clearly doesn't work. For his own safety, I have to rip this off like a bandage. "You're just some loser kid who saved me from a beesting. Other than that, you don't mean anything to anyone, especially not me."

Before he can answer, I storm off. No, Anton, don't look back at him; this isn't some romantic comedy. I turn the corner at the end of the corridor and break into a sprint. The minute I'm alone, I bring my palms to my eyes. Now I'm crying. Why am I crying? This isn't like grieving Nanna; I'm less certain that these tears will someday turn into happy ones. But I try to reassure myself that it's done now, the worst part is over. I push down all the sadness and guilt and regret and try to pretend it never happened. I've always been good at that. Then I stand up straight, clear my throat, and go to join Kehinde and the others outside.

I can't join in with the chat. While they're all going on about some kids who gave Caleb a dirty look at the bus stop, I'm sitting gazing into space. Across the playground, Rochelle and her math geeks are walking toward the library. Rochelle's staring at me, turning back every few seconds. She knows I ain't been chilling with my crew for some time; she must be proper baffled. She sends me a message.

> Are you OK?

Then later she calls me. When I don't pick up, a string of messages follow.

> How could you?

> I don't ever want to talk to you again

> He looked up to you.

I close the thread immediately. So she's spoken to Matthew.
    When I look again later, she's deleted the first three, and all I have left from her is, "He looked up to you."

The next day is rough. Sitting with the guys in homeroom feels foreign. I got nothing to contribute, and Kehinde's loving it. The way he smiles, but he's dead behind the eyes, it's creepy. He knows I ain't going nowhere; man's got me right where he wants me. Turns out Mum was right all along about who he is and what he's like.

Once or twice, the other two try to bring me into the conversation, but I just give one-word answers. It's bad enough I ditched Matthew, my only real friend; now it's like I'm sitting here getting mocked for it.

Mr. Benjamin asks me why I'm not sitting in my usual seat in the third row, and the whole class gasps when I tell him to get lost. Matthew and Rochelle are sitting side by side, and I see her rub his shoulder when the back row laughs with me. Even Mr. Benjamin looks a little hurt, but he chooses to carry on the lesson instead of kicking me out the class. That makes me feel worse. Just when I was making progress, bang, half a doughnut, U-turn. The dark cloud that I thought I got rid of is back with a vengeance. But you know what? I deserve this. All that time I spent hyping up Kehinde, watching him bully kids like Matthew, mouthing off to teachers for a laugh, this is what I deserve.

The whole of this week I been thinking about Matthew and Rochelle, no matter how much I try not to. TGIF now, though, cuz these last few days have dragged on like a cricket match. The streets feel different on a Friday afternoon; there's optimism in the air that just doesn't exist on a Tuesday.

I'm passing by the Poundshop on my way home when I spot something, or someone, out the corner of my eye that makes my insides leap. Nanna, sitting at the back of the bus that just went past, wearing her hat, staring out the window at the world going by. Like a shock of electricity, my legs bolt into action. I sprint after the bus, trying to catch another glimpse of her. I just about make it to the bus stop before the driver pulls off again. I'm pounding on the door, couldn't care less about causing a scene or the bus driver biting his tongue as the doors hiss open. My soul is vibrating; Mum's never gonna believe this.

Making my way slowly to the back of the bus, the pounding in my chest fades away immediately when reality hits. It's not Nanna at all. It's just some little old lady wearing a similar hat. Actually, up close, she barely even looks like Nanna. I take a seat opposite this complete stranger, tryna style it out. I must be staring, though, because she looks at me kinda funny. It's all too much in such a short amount of time. There's a shudder from within, and my lip wobbles, and my eyes just go. Tears just rolling and rolling; they won't stop. The lady now looks worried.

"You OK, son?" She pulls out a packet of tissues and offers me one. I tell her she just reminds me of someone I know. And as I step off the bus at the next stop, something clicks. I do have feelings, and it's time to face them instead of burying them. I can try to manage them, think on them, pretend like they're not there, but there's no denying it. I can't hide from my emotions anymore.

I sprint home and kick my shoes off by the front door, but instead of going to the kitchen or my bedroom, I'm standing in front of Nanna's room. I can hear Mum pottering in the living room, probably with her headphones in because she didn't hear me come in. She's left Nanna's door ajar again, and the minty smell hits me straight in the heart. My hand is shaking before I've even reached for the handle. This is a million times harder than walking into the petting zoo. Deep breath.

I step inside, expecting some kind of force field of grief, like a vampire breaking into a church. But it's just a room. Her wallpaper, her trinkets on the cabinet, pictures of me and Mum and Granddad in flimsy photo frames. I sit on the bed, the loud springs creaking as my butt bounces slightly. It's the little TV screen at the end of the bed that gets me. She's always had her own TV in here, but she chose to watch her shows in the living room to be closer to me and Mum.

That's the kind of person Nanna was.

"She was very proud of you, Anton, of both

of us." Mum's silently appeared, leaning up on the doorframe. I don't know how long she's been standing there, but I do know I feel safer with her here, more secure in a way.

"Why did she have to go, Mum?" I still can't say the word *die* out loud; it's like my mouth and my brain don't cooperate on that one. "She didn't do nothing to anyone." Now my voice is quivering. "If I'd known she was ill, if I'd seen something, done something, maybe she'd still be here." Mum shakes her head and comes inside, the bedsprings complaining loudly again as she sits down next me.

"You couldn't have stopped it any more than you can stop the sun from rising. I know it's tough, but grief is hard enough without adding the burden of blame. This was an accident, completely unforeseeable, and she wouldn't want us to tear ourselves apart in her name." Mum squeezes my leg and rests her head on my shoulder. "People come and go, Anton; that's just the nature of life. Death is inevitable; but happiness isn't. And a loving family isn't, either. That makes us incredibly lucky, don't you think?"

"Yeah," I concede. "I just miss her so much, Mum."

"Me too."

Mum does a tiny sniffle, the most discreet little noise of someone crying. Someone who's been so strong for the last few weeks, years even, whose best friend in the world has gone and isn't coming back. And just hearing it, something in my heart breaks like a glowstick, the cold phoenix rising up, but joined by a golden one. I'll never see Nanna again, but I've got all these memories that I'm so grateful for. Matthew was right, like always. I couldn't have ever asked for a better Nanna. I won the lottery with her.

Mum composes herself and straightens up a bit. Before she leaves me to have a minute alone, she says one more thing.

"Life is so short, you know; it's *so* short, a simple amalgamation of the choices we make. If you're lucky enough to experience a second of joy, let alone a lifetime of it like your Nanna, then those are the moments you hold on to."

In my own head, once she's gone, I'm tryna figure out this whole thing. Mum's right; when you boil life down to a collection of decisions, you can kinda see a person's whole life history like a map. Nanna's decisions brought her joy; she practically dedicated her life to it. That's why she chose to move in with us when Dad messed up our lives and Mum needed the childcare. The thought keeps popping up in the back of my head. *What do my decisions say about me?* I know which ones have brought me the most joy in these last few weeks. And which ones haven't.

It suddenly makes sense. Lining up in my mind like dominoes. Matthew, that annoying little bundle of sprinkles and stupid rhymes, he's the best friend I've ever had, and I'm choosing now not to lose him. Kehinde and them man think they're gangster, but they're cowards and they won't touch Matthew. I won't let them.

Right. Decision time.

St. Luke's grand opening is on Sunday. There's not much left to do, but me and Matthew started the project together, you can be damn sure we're gonna finish it together. I'm almost faint from how relieved and sure I am.

I make a promise to be someone Nanna

would be proud of, who my mum can be proud of, and more important, someone that *I'm* proud of. I know what that person looks like, what they do, what their life is like. I know I'mma sway left and right while I try to get there, but it's completely doable. Standing up from Nanna's bed, I got one thought in my mind: Time to go become that person.

I texted the guys, telling them I want to meet. This can't wait until Monday morning; I ain't a coward that puts things off. I'm calling Matthew in the meantime, but it keeps going straight to voicemail. So I try Rochelle instead.

"What do you want, traitor?" Her first words when she answers. I'm just thanking the heavens that she picked up.

"Is Matthew with you?"

"What do you care? After what he told me, you don't deserve to know where he is."

"Look, I know I messed up. I'm tryna make it right. Please, Rochelle." My days, I can't believe

I'm actually gonna say it out loud finally. "He's my best friend. I need to fix this."

She does the longest sigh. "You're not gonna hurt him again?"

"Never," I reply.

"And you'll hang with him at school? You'll start acting like an actual friend?"

"Yes, yes, I'll do all those things." There's no way I'm going back to being some loser who pretends not to care. "All this time I was trying to show him how to be like me, when I should've been trying to be more like him."

Rochelle's silence cuts me deep, and I punch the air when she finally responds.

"He's at that hall you've been decorating. Told me and Fernanda it was his happy place and he needed to be there." This guy is so endearing.

"Thanks, Rochelle."

"Don't let me down."

"I promise I'll try not to."

"That's good enough for me, Anton. Now go make this right."

It took them a while, but Kehinde eventually gets back to me, saying to meet at Marcus's place. Marcus's flat is the same size as mine, but he lives with both parents, two brothers, and a sister. All the windows are wide open to let some air in, but it offers all the fresh air of an old Labrador coughing on you. Matthew calls them labracadabradors because they're such magical beasts. Lol. So silly.

Me and Marcus are cramped up in his bedroom, which is basically a bunk bed, a double bed, and just about enough space for a wardrobe with no doors. We're playing *FIFA* while we wait for the others to get here. I'm not sure if I should bring it up to Marcus first or wait till we're all together.

During our first game, Marcus checked his phone three times in five minutes. He's got it angled so I can't see the screen. Hmm. We play another match, more or less in silence. I forfeit after that; the only thing on my mind is that I'm telling them to leave Matthew alone. If not, I'll sick Mr. Wall on them.

"You got an iPhone charger?" I ask. I'm on 2 percent.

"Nah, I don't know where it is." He didn't even look. Saying that, he's barely looked at anything but the screen since I got here. Yeah, something's not right.

"Where are the others?" He keeps telling me they'll be here later, but the way he's avoiding eye contact, it's bare suss. I take a deep breath as it all starts to fall into place. "They got you to distract me, didn't they? They're not coming." He doesn't confirm or deny. He could have easily said, "They'll be here in ten minutes," or something, but Marcus is too simple to think like that. I stand up to block the TV. "What are you not telling me, man?"

"Anton, I can't, fam." He's biting his bottom lip. Marcus has always been a tiny bit softer than the other two. I wonder what kind of person he'd be if he got out from under their shadow. But I don't have time to pander to him right now.

"Listen, I'm done playing with you. Is it something to do with Matthew?" I grab him by the collar. Once upon a time, I would've grabbed him by his oblong head, but that ain't me no more. He tries to grab me back, but I firm my grip. If Matthew's in trouble, I ain't got no time to be playing games. But he's not giving up that easily and we scuffle a bit.

We're not getting anywhere. What would Matthew do? I release his collar and take a step back. "This isn't about me anymore, Marcus. You're smart enough to understand; Kehinde is going down a path you don't wanna follow."

Marcus falls back onto his bed when I say that and looks down into his lap. "They'll know I told you."

"Cool, let them know. You're your own man. I know you, I know your family, you know what the right thing is."

He grabs the sides of his head. Quietly, he says, "The hall. The one you've been working on. They're going to trash the place."

I let out a single, loud shout that would put Matthew's whistle to shame. "That's my mum's job he's messing with!" I don't believe this; the grand opening is in two days. "Marcus, that hall is for the community. It's for vulnerable people. It's *important*."

He sits there, shaking his head. Clearly Marcus isn't coming with me to stop them. I'm dodging and sidestepping his little brothers in the corridor, sprinting all the way downstairs. It's only when I reach the bottom that I remember what Rochelle said on the phone earlier. Matthew's at St. Luke's. I push myself to run even faster.

AGH, STUPID PHONE. I tried calling Mum, but it died after two rings. There's no time to stop off home—who knows what Kehinde and Caleb are doing to Matthew right now? As I approach St. Luke's, I can see the lights are on inside. Even though I'm dripping with sweat, I run through the parking lot and burst through the door.

What I see sickens me to my stomach. Beyond the workbenches scattered about the place, the discarded rollers, and piles of planks and dust, is Matthew, terrified, in a corner. He's trying to hold off Kehinde and Caleb with a broom, while they're openly laughing and taunting him.

Kehinde's holding a bucket of paint, and Caleb's waving a discarded plank of wood. Matthew seems unhurt, though. Other than being quite scared and a bit tearful, I think he's OK.

"Anton!" Matthew exclaims when he sees me, with all the relief of someone who's just been saved by Superman.

"Leave. Him. Alone," I growl, my fists clenched, ready for what happens next.

Caleb turns to Kehinde, waiting for instructions. "Marcus must have snitched," he says. Damn right Marcus snitched.

Matthew screams, "No!" as Kehinde takes his paint pot and throws it, hard, at the freshly painted walls. There's a loud *bang* and a clang of metal, and we look on helplessly as red paint splatters and drips down weeks of hard work. It goes all over my mural, completely ruining it. Kehinde goes to grab another one, but I run over and tackle him to the floor before he can pry the lid open. I'm trying to hold Kehinde down, but he's nowhere near as easy to grab as Marcus. He knows how to slither and slip his way out of things. I take a punch in the jaw that knocks me sideways. Now I'm the one in a headlock, scrambling to get out of it. Caleb rushes over to help Kehinde, but Matthew jumps in the way.

"Oh no, you don't." He brings up his hand in a karate-chop motion. "Hi-ya!" He swings his open palm and misses by six feet.

Caleb looks confused for a millisecond, then responds with a punch to the eye. The *smack* can be heard over my tussle with Kehinde. Through a gap under Kehinde's arm, I can see Caleb swinging more blows at Matthew, standing over him while Matthew shouts at the top of his voice, "Grayskull, bless my strength."

Sigh. With my free hand, I find the fleshy bit of skin behind Kehinde's knee and pinch it as hard as I can. Desperate times call for dirty tactics. He lets out a wail, and I feel the grip loosen around my head. A well-timed punch to the ribs, and a kick between the legs, and suddenly I'm clear of him.

As soon as I'm on my feet, I rush over and yank Caleb by the back of the collar, sending him sprawling into a worktable. He squares up and comes back for round two. He only stops when he sees Matthew pointing his phone right at him.

"Yo, what you think you're doing? Stop filming me."

"It's just gone to my friend." Matthew turns the screen around to show that the video's been sent to Rochelle. "The next move is yours. If I were you, I'd run before she sends it to the police."

Caleb turns to Kehinde, who's nowhere to be seen. When Caleb realizes he's completely alone, he bolts for the door. Coward. I immediately turn to Matthew, grabbing him by the shoulders to check the damage.

"Bro, you OK? Are you hurt?"

"Physically, yes. I got punched in the face. Emotionally? I started healing when you came and rescued me."

We're both a mess. All scratched up and beaten, covered in dirt and paint. And for a brief second, we both start laughing. How we both survived that is unreal.

"Oh, Anton! Did you see my karate move? I—"

It's not over yet, though. "Wait, Matthew, something's up.... Can... Can you smell burning?"

Matthew sniffs the air, and just then I notice smoke wafting across the floor. It's coming from the room we've been working on, just the two of us. There's a noise from inside, Kehinde desperately screaming and pounding on the door. He must've locked himself in.

"Anton, that's the only room without a window." Matthew's eyes are wide and filled with fear.

The burning smell gets more and more intense.

"Matthew, call 911! Now!" I shout. "Kehinde, you need to wiggle the handle," I yell, but he can't hear me, he's too busy panicking. Thick dark smoke is creeping out from under the door now, and that's when my brain gives up. I can't think. I'm frozen in fear while smoke billows around my ankles. And then Matthew's voice snaps me out of it.

"We need to bust the door open." He's holding a fire extinguisher, which he hands to me. "But I'm not strong enough. Smash it above the door handle." Suddenly wired, I throw my shoulders back, and with all my strength, I crash the extinguisher where he told me to. There's a loud *crack* and the door breaks, sending all the smoke straight into our faces. Coughing and tearing up, I hit the door again, and this time it swings open. Oh, thank God.

Kehinde's in a crumpled heap in the doorway; he's buried his head in the neck of his T-shirt. Matthew springs into action, grabbing him by the ankles and dragging him to safety. I hold up the fire extinguisher and start spraying frantically in the direction of the thickest smoke: a waste bin in the corner of the room. The flames disappear almost immediately, and the smoke goes from black to a chemical white. My entire body is tense, my airways are blocked up and stinging. When there's nothing left in the extinguisher, I carefully back out of the little room.

The main hall is empty now, and I find Kehinde lying on the ground outside, spluttering, while Matthew flags down the fire engine. The adrenaline still feels like a sugar rush. Everything's in slow motion.

By the time my pulse slows down to four

hundred beats per minute, the scene has changed. The firefighters are dousing the room with a hose. Some paramedics have arrived, too, and are checking Kehinde for smoke inhalation in the ambulance. Then Mum is rushing in and grabbing me into the biggest hug, kissing me all over my head and face, and I just let her. She pulls Matthew into a hug, too, holding his cheeks so she can observe his black eye. I can tell he's slyly enjoying the attention.

We're both falling over ourselves to tell her what happened. I'm explaining how Kehinde and Caleb came to destroy the place, and then we fought them off, mainly me because Matthew's karate chop hit thin air, but then he saved the day. He chimes in to tell her that I protected him and put out the fire single-handed, and, yeah, I get pumped a little.

With the firefighters in the room, we go to inspect the damage. Aside from the mess in the main hall, there are dirty black stains all over the walls and ceiling and carpet of the quiet room. The place is supposed to have its grand opening in two days. Mum says she can call an emergency contractor to come and fix the door tomorrow and keep the room locked on Sunday. I love how she sees solutions instead of problems everywhere she looks. But I'm still gutted my mural got ruined. Hopefully I can redo it tomorrow. It's gonna be a long day, but I think it's doable.

Matthew's called his mum to come pick him up. While we're waiting for her car to pull up, I have to apologize. I can't let him go without addressing it.

"Bro, about the other day, all those things I said, I take it all back; I didn't mean any of it." I bite my tongue and look up at the sky. "I told myself I was protecting you, because Kehinde was threatening you, but, like, I was just being hella weak. I didn't want to hurt you, I swear. I'm really sorry."

"Anton, you saved me tonight. If you hadn't turned up, who knows what would've happened?" He looks at the ground, and in the dim streetlights, I can tell he's confused. We must look a right mess, clothes all torn, bruised faces. He wears it well, though, better than I expected. "Now that you've saved *me*, and Fernanda's kind of my girlfriend, does that mean that we're even and you don't have to be my friend anymore?"

"Man, that stopped being the reason for our friendship a long time ago." And then I tell him what I know he's been wanting to hear for weeks. "You're my best friend, Matthew."

He looks me in the eye with a big grin on his swollen face. "Really, truly?"

"Yes." Sigh. I reach out to pat him on the shoulder. Instead, he opens his arms wide and we hug it out.

"And the best friends settled in warm embrace," he whispers in my ear.

"OK, stop hugging me now." I step back. "You see what you did? You made it weird. You're on a hug ban until you think about what you've done." We both laugh. And when his mum's headlights snake their way toward us, I can't help thinking about how much fun we're gonna have tomorrow.

IT'S ALL HANDS on deck the next day. Rob and Jess called every available Happy Camper to come help out. The Safe Havens people are on their way. Rochelle's here, too, and Fernanda, and even Grace came out from her lair. Mum's bossing it, racing around in her high-vis that lets you know she's top dog around here. She's pointing, shouting, instructing, making sure everything's perfect as can be for the opening.

After painting a fresh base coat in both rooms this morning, we're taking a break to let it dry. Fernanda's sitting on Matthew's lap, and that Sebastian kid is showing Grace how to make a friendship bracelet. Me and Rochelle are sitting next to each other. I'm very conscious of how close our knees are to touching. Matthew's recounting last night's events, in the most Matthew way.

"Oh, Fernanda, my dear, I was so brave; you would've been so proud. I didn't even need my whistle, not when I have these in my arsenal." He holds up his soft hands in the karate-chop position.

"Aww, *mi amor*." She kisses the top of his head.

Rochelle silently raises her eyebrow at me, and I shake my head. We both know he's about as lethal as a newborn baby.

She leans across and whispers, "Thank you for protecting him." I nod and smile. "Was he helpful?"

"Yeah, he kinda saved all of us," I admit. "But in the fight, well, let's just say it was like watching an ice-cream cone fighting the sun."

She giggles and squeezes my knee. Now I'm the one who gets all giddy.

"I do love that little weirdo," I say. Matthew's

pretending to catch the kisses that Fernanda's blowing and then rubbing them all over his face, and somehow it turns into a game of peekaboo. I'm way more entertained than I should be. "He's a geek, but he's happily geeky. Man's always gonna be himself."

"And what about you? You're not a geek, and you're not a bully, either, so what are *you*?" Rochelle asks.

"I dunno. I'm just me, I guess. You think that's good enough?"

"I really do," she says, positively beaming.

"Double-bubble promise?" I ask. What have I become? We both fall about laughing, and Rochelle starts nodding.

"Double-bubble promise," she says.

The grand opening is a super success. The whole community turned up to show their support. Mrs. Campbell from two doors down came through with huge trays of jerk chicken and rice and peas. The family at the end of the road brought homemade banoffee pie. Basically, there was so much food that we had to bring out extra tables.

Mum's colleagues were there, along with Joshua Nikos and his crew, and a reporter and photographer from the local newspaper even covered the event. Matthew kept trying to creep his way into all the pictures, but the only one they got of him was midmoan when he spilled ketchup on his pants.

"Oh no, my chinos." He had an epic meltdown. "Anton, you don't think they saw, do you?"

"They definitely did."

A bit later on, I'm in the bathroom while Matthew washes the stain off in the sink.

"Hey, Matthew. Thank you. Not just for helping out here, but for getting me to start believing in myself. I appreciate it, really." I'm proper being sincere.

"You are most welcome." He smiles at me. "And you've helped me, too. You showed me how to be brave, how to stand up for myself, and how to be more confident. I wouldn't have a group of friends if it wasn't for you." Weirdly, he taught me all those things about myself, too. And I even got an upgrade on my crew out of it.

"That's cool, man; thank you for saying that. But could you make less eye contact with me when you're standing there in your underwear?"

He apologizes and happily goes back to scrubbing his trousers. I do rate him; lots of people say they don't care what others think, but Matthew puts that into practice.

Back in the main room, people are smiling and laughing as they help themselves to food. I am proud of my mum, for real. She's having a laugh with Rob over in the corner. Looking around, I can't believe this place was some run-down shack, just crumbling walls and a roof, before she brought it to life. The way people talk about it, a safe haven for women, a place where families can feel secure, shows me that it's more than just a building.

And it also reminds me of Nanna; at first glance, she was just some random lady, a purple coat and hat on skin on flesh and bones and muscles, darting around the supermarket. But to me she was so much more, a true superhero.

Kids who have never met before are shrieking loudly as they run around playing, and everyone sitting down has a person or a group to talk to. Joshua Nikos, who's walking past, catches me standing there, taking it all in.

"This is all pretty special, isn't it?" I say to him. "St. Luke's weren't ever like this before."

"Yeah, it really is," he replies. "It's amazing what hard work and care and a few licks of paint can do to a place. Nothing is beyond redemption, Anton." I hear that.

"Hey, thanks for helping me out, before, that thing with my dad. And thanks for dedicating your time here."

"We all did, including you. You should be really proud of yourself." I'm not sure if I am, not fully, anyway, not yet. But one thing I am proud of is the people I'm choosing to surround myself with. I look over at Rochelle, Matthew, and Fernanda, and even Grace, all sitting together chatting and eating. One last handshake with Joshua Nikos, and I go over to join my people. A quarter of them are Happy Campers. Who'd have thought it?

EPILOGUE

SCHOOL LOOKS COMPLETELY different in the last term before the holidays. I got another B in English, and a B in math that feels like even more of an accomplishment. I locked in my exam subject options officially, too. Mum took me to a fancy Spanish restaurant to celebrate. It was also Nanna's favorite place to eat. From now, every time we have great news to celebrate, we'll be coming here. Mr. Wall mentioned he might make me a hall monitor next year, if I keep up the good work. Looks like we might have something else to celebrate in the autumn.

St. Luke's has been up and running for a minute now, and I had no idea it would be so busy. Rochelle says it's bittersweet; the fact that it's busy means there's a lot of vulnerable women out there. I'm just happy they've got somewhere to go. There's a lot of support groups and workshops around rediscovering who you are. Tons of tears and that. I weren't happy at one girl who was tryna steal the toilet paper from the bathrooms, but Mum sent me to the store to buy the girl a bundle pack. She said anyone that desperate needs compassion, not judgment, and I felt proper bad after. I guess I got a lot more to learn.

We named the quiet room after Nanna, which is ironic because she was the loudest person I've ever known. And for my birthday, my new squad put their money together to buy a shiny new plaque for her and everything. Can't lie; I did cry a bit, especially when Mum came and put her arm around me as we hung it up. Whenever I see it, I think about my silent promise to Nanna, about striving to be someone she can be proud of. I'll always make an effort to keep that promise.

As for my dad, I ain't seen him since our last meeting. But Joshua Nikos was right, nothing or nobody is beyond redemption. I guess I'm living proof of that. I know my dad probably won't change. But he might. And Nanna always taught me to believe the best in people. So who knows what'll happen in the future.

Matthew and Fernanda are still going strong. The way they talk to each other makes me a bit nauseated; can't lie. It's like they've both been doused with lavender spray. It's all kissing each other's hands and sitting on laps and that. Sometimes Matthew sits on her lap while she curls a finger in his hair. Bless him, he's more smiley and bouncy than ever. I dropped out of the Happy Campers; it wasn't really for me, but I still walk him over sometimes, just to pop in and say hi to Rob and Jess.

As for my old crew, they've completely disbanded. Marcus was the first to leave; I've spotted him chilling with the skater kids at the back of the school. He's grown out his hair into a bit of a messy Afro, and his style's changed. He does seem more relaxed now. We give each other a nod when we pass in the corridor, and he's the only one who didn't unfollow me on Snapchat. Maybe next year we'll be in art class together.

Caleb and Kehinde got suspended for the part they played in the St. Luke's incident. Mum didn't want to press charges, though, because she didn't want to ruin their lives at such a young age. Caleb didn't come back, and I heard his family were changing schools after the summer. Kehinde mainly rolls around on his own now. I don't hear from him at all. My phone is very grateful.

I have a new squad now. Me, Matthew, Rochelle, Fernanda, and Grace. I don't even mind Grace that much anymore. She's just a bit grumpy and has a hard time with outwardly expressing her emotions. Happens to the best of us. Joining a new group chat was strange, but fun at the same time. I'm glad to not just have angry podcasts in the group chat anymore. Instead, we exchange fail videos, jokes, memes, and celeb gossip. Fernanda's even trying to get Matthew into football, and I'm here for it.

Me and Matthew are walking to the bus stop after a day in the park. We're chatting about summer plans, and he asks if I want to join him and his family in Spain this summer.

"Is Rochelle going?" I ask, half jokingly.

"No." He laughs. "Just us, I'm afraid. Hey, are you ever going to ask her out?" He does a cheeky half smile. "I have a feeling she might be into you, too, just from some of the stuff she says to Fernanda." Look at this guy. Five minutes in a relationship and he's already a guru.

I shrug. "If it happens, it happens. All I can do is be myself around her. If we do end up getting together, it'll be magical." Oh God, I sound just like him. I look at my watch and see it's still early in the day. I got a few hours to kill before dinner.

"Mind if I come over? We can watch a couple of episodes of that *Drag Race* show." Can't lie; that show got me invested. The queens are bare savage with their takedowns, proper lols, and some of the design challenges can be pretty stressful.

"Absa-daba-lutely, you can come over." He doesn't even try to hide his excitement. "Are you staying for supper?" I love that he says "supper" like a Victorian nanny with typhoid. Last week,

I had a Pop-Tart after dinner and he called it "pudding." He always gets me with those random ones.

"I'll text my mum and ask her," I tell him, pulling out my phone.

"Great," he says with a smile. "Maybe we can play that card game I was telling you about. You can be a sorcerer; I'll start you on level one."

"I can watch you play, learn the rules and that."

"Yayzies! And after that, we can listen to ABBA through the new speakers. I've downloaded their live set in Bucharest that'll blow your socks off."

Oh, Matthew, I can't think of anything worse. And at the same time, I can't think of anything better.

ACKNOWLEDGMENTS

My greatest thanks go to the following people:

My cousin Lilly, a.k.a. Chambooboo, I told you you'd be first in my list of acknowledgments. If you ever write a book, I'd like it dedicated to me in return. Unless it's a cookbook, a dictionary, or a biography of Harry Styles.

My team at Hot Key. Ella, whom I see as a teacher, friend, and cowriter, as well as an editor. I came up with a funny story, but your input is what made it worth telling. If *King of Nothing* teaches anyone to be more respectful and thoughtful to women, then it's thanks to you.

Pippa Poole with an *e*. Because that's how it's spelled. My wonderful, hardworking publicist with a great surname. Every table you sit at is a Poole table.

Jas Bansal for spreading the word.

Dominica Clements. When people say they read books from cover to cover, you are the first and last point of contact. The words I've written are but a "cover sandwich," and what a beautiful one you've crafted for *King of Nothing*.

Tosin Akinkumi, thank you for illustrating so beautifully and expertly. You can find Tosin's Instagram here—@artbytosin—and see many more examples of this incredibly talented illustrator's work. I recently tried to do a finger painting but ended up painting my thumb by accident. I'll leave it to the professionals.

Talya Baker, how ironic that you're a baker yet we meat again. Thank you for fine-combing this manuscript and making me look competent. Details are of the upmost importance; without them we wouldn't have a proper functioning societt+y.

Many thanks to Margaret, my homie away from home. This book doesn't happen without you. Anyone who enjoys it has you to thank.

Roddyna Saint-Paul, thanks for a roddy good time! May you always find ten dollars in your pocket, adjusted for inflation depending on when you read this.

Esther Reisberg, my job is easier because of you. I shall always root for you. Like ginger. And you, too, Lindsay Kaplan and Bunmi Ishola.

Tracy Koontz, thank you for all your hard work. Tracy means more to me than Trey Songz; he never worked on this book.

Gabrielle Chang, the designer, thanks to you the book wouldn't be finer. I wouldn't Chang a thing.

Kingsley Nebechi. This guy is a giant, both in talent and in height. You can find Kingsley's art @kingsleynebechi on Instagram.

And my family and friends. Benjamin, your laughter let me know I was on the right path.

Sebastian, I'm sorry for naming such a dweeby character after you, but in my defense.

OGC, this is all a continuation of what you started. Love.

The Darley Anderson Children's Book Agency #teamDAkids.

Granddad, John Lessore, your bloodline shall continue throughout the ages.

The rest of my family, you bunch of pirates and degenerates. Thanks for the love.

My close friends, you know who you are. I hope. Therefore I am.

Judi Mouton, merci! They say that French people are obnoxious, annoying nationalists who sit around eating snails. But I've never seen you eat snails.

Dwayne Johnson, a.k.a. The Rock. For no reason, just seeing if this makes it into print.

Tia Fisher, an outstanding author who relentlessly championed my last book, I hope you enjoyed this one almost as much. I'd recommend Tia's book, *Crossing the Line*, to anyone looking for their next read; it's pretty special and one of my faves. Shout-out books.

Carol Roberts, a.k.a. Didi, your kind words and support have meant the world to me.

And most important, Gary von Shmickelbach. My best friend, my brother, I could not have done this without you.

CLARE WALLACE

Nathanael Lessore is a British author who can prove it with his passport. His dad is French, and his mom is from Madagascar (the place, not the movie). Growing up on a block in Peckham, Nathanael's childhood was a vibe. The neighbors were fun, loud, unpredictable, and unique. But most importantly, they were a community. And Nathanael will always authentically represent South London's diversity and togetherness in the stories he tells. When he's not writing, Nathanael enjoys stargazing at the moon and standing in doorways. If he wasn't a writer, he would've joined the NFL (if not for his lack of talent and basic understanding of the game). His first novel, *Dropping Beats* (published as *Steady for This* in the UK), won the Branford Boase Award and was shortlisted for the Carnegie Medal.

More hilarious and heartwarming stories from NATHANAEL LESSORE

CELEBRATING 100 YEARS OF PUBLISHING

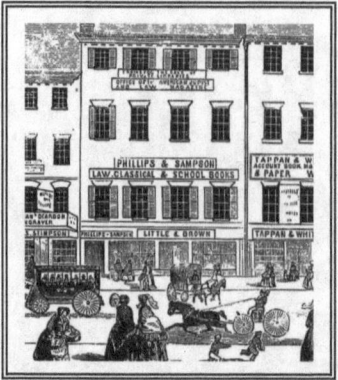

Dear Reader,

You may have noticed the words "Little, Brown and Company" on the title page of this book and wondered what they mean. Well, Charles C. Little and James Brown were the founders of this publishing house, and the "and Company" is all the editors, designers, marketers, publicists, salespeople, and more who help produce each book and bring it to readers like you. Little, Brown was founded in Boston, Massachusetts, in 1837, and some of its early publications included *The Writings of George Washington* and *The Works of Benjamin Franklin*. The catalog grew to feature works by Emily Dickinson and Louisa May Alcott, among many other notable authors. In 1926, recognizing that the literature we read when we are young has a deep and lasting influence and requires expert curation, the company appointed an editor to lead a dedicated children's department.

In 2026, Little, Brown Books for Young Readers celebrates one hundred years of excellence in publishing. Today, we are a division of Hachette Livre, the third-largest publisher in the world, and we are based in New York City. Our staff has grown from a team of two to more than one hundred people. And with the changes in technology, our books are read by more readers, in more ways, and in more countries than ever before. However, one thing has not changed: our commitment to providing a supportive home for all creators and superb stories for all readers. Thank you for being one of them.

Megan Tingley
Megan Tingley
President and Publisher

LITTLE, BROWN AND COMPANY
BOOKS FOR YOUNG READERS

To learn more about Little, Brown's history, authors, and books, please visit LBYR.com.

www.ingramcontent.com/pod-product-compliance
Lightning Source LLC
LaVergne TN
LVHW031535060526
838200LV00056B/4512